SOPHIE BRIGGS AND THE SPIKE OF DEATH

SOPHIE BRIGGS AND THE SPIKE OF DEATH

THE SCHOOL OF ROOTS AND VINES™ BOOK ONE

MARTHA CARR

MICHAEL ANDERLE

L M B P N

DISRUPTIVE IMAGINATION

This book is a work of fiction. All of the characters, organizations, and events portrayed in this novel are either products of the author's imagination or are used fictitiously. Sometimes both.

LMBPN Publishing
PMB 196, 2540 South Maryland Pkwy
Las Vegas, NV 89109

Version 1.01, August 2022
ebook ISBN: 979-8-88541-231-5
Print ISBN: 979-8-88541-847-8

THE SOPHIE BRIGGS AND THE SPIKE OF DEATH TEAM

Thanks to our Beta Readers
Larry Omans, Angela Wood

Thanks to our JIT Readers

Dave Hicks
Jeff Goode
Christopher Gilliard
Diane L. Smith
Dorothy Lloyd

Editor

SkyFyre Editing Team

CHAPTER ONE

It was finally time for school.

Sophia Briggs could hardly breathe as she pressed her face against the minivan window. Outside, tall, hearty maples and oaks towered on either side of the snake-like two-lane state road that wound and curved with a dozen glistening creeks.

It had been a long wait since her after-hours exam in the gym of the public school three months ago. She'd proven her elemental gift of life and passed with flying colors, not surprising anyone.

She'd always been a healer, a helper, a grower, just like the rest of her family. She loved the forest, the trees, and the way their branches and leaves beckoned to her, and how trees seemed to whisper to one another.

Now, on her way to the School of Roots and Vines in Bardstown, Kentucky—near her home in Louisville—she could learn even more, expand her gift, and hopefully, figure out her place in the world.

She suppressed the urge to bite her lip for the

hundredth time. It wouldn't make time go any faster, and besides that, she didn't want scarred and sore lips on her first day.

As the minivan rounded a curve, Sophia spotted the brown, reflective material of an informational sign, its words hidden behind a curtain of dark green ivy.

The van slowed, then stopped. Joyce Briggs, Sophia's mother, heaved a sigh.

"Well, the GPS said this was the way to go." She turned toward the backseat, her dark brown eyes the model of Sophie's. "Sophie, hon, let me see your syllabus. I'll double-check the address."

Sophie grabbed her backpack, rifling through her welcome folder.

"I *know* where I'm going, Joy." Walter Briggs tapped the GPS, which was no longer responding. "What's the matter with this thing?"

Amelia, Sophie's ten-year-old sister, suddenly squealed.

"Look!" She pointed to the brown sign.

As they all watched, the ivy parted, revealing bold white letters: *School of Roots and Vines, 1 mi.*

Sophie smiled, a thrill racing up her spine.

"Step on it, Dad!"

As they traveled, the serpentine curves in the road turned one mile into what seemed like ten. Sophie tucked her long, dark hair behind her ear and tapped her foot, staring ahead as far as she could see. It was useless. The trees, in the fullness of their late summer foliage, provided a solid wall on all sides.

The road abruptly straightened, losing a lane as it approached a towering pair of iron gates dripping with thick, verdant vines and ivy. A bronze plaque shimmered on the gate, and antique serif letters spelled out *School of Roots and Vines: A Boarding School for Young Elemental Talent.*

Sophie gulped as the car slowed and the gates began to open. It hadn't seemed real somehow until now.

The van moved forward once the gates had opened completely. Sophie noted the trees flanking the road seemed to lean toward them as they drove past. She smiled—it was as if the trees wanted to welcome them to campus.

Trees gave way to a sprawling lawn dotted with several smaller buildings and what looked like a huge amphitheater in the distance.

But front and center stood a structure that Sophie found strange and unfamiliar. At first glance, it looked like the largest and most central building. Looking at it again, Sophie gasped.

A magnificent oak tree the height of a skyscraper towered in the center of the campus. Its upper leaves, well above the main canopy of Bernheim Forest, glistened in the sunlight while its lower leaves shifted cheerily in the breeze.

Lower down the massive trunk, at the ground, Sophie could see people busily going in and out of grand double doors—the main entrance, she realized.

"Wow," Sophie murmured.

"Is that all *one* tree?" Amelia asked.

Sophie nodded, joy and awe swelling in her chest. "I think so, Millie."

Walter parked the van behind several other vehicles along the main drive and turned around in his seat. "You ready, girls?"

Sophie's heart raced as she grabbed her backpack. "Yep!" She slid the van door open and climbed out into the dappled sunshine, helping Millie out next.

Both girls stood gawking at the tree for several moments. Standing in front of it made Sophie feel microscopic.

But one small branch near the bottom, tousled in an unfelt breeze, lost a dark green leaf which fluttered in Sophie's direction, brushing her cheek as it fell.

"I think it likes you," Millie giggled. "It just gave you a kiss."

Sophie rolled her eyes. "Great. My first admirer at school is a tree."

Still, a smile lingered on her lips, and she tucked the leaf into her pocket.

Sophie swept her gaze toward the center of campus, right in front of the tree, where a maze of flowering bushes clustered beautifully at its base.

At the top of the steps leading into the massive tree-building, an older woman dressed in black and hunter-green was working. Her graying hair had been braided and rolled into a tight bun at the base of her neck. She swept her fingers through the air, and in response, little bursts of wind pushed fallen leaves off the steps.

She glanced up, as if feeling Sophie's gaze, and gave half a smile before turning and ushering another family into the school.

"I bet she's the boss. Mom and Dad said she was awful strange when they talked to her," Millie whispered.

"I think you mean 'headmistress,'" Sophie corrected. "And you're probably right."

She'd overheard her parents talking about Norma Case, the woman who'd ruled the school for so long that no one remembered who had come before her. Sophie made a mental note to try and stay on Headmistress Case's good side. She'd bet anything that her wind powers extended far beyond leaf blowing.

"Hi, there!" A friendly-looking teen with sandy blond hair jogged in their direction. "Welcome to Roots and Vines. My name's Bradley. You folks look like you could use a hand."

"I'm all right," Walter grunted, pulling Sophie's bags from the back of the van.

Bradley chuckled, holding out a map. "I meant finding your way around."

Walter's cheeks reddened. "Ah."

"That'd be wonderful," Joyce said, accepting the map. As she opened it and Sophie peeked over, the illustrations moved almost like a holographic picture. The bed icon marking the dorm building switched back and forth between pink, showing the girl's building, and blue for the boys, on the opposite side of the massive tree. The icons for each elemental building similarly changed color or repeatedly flashed, showing emergency meeting locations, where to find safety officers, or simply where to use the restroom.

"Neat," Millie said, a note of awe in her voice.

"Would you folks like a tour?" Bradley glanced at Walter, sweating with the strain of Sophie's multiple bags. "And maybe a dolly?"

"That'd be great, thanks," Walter said.

Once Sophie's bags had been loaded onto the dolly,

Bradley led them to the girls' dorms, pointing out important sites along the way.

Sophie couldn't help but notice that the mums and tiger lilies planted in the central garden leaned toward the Briggs as they walked by. She smiled back at them, stretching out her fingers to touch their petals. In response, their stalks grew a couple of centimeters, and the blooms moved in the light breeze as if dancing.

"Obviously, this here is Thicket Hall." Bradley gestured up at the magnificent oak school building. "Heart and soul of the school, that is."

Sophie smiled up at it as she walked, feeling for the leaf in her pocket.

They continued up an old-fashioned stone walkway that cut through the great lawn like a highway system, with branches leading in all directions.

"This here's the fire elemental building," Bradley said, gesturing toward a stout brick building off to their left. Black singe marks demarcated the outside of the door frame. "It used to have a thatched roof. You can imagine how well that went over."

"It...wait for it...went up in smoke!" Millie burst out laughing at her joke while Sophie just shook her head and ruffled Millie's dark, wavy hair.

They walked down the sidewalk that rounded the gigantic tree. Sophie could see a lake—or maybe a pond—behind another brick building.

"That's the water elemental building. Any excess water leads out to Crystal Pond there."

Sophie noticed the notches around the base of the building, trickling water into a gutter-like aqueduct feeding the pond. She heard a squeal from inside, and a sudden burst of water flowed from the notches into the aqueduct.

"Uh-oh, somebody just got soaked," Millie said.

"Then there a way off, you can see the air elemental pavilion. It's made breathable, you understand."

"I'll say," said Joyce.

The pavilion's sides could be closed or opened, Sophie saw, by pulling wooden panels across the open spaces. It was currently open on two sides, and several teens gathered inside, spinning up weak vortexes in a sandbox.

"Then there's the life elemental greenhouse." Bradley had stopped. He pointed off the sidewalk to the right, across the huge circular lawn, and near the top of a gentle hill, where Sophie could just see the glass walls glinting in the sunlight. Her heart buoyed—that's where she'd spend her time learning, growing, healing.

Walter clapped Sophie on the shoulder. "Good memories in that place, Sophie. You'll have so much fun here."

"I know I will, Dad," she replied, patting his hand.

"This way to the girls' dorms," Bradley called. They followed him down a narrower sidewalk that branched off to the right, behind and past the fire and water buildings, to a beautiful, long building covered in natural stone. He stopped at the entrance and flipped through a tiny notebook he'd pulled out of his pocket.

"Might I ask your full name so I can give you your room number?"

"Sophia Briggs," replied Sophie, and Bradley flipped a couple more pages.

"Ah, here you are. Room 318." He handed her a slip of

paper. "Just show this to Rhonda at the front. She'll get you your key."

"Thanks for the tour!"

"No problem." Bradley smiled at Walter and Joyce. "You must be so proud of your daughter. Not everyone gets a chance to learn here. She must be one of a kind." He winked at Sophie, then gave a short wave and jogged off to help someone else.

The Briggs' glanced at one another. Her parents' apprehensive smiles made Sophie's heart ache.

"Don't worry, guys. You can still help me get settled."

Joyce smiled, her eyes already watering. "Of course, hon."

Sophie retrieved her room key from Rhonda and found an elevator so Walter could bring her bags up to the third floor. They all piled in, taking in the bright wood paneling and the aroma of lemon and pine.

Once on the third floor, they followed the gleaming wooden signs to room 318. Opening the door, Sophie gaped.

"Whoa!" Millie cried.

Her sister was right. The oak walls practically shimmered with polish, and the iron chandelier hanging from the ceiling cast a friendly yellow light on the large, open room. Sophie counted four beds, each with a tall, sturdy dresser next to it and a beautiful quilt spread across it. Against the far walls stood four hutch desks with high-backed, ornate chairs.

"You gonna let us in?" Walter asked.

"Oh, yeah." Sophie stood aside as her father pushed the dolly into the room. Joyce went to the window against the back wall, stroking the leaves of the ivy plant sunning there. Its leaves curled around her fingers as she sang to it.

"I think you should take this bed," Joyce said, pointing to the bed closest to the window, on the right side of the room.

"Well, it's also the only bed not taken yet," said Walter, dumping Sophie's bags onto that bed. Sophie glanced at the other beds again, noting luggage sticking out from under the quilts or school supplies laying out on the desks.

"Hi," said an unfamiliar voice. Sophie turned to the opposite wall. A girl with short, dark hair and lots of earrings stood in a doorway she hadn't seen. "What's your name?"

"I'm Sophie," Sophie said.

"Leslie, nice to meet you. I've got that bed." She pointed to the bed next to Sophie's. "Don't worry. I won't snore."

Sophie smiled, then gestured behind Leslie. "What's that room?"

"Oh." Leslie beckoned her over. "It's the bathroom. Come look."

Sophie stepped into the large bathroom. Soft globe lights adorned the mirror, set in the same iron as the chandelier in the main room. Instead of wood, glistening natural stones formed tiles along the floor and walls. A walk-in shower stood on each side of a double sink, and two doors demarcated where the toilet stalls were.

"Wow. Nice and roomy," Sophie said.

"Yep. Pretty cool!" replied Leslie.

"What's on the other side?" Sophie pointed at a door on the opposing wall.

"Oh, that's the other room we share this bathroom with."

Sophie frowned. The bathroom didn't seem so large now. Voices had grown louder from her room, and she and Leslie stepped out.

Three pairs of adults, along with Walter and Joyce, mingled in the center of the room.

"Oh, there's my folks." Leslie pointed to a slender woman with dark hair and a man with bright red hair and an even brighter smile as he looked at Leslie.

"Come here," he beckoned.

As Sophie watched in awe, Leslie's mother swirled a water bottle, the liquid inside forming a seahorse that reflected the light from the window into rainbow colors.

"Take care of yourself, ok?" her mother insisted.

"I'll be fine," Leslie said, rolling her eyes. She took the bottle from her mother and swirled it, adding a starfish and jellyfish to the seahorse. "I'm a water elemental. I'll just send a hurricane upon anyone who dares to try me."

Sophie chuckled, as did Leslie's parents.

"We know you'll be fine," Leslie's mother said, ruffling Leslie's short hair. "It's your father I'm worried about."

Leslie's dad wiped a hand down his face, his eyes reddening. "Don't be silly."

Sophie saw her mother waving at her and went to her side.

"Sophie, this is Janet and her parents."

A shy girl with cute cat-eye glasses and mousy brown hair in a ponytail waved at Sophie.

"Nice to meet you, Sophie." Janet's northern dialect

came through strong, and Sophie wondered where she was from.

"You too, Janet." She shook Janet's hand, noting the charm bracelet on her wrist with a Michigan charm. So that solved the mystery. "What's your gift?"

"I've got earth." She shook her charm bracelet. "See this little terrarium? I made it for my exam."

Sophie peered at the tiny crystal globe filled with minuscule rocks and one little succulent.

"Wow. That's neat."

Janet beamed with pride. "And I made my Michigan charm, too. It's earth from our front lawn. So, I never feel like home is too far away."

"I love that," said Sophie.

"Hi!" Another girl bounced into the room, her blonde hair in a wispy French braid down her neck. "I'm Brianna." She twirled her fingers, sending a breeze swirling around them.

"Air, if you couldn't guess," said her dad, his blue eyes practically glowing with love.

"Nice to meet you. I'm Sophie, and this is Janet." Sophie gestured politely toward Janet.

"And I'm Leslie." The dark-haired girl had managed to shoo her parents away and joined the circle in the center of the room. "My gift is water."

As the other three girls introduced themselves, Amelia tugged on Sophie's sleeve. Sophie turned to see her parents gazing at her, their expressions torn between pride and sadness.

"Anything else we can help you with?" Walter asked.

Sophie shook her head. "I think I'm good to go."

"It seems you have some lovely roommates," Joyce added, nodding toward the chatting girls.

"Yeah, I'm sure they'll be great," Sophie said. As much as she loved her parents, there was so much more she wanted to explore—especially the giant tree-building. Excitement was building in her chest again.

"We're gonna miss you, Sophie." Amelia wrapped her arms around Sophie, then whispered, "Call me and tell me about *everything*."

Sophie laughed and hugged her sister tight. "You know I will, Millie." Then she looked up at her parents, noting her father's surreptitious glance toward Sophie's backpack, which suddenly had dollar bills sticking out of the top pocket.

"Dad."

"What? Maybe you'll want a snack, or run out of pencils, or—"

"I'll be okay," Sophie said, hugging each of her parents and herding them toward the door. "You know that."

"Yes," Joyce said, pausing to tuck Sophie's wavy, dark hair behind her ear. "We know."

Then, with one final, lingering smile, Joyce, Walter, and Amelia headed off down the hall.

A tinge of nostalgic sadness swept through Sophie as she waved after them, but the voices of the chatting girls behind her quickly reignited her excitement.

It was finally time for school.

CHAPTER TWO

"I've got it from here, Mom. It's okay." Brianna's parents reluctantly left the room. The bubbly blonde sent a whirl of wind closing the door behind them, then turned back to Sophie, Janet, and Leslie. "Sheesh. Thought they'd never leave."

The four girls giggled. Janet went straight for her matching luggage, pulling the zipper on the biggest suitcase. "Time to make this place our own!"

Sophie and Leslie followed suit, pulling out their belongings and arranging them into the dressers and onto the desks.

Sophie found her potted plant, a purple African violet, and placed it on her desk nearest the window. She knew it would need lots of sunlight, and while most African violets hated cold water, she knew this one liked its moisture at room temperature—preferably out of Sophie's water bottles. She pulled a few bottles out and tucked them in her hutch, then touched the deep purple blossoms of the plant.

The purple deepened in response to her touch as if asking a question.

"We're in a new place now, Vi," she whispered. "But we're all right. I'm still gonna take care of you."

One hairy leaf brushed her finger—an affirmation. Sophie smiled.

"Aww, Bluebell. I miss her already." Brianna put a framed photo of a corgi on her desk, staring at it with her hands clasped.

"Cute dog," Leslie said.

"Isn't she?" Brianna fawned.

Janet placed a coffee mug on her desk, then filled it with ten freshly sharpened pencils.

"You can never have too many pencils," she declared, placing each tip-up.

"Won't you poke yourself leaving them that way?" Sophie asked.

"Maybe, but it's better than having a broken pencil tip." Janet shuddered.

Sophie smiled and turned to her belongings. She stuffed the extra money from her father into the top drawer of her desk, then pulled a bag of new notebooks out of her backpack and tossed them on her desk, followed by the welcome folder.

"Don't you just love new school supplies?" Janet sighed.

Sophie eyed Janet's neatly filed notebooks, tucked lovingly into the hutch, then glanced at her own messy bag of notebooks sprawled over her desk.

"Uh, sure," she said with a nervous chuckle. "They're great."

"I agree with you, Janet," said Leslie. She stacked her

composition notebooks on their side, then scrawled her initials onto the spine of each, using a different colored marker for each one. "Makes my 'chi' happy. Or whatever that saying is."

"How did you guys feel about the entrance exam?" Sophie asked, self-consciously straightening her notebooks.

"Oh, it was nerve-wracking!" Leslie said. "How can I show them what I can actually do when I'm so nervous?"

"Same," Janet said. "I hate being put in the spotlight."

"It was a piece of cake," Brianna said, unwrapping a snack cake and taking a huge bite. "You could say I blew them away."

They all laughed.

"What about you, Sophie?" Leslie capped her markers, glancing at Sophie for an answer.

"Well, I felt..." She struggled for the right word. "Known? Um, normal? Accepted. That's it."

All three girls nodded in response.

"Like you finally figured out that what makes you special is also what makes you fit in," offered Janet.

"You're good with words, Janet." Brianna sighed.

"Well, you're something of a comedienne yourself," Janet replied. The girls shared another laugh.

"Did you all get an eyeful of Jeremy?" The girls had been unpacking quietly for a moment, but Brianna's question only seemed to deepen the silence as all three girls blushed.

"I mean, our student guide was okay looking, I guess," Sophie said, remembering Bradley winking at her. "He was probably a senior, though."

"Oh, man," Brianna said, throwing herself dramatically

onto her bed. "Jeremy was like the sunrise. And I mean, like, the sunrise over the Rocky Mountains. That kind of sunrise. Not like a sunrise behind a bunch of crappy gray clouds. We get those a lot where I live in Oregon."

Janet gave her the side-eye.

"What?" Brianna threw a soft wind-ball at Janet. "I'm just trying to be good with words. Like you."

Janet blocked the wind-ball with a stony sheen over her hand.

"Just stick to words like 'cute' or 'hot,' okay?"

"I will say there was one good-lookin' feller. He wasn't a guide or anything, but dadgum." Leslie slapped her mouth, her eyes wide. "Doggone it! My Tennessee is coming out."

Sophie snorted, and soon all three girls were cackling with laughter.

"So, do any of you have Professor Rogers in first block?" Janet gestured at the laminated, color-coded schedule tacked to a corkboard she'd put on the wall next to her desk.

"Yep," said Leslie, who'd draped a Minky blanket over the back of her desk chair and was now sorting her clothes into her dresser.

"What are you talking about?" Brianna was on her third snack in an hour. "I didn't even know we had our schedules already."

"I think it's in the welcome folder," Sophie said, pulling her folder from her hutch. Flipping through the crumpled papers, she finally produced her schedule. "Oh! I do."

"Great!" Janet beamed. "We can all sit next to each other."

"Sure," Sophie said.

"I've got…who was it? Rogers?" Brianna squinted at her paper, which was covered in teeth marks and water spots. "Sorry. Bluebell chewed this up, and it's hard to read."

Janet joined Brianna, adjusting her glasses. "Yep. Looks like all of us are with Professor Rogers in first block." Janet gingerly took Brianna's schedule, grimacing. "I'll...um. Make you a new one."

"Oh, thanks, Janet!" Brianna threw her arms around Janet's neck, nearly knocking her glasses off. "You can make it all pretty like yours."

Janet didn't say anything, but she smiled as she fixed her glasses.

"I can't wait to see what's inside the life building," Sophie said. She'd gotten her desk to a point where she could at least find everything, and her clothes were put away for the most part.

"Why don't we go look?" Brianna brushed some crumbs from her shirt.

Leslie stood up from her desk. "I could use a break from all this labeling."

Janet looked longingly at her folders. "But I just started—"

"It'll still be here when you get back," Brianna said, pushing her toward the door.

"Um…" Janet sighed again. "Okay, but just for a little while."

The four girls headed down the hall and piled into the elevator. Brianna patted her pockets, then smiled, satisfied. "Got my snacks. We're good."

The elevator doors opened as they reached the bottom

floor. Standing outside the doors where another group of four girls.

"Hurry up and get out," said a tall girl with dark, shiny hair that reached her waist. Her amber-colored eyes bore into Sophie's. The toe of her nude-colored high-heeled shoe tapped impatiently. "We need to get upstairs."

Sophie furrowed her brows. Attitude, much? "Okay. Just give us a sec."

Sophie moved to get off the elevator, but indignation crossed the tall girl's perfectly manicured features. She snapped her fingers, and a small flame danced to life in her palm. The two girls next to her gasped softly in admiration.

But one girl with dark braids, standing behind the other three, crossed her arms and rolled her eyes.

"Listen up. I'm not in the best mood, okay? I'm having to share a bathroom with seven other girls, a bedroom with three other girls, and I have NOWHERE to put all my stuff, okay? So just move it along."

The elevator door suddenly began to close. Sophie jumped back. The tall girl's flame went out as she stared at Sophie, shock and anger boiling in her eyes.

For a split second, Sophie watched the girl with the braids, who'd moved closer to the doors. She made eye contact with Sophie and gave a thumbs-up.

"Don't you dare!" The tall girl's palm brightened, and she drew her arm back as if to fling something at Sophie.

The doors closed just as she released her arm.

Sophie hurriedly pressed the button for the second floor.

"Soph." Brianna giggled. "Did you close the door on her?"

Sophie realized she stood nearest the button panel. She shook her head violently. "No. No, it wasn't me. I think the door just timed out or something."

She couldn't shake the image of the girl with the braids giving her a thumbs-up. Had she done it? If she had, it was a brave move on her part. What would the tall girl do to her if she found out?

"Well," said Leslie, barely hiding a smile, "you're gonna be on that girl's hit list."

Sophie sighed. That was just great. She'd already made an enemy, and it wasn't even the first day of classes yet.

But glancing at her smiling roommates, she knew she'd made many more friends. Maybe even the girl with the braids was her friend—or at least united with them against the tall girl's entitled attitude.

She dug in her pocket, feeling for the little green leaf, and smiled. All in all, it hadn't been a horrible start.

CHAPTER THREE

"Dude." Brianna stared wide-eyed at the fire building Sophie had seen on her way in, covered with soot and scorch marks.

Janet hugged her arms nervously. "Let's hope their practice sessions don't often escape. Otherwise," she said, glancing around and noting their position directly in front of the burned front door, "we're directly in the line of fire. Quite literally."

Leslie scooted up the path. "Yeah, I'm just gonna avoid that."

"I wanna go in," said Brianna, her brown eyes alight with curiosity. "Who's in?"

Janet and Leslie both shook their heads.

"Sophie?"

Sophie sighed, then shrugged. "I'll peek inside with you, I suppose." She just hoped Miss Tall Prissy Pants wasn't inside.

As she and Brianna approached the door, someone from within started yelling.

"Put it out, put it out!" A young boy with brown curly hair hurtled out the front door, nearly knocking the girls over. One of his curls was aflame, and he desperately beat at it, then looked around for help.

"Hold still." Leslie pulled out her water bottle, opened the top, and then swirled her fingers, releasing them in the boy's direction.

The water spiraled out of the bottle toward the boy's flaming hair, but the boy took off down the path, screaming even louder.

"Well, heck," Leslie scoffed, letting the water fall useless to the ground.

"I got this," said Brianna. She swung her arms as if hugging the air, then pushed out with both hands. The wind blew past Sophie's ankles, rushing down the path after the boy. The sudden gust shocked him into standing still, and finally, the air rushed past his head and face, putting out the flame.

"You're welcome," Brianna called.

Sophie laughed, then stepped back from the door of the fire building.

"Maybe we should move on?"

"Fine." Brianna huffed. "But just think what might have happened if I hadn't been there."

On they walked until they reached the water building at the edge of Crystal Pond.

"Look at that." Leslie stood back and took it all in, then glanced at the other three girls. "Y'all interested in taking a look?"

"I feel safer about this one," Janet said.

Sophie followed Leslie into the building. To her

surprise, there wasn't water everywhere. The practice rooms, they discovered, were confined to the back of the building nearest the pond. Sophie did notice, however, that large towels were hanging from almost every door they saw.

As they walked upstairs toward the classrooms, Sophie noted several portraits lining the walls of the staircase, each with a silver plaque underneath. She read the names of a few. "Marina Yew, Late Professor of Water Ecology" and "Philip Nettles, Water Combat Instructor Emeritus."

"I've heard of him," Leslie said as they passed Philip Nettles' plaque. "Mom said she had him as an instructor, and he was the best. Hard on you, but the best."

"I wonder what kind of cool professors have had the life gift," Sophie thought aloud.

"One of the greatest was Dr. Kendall Bright," Janet said matter-of-factly. "She was not only the first female Dean of Life, but it was also said that her gift helped save Bernheim Forest from a horrible disease that threatened a huge fraction of its flora."

"Is there anything you *don't* know?" Brianna teased.

Janet pushed her glasses up and gave a smug grin.

After Leslie's curiosity was satisfied, they left the water building and headed up the path toward the air pavilion.

"I like that ours isn't all closed up," Brianna said.

"Ours isn't either," Janet retorted. "It's back toward the edge of Bernheim. It's like a big arena. I mean, not the one that we all practice combat in—"

"But is it a big, beautiful pavilion, though?"

Janet rolled her eyes.

"Didn't think so."

As Janet and Brianna continued arguing, Leslie tilted her head at Sophie.

"Hey. Let's go check out that barn."

Now that she was closer to the top of the gentle hill, she could see past the air pavilion and past life's greenhouse to the barn Leslie had mentioned. It had a little shed or workshop attached to it.

"Do you think that's death's building?"

Leslie shook her head. "Doesn't strike me as deathly."

Sophie shrugged. "Ok. Let's check it out."

It took them a few minutes of walking to reach the barn. Sophie could hear mooing and sheep bleating. The attached workshop building had its door open, and Sophie peered inside as they approached. She was just able to make out a large figure and steam drifting out of the open window beside the door.

"Who's that?" Leslie asked.

"Don't know." Sophie veered toward the workshop. "Let's go see."

The smell of burned plant matter stung Sophie's nose as she entered the doorway. Against the far wall, a tall, stocky man stirred something in a pot on a stove. His back was to the girls, and Sophie took a couple more steps inside.

Shelves full of tools and instruments Sophie had never seen before lined the walls, interspersed with full bookcases. She read the titles of a few books. *Proper Care and Maintenance of Mature Oaks, The Complete Guide to Maple Husbandry,* and *Common Deciduous Pests and How to Control Them* caught her eyes.

A feeling like friendship clicked in Sophie's heart, though she didn't even know the man at the stove. If he cared this much for trees and plants, he *must* be a good person and a kindred spirit.

As they stepped closer to the stove, Sophie noted dozens of bottles, both clear and amber, labeled with peeling, faded paper and scrawled on with illegible handwriting.

"Argh!" the man at the stove screeched, startling Sophie and eliciting a squeal of surprise from Leslie.

He whirled to face them. Sophie glimpsed his bulbous nose and deep-set hazel eyes before he launched into a tirade.

"What on earth are you girls doing in here? Golly gee, can't you see I'm cooking something here? Done burned myself, and now you kids come in here and scare the bejeebies out of me."

"Sorry! We're sorry. We just—"

"I know. Just curious. Like all kids your age." He pointed a dripping wooden spoon at them. "Curiosity killed the cat, you know."

As if in response, a pitiful meow sounded from the corner.

"Well, except that one." The man walked over and scratched a tabby cat behind the ear. The cat stood up, stretched, then limped over to Sophie and Leslie, rubbing against Sophie's leg.

"What's his name?" Sophie picked him up, examining the paw he'd been guarding. A brown burr had gotten stuck between his toe pads, and Sophie murmured to the cat as she gently dug it out.

"Mincemeat," the man replied, watching her with interest.

"Aww, Mincemeat, what an awful name for a cat," she cooed as she pressed her fingers to the injured paw, closing the tiny wound.

"Hey now," said the man. "Named him myself."

"There." Sophie set him on the ground, but Mincemeat continued to rub against her legs, mewing happily.

"Did you just...heal that?" Leslie grinned. "That was cool."

"What'd you do there?" The man bent down to scratch Mincemeat's ears, picking up his paw.

"He had a burr in his foot. I got it out for him and made sure the wound was closed." Sophie shrugged. "My gift is life."

"Ah." The man straightened and gave a nod of appreciation. "Thanks for that. Say, you girls got names?"

"Sophie," said Sophie. "And this is Leslie."

"Name's Roscoe. I'm the caretaker for the animals as well as Thicket Hall."

A surge of excitement rushed through Sophie. "Wow. That's a big job. How do you do it?"

Roscoe herded them toward the door.

"Listen, I'd love to chat some more, but I've got to do the rounds with the animals, and you girls need to get out of my workshop before you touch something you're not supposed to."

"We can help!" Sophie offered. "I want to know more about what you do for the tree."

Roscoe snorted. "You wanna feed horses and clean up after goats just to hear me talk about trees?"

Sophie nodded vigorously.

"I just love trees. They're kind of my thing, you know?

And they're alive in a unique way. They even have their network of roots to communicate with each other. And if one tree is lacking, the others around it will help it. I mean, what other plants do that? Plus, sometimes, I even feel like I can hear them." Sophie laughed, then rubbed her arm self-consciously.

Roscoe and Leslie stared at her as if she'd lost her mind.

She cleared her throat. "Anyway. So, yeah. I'd love to hear what you do for the trees, if that's okay. And I'll help with the animals so you can talk."

Roscoe raised an eyebrow. "Well, you'd be the first person to ever ask me about my work. Most kids just leave me alone, but I can see we share an interest in trees." He coughed. "And what about you?" He glanced at Leslie.

She shrugged. "I'm game, I guess."

Roscoe sighed. "All right."

As they walked through the barn, throwing fresh hay to the horses and gathering eggs from the chickens, Sophie interrogated Roscoe about anything she could think of, but most especially about Thicket Hall and its history.

"The tree's older than anyone can remember," Roscoe said. "I mean, if you count just the rings you can see from the inside, it's got to be at least 700 years old."

Sophie's mouth fell open. She could only imagine how much that tree had seen and experienced, how far its roots traveled, and how deeply they were implanted in the earth.

"When was the school established?" Leslie asked.

"In the late 1800s," Roscoe said, scratching his head as he bent to give the chickens their feed. "Can't remember the exact year, but I'm sure that'll be something you have to memorize for your very first test here."

"So, this tree was already this big over a century ago," Sophie pondered aloud. "Has it kept growing, even though there's an entire school in it?"

"Absolutely it has," Roscoe said. He handed Sophie a bucket of some sort of pellet food and led the girls through the barn to the goats' enclosure. Dozens of little bleating faces clamored against the gate, eyeing the bucket Sophie held. "In fact, my entire job is to make sure that tree keeps growing and stays healthy."

"Oh." Sophie breathed. "How do you maintain a tree so large? Are you a life elemental, too?"

"No." Roscoe looked away from her, examining the goat's water trough, though his dejected tone told Sophie her question struck a nerve. "I just have a green thumb and a passion for oaks."

"You know," Sophie said, handing him the bucket of food, "that's even better than a gift in many cases."

Roscoe looked at her, the hardness in his dark eyes lifting somewhat.

"Yeah, well. I'm good at what I do, and I like it. So that's why they keep me around."

"Um, hi."

Sophie, Leslie, and Roscoe all whirled toward the new voice.

The girl with the braids, the one who'd given Sophie a thumbs-up at the elevator, waved shyly at them. She glanced at Sophie and smiled.

"Sorry. I hope I'm not intruding. I just love animals, and I overheard you all talking while I was saying hi to the horses."

"If one more first-year scares me out of my wits today," grumbled Roscoe, but Sophie touched his arm.

"It's okay. We know her."

"Joy." Roscoe stalked off.

Sophie smiled at the girl. "Don't mind him."

The girl stepped forward and shook Sophie's hand, then Leslie's. "I'm Charlotte. I think we might actually be in the room next to yours." She jerked her head toward the entrance to the barn, where two more girls were making their way past the horse's stalls. "I met Brianna and Janet already."

"Hey, guys," Brianna called.

"I'm Leslie," Leslie said, addressing Charlotte.

"I'm Sophie," Sophie added with a smile. "Nice to meet you, Charlotte."

Charlotte gave a wide smile.

"Trust me. It's way nicer to meet you. My roommates are..." She rolled her eyes. "Well, not like you guys."

"Yeah, what's with that Olivia girl?" Brianna said. "Thinks she owns the place or something."

"Or something is right," Charlotte said. "Comes from old money and an old, well-established fire family. Headmistress Case doesn't care. I heard Olivia complain about the whole thing—her parents asked for special treatment, and Headmistress turned that down."

Sophie stifled a snort. "No wonder she was in a bad mood."

"We're gonna go check out the earth building," Janet said, then smiled at Charlotte and waved. "It was nice to meet you. We should hang out again sometime."

"Agreed," said Charlotte.

"I'm coming with y'all," Leslie said. "No offense, Soph, but I'm getting tired of smelling horse manure."

Sophie laughed. "No worries, Leslie. Thanks for coming with me."

The girls waved, and soon it was just Sophie and Charlotte in the barn, with Roscoe still bustling past from time to time.

"So, what's your gift?" Charlotte asked.

"Life," Sophie said.

Charlotte's brown eyes lit up. "Mine, too! I especially love horses. Back in Lexington, we had a horse farm. I was always out making sure they were shod correctly, giving them baths, healing up any little wounds I'd find. Made a lot of equine friends that way. Kind of why I ended up wandering in here." She chuckled.

"I always loved driving by those horse farms. Just so picturesque, and then you'd see the horses running in their big open fields." Sophie sighed happily.

Charlotte nodded. "My favorite place to be."

"Well, I was just asking Roscoe about Thicket Hall. He takes care of it."

Charlotte's eyes widened. "What? You can't be serious. One person taking care of that gigantic tree?"

"Yeah, and my job would be easier if you kids would stay out of my hair. Or at least help like you said you would." Roscoe bumped into Sophie as he passed by, hard enough to make it seem purposeful.

"Sorry!" Sophie grabbed a rake.

"I'll help, too," said Charlotte, grabbing a horse brush.

The girls worked alongside Roscoe in amiable silence,

raking the dirty hay out of the horse's stalls and giving them all a good brush down.

"You know," said Roscoe, "the barn workers will be awfully glad you did all this for them."

Sophie paused, looking up to give Roscoe a questioning look.

"You didn't think I did all this by myself, did you?" Roscoe let out a good-natured guffaw.

"But why did you let us help you if it's someone else's job?" Charlotte asked.

Roscoe shrugged. "Sophie here offered. I wasn't gonna turn it down. Besides," he glanced at his watch, "they don't come in for another hour or two."

Sophie rolled her eyes and moved to continue raking.

The next instant, she dropped the rake and took off running for the barn door.

"I didn't mean to upset you!" Called Roscoe.

"Sophie!" Charlotte cried, running after her. "What's the matter?"

Sophie felt fear, raw and primal, coursing through her. She needed to find the source and fast. Whatever it was needed her *right now.*

She rounded the corner of the barn, turning left, then wheeling back and turning right. There, about twenty yards ahead, two small animals, tails straight up and hairy, back arched.

Sophie recognized the tabby cat instantly. Mincemeat. The other animal, a much larger raccoon, clearly had the upper hand if the terror radiating from Mincemeat was anything to go by. If she didn't act fast, Mincemeat would become mincemeat.

She noted a few tall sprigs of grass near the animals. She stretched out her hand and twisted her fingers upward, calling the roots of the dormant daffodils to dig deep and its leaves and shoots to reach high.

Slowly and dazedly, the daffodils obeyed her, sprouting into life right in front of the raccoon's face. It sniffed, then sneezed, backing away slightly. Its tail twitched in confusion.

Sophie pushed harder, and the grass around the daffodils began to spiral up toward the sky.

Now thoroughly freaked, the raccoon backed up, then took off running around the barn.

Sophie closed her fists and her eyes, bringing the flow of magic to a stop, and breathed deeply. If she tried to stop it too quickly, it could backfire, so she pushed Mincemeat's lingering terror out of her mind and focused on tranquility, slowing, then stopping, like gradually turning off a faucet.

Releasing a breath, she opened her eyes. The plants had stopped growing. The tall grasses and weeds, along with the out-of-season daffodils, made her chuckle. If anyone happened across this patch of flora, they'd be sure to leave scratching their heads.

"Sophie. That was amazing!" Charlotte giggled.

Sophie smiled. It had been pretty cool, hadn't it?

Mincemeat slunk through the weeds and wound himself around Sophie's ankles. She lifted him into her arms and scratched under his chin, earning her the rich, velvety sound of Mincemeat's satisfied purring. He licked her fingers with his scratchy tongue and looked directly into her eyes.

Sophie stared back into those little blue cat eyes. Mincemeat didn't blink, didn't move, for several seconds, just stared. As if he were trying to tell her something, trying to thank her.

"What's all this?" Roscoe rounded the corner of the barn, noting the daffodils and tall grass with furrowed brows. "Listen, if you want to make my daffodils sprout, you need to wait until spring."

Mincemeat leapt from Sophie's arms and ran to Roscoe. Sophie shook her head, clearing away the excitement of what had just happened—and the mystery of Mincemeat's staring.

"Everything good, Sophie?" Charlotte touched her arm gently.

Sophie took in a deep breath and smiled. "Yeah, I'm good. Sorry about the daffodils, Roscoe. A raccoon had Mincemeat here trapped, so I did what I had to."

Mincemeat seemed to meow his affirmation. Roscoe picked him up and scratched the tabby's ears, then looked at Sophie, a question in his deep-set eyes.

"You're an interesting one," he said. "Twice today, you've helped my cat, and I had no idea he needed me."

"I'm also apparently the only one who's ever asked you about your job," Sophie said. "So yeah. I guess I'm a weirdo."

Roscoe chuckled, still holding Mincemeat.

"I guess you are."

CHAPTER FOUR

Norma Case strode briskly into her office. Three professors, the three she most trusted, followed closely behind—Violet Rogers, Professor of History, Byrne Murphy, Professor of Mixed Elemental Cooperation, and Clarice Nelson, Professor of Elemental Sciences.

To all outward appearances, this wasn't a special meeting. She called this squad of professors together at the beginning of each school year, and this year was no different.

But it was different in ways Norma hadn't quite put her finger on yet.

Once all three professors were inside, Norma nodded to Byrne, who touched his fingers to the door.

Interlocking stones sprung up and covered the door like a turtle's shell except for the lock. It then spread to the walls, essentially creating a soundproof room where they could speak without fear of being overheard.

As a final touch, Norma turned her key in the lock, then sat behind her desk.

Clarice collapsed onto the loveseat near the window.

"I don't know about you all, but I'm *exhausted.* All this first-day stuff..." she yawned. "Do we *have* to have this meeting today?"

"The answer is yes, we're all tired, and yes, we must have this meeting *today,*" Norma said calmly, though her fingers clenched in anger at Clarice's carefree attitude. "It's when we are off guard—a.k.a., tired and extremely busy with other things—that catastrophe could happen."

"There've been rumors in town," Violet Rogers added. "They say there's something happening under Thicket Hall. They think maybe this year will be the year it'll be compromised, that maybe someone will try and hurt it. Maybe one of the first years."

"There are rumors like that every year," scoffed Clarice. "Nothing ever happens." She pressed a hand to her mouth, failing to suppress another yawn.

Norma whirled her fingers, blowing a sharp gust of air through Clarice's wispy bangs.

Clarice sat up straighter, scowling.

"That's right," Norma said. "Nothing ever happens. And I'd like to keep it that way. Hence why we're here."

"Yes, Headmistress." Clarice folded her arms and examined the embroidery on the arm of her sleeve.

"What else can we do to help Roscoe?" Violet asked. "It's hard to send help when so few of us know the true purpose behind what he's doing. If anyone we don't trust completely gets too nosy..." Violet shuddered. "That's information we obviously don't want to get out. Anyone who knew how to take care of Thicket Hall could also harm Thicket Hall irreparably."

"Well, it's no secret that Thicket Hall is a treasure," Byrne said. "It could be as simple as asking his barn hands to be vigilant. If they see something, say something. That kind of thing. They wouldn't have to know what or why. Just anything that seemed threatening."

"Yes," Norma said, "Except the biggest threats to Thicket Hall are the ones we can't see. Things like ancient highways of power unable to be contained—or someone discreetly rendering them unstable with powerful magic, whether that be life *or* death magic, as in the past, or any of the others."

All three professors nodded soberly.

"That's *why* we keep the secret, of course," Violet added. She stood and plucked a twig from Norma's potted bonsai. "If anyone knew what the tree does, the raw power it contains, this world would quickly be turned upside down." The twig caught a spark from Violet's fingertips and burst into flame. Violet sprinkled its ashes for effect. "Lest we forget that a mere five years after its establishment, The School of Roots and Vines suffered its most famous and devastating breach."

"Spare us, Violet," Clarice said, waving her hand. "We know that story already."

"It bears repeating," Violet snapped.

Byrne looked pleadingly at Norma.

"Now, my honored guests," Norma chided. "History will repeat itself if not learned and heeded." She nodded at Violet. "Go ahead."

"Thank you, Headmistress." Violet cleared her throat.

Byrne and Clarice exchanged weary glances.

"In the year 1896, one mistake caused more chaos and

destruction at the School of Roots and Vines than any year before or since. A talented senior death student, under the guidance of his power-hungry father and with the help of several of his friends of varying elemental skills, struck the tree's roots from within the Secret Cavern. They'd learned the location of the Cavern from a simple conversation with a careless groundskeeper back when the tree's importance was common knowledge to all staff."

Violet stared hard into each of their faces as she continued. "This breach of confidentiality led to the deaths of two professors, three of the students, and the largest outbreak of raw elementals in this state's recorded history. It took the entire staff and faculty, not to mention half of the graduating class, to contain the outbreak and prevent the elementals from destroying Bardstown. This is on top of the havoc wreaked by the tree's inability to contain and filter the channels of magic beneath it due to its wounds. Fire elementals suddenly found their magic directing the water in the pond. Air students would try to blow debris off a survivor, only to light the debris on fire."

Violet shook her head sadly as she paced. "This school was almost shut down in its infancy due to the Elemental Safety and Containment Board's investigations. All of this is from *one* absentminded disclosure of what should have been top-secret information. *That's* why we have this meeting every year. *That* is why I repeat this story every year without fail. To forget is to let our vigilance grow cold." She gave an extra hard glance to Clarice, who dipped her head.

Norma nodded in thanks to Violet, who took her seat next to Byrne.

"I will add to Violet's reminder of the past that there are also present signs and symptoms we shouldn't dismiss," Norma said, steepling her fingers in front of her on the desk. "It's true there are rumors every year. This year, they seem more…detailed. More precise. It's troubling, to say the least." She glanced at Violet. "There are actually many parallels between the rumors this year and the events you just described. Some of them include ambitious first-year students, from which there are plenty to choose this year. Some involve trespassers from outside of the elemental community. Some even suggest there is a secret about the tree, hidden from the public."

"That's hitting dangerously close to home," Byrne said, shifting in his seat.

"Correct," Norma said. "I don't advocate for adding more personnel to the list of confidantes. The more people know, the higher the risk grows of secrets getting out. It's becoming clear we need to up our protections and our surveillance."

"One thing we can do is, like Byrne said earlier, just having faculty—cooks, student guides, everybody—watch out for anything or anyone suspicious around the tree." Clarice shrugged. "It may not be perfect, but it's better than the four of us having to constantly be on watch."

"Then maybe we—the four of us and Roscoe—can focus more on the unseen threats," added Violet. "We can be on guard for elements getting out of alignment, powers suddenly becoming stronger than students can control—things like that."

Norma nodded. It wasn't a perfect plan, but it would

free up their bandwidth, and hopefully, create a protective community environment around the tree.

"I like this plan," Norma said. "I've been protecting Thicket Hall and the Bardstown area for a *very* long time. I'd rather we not fail now."

Byrne leaned over to Violet, a playful glint in his eye. "You brave enough to ask her how long?" he whispered, not realizing Norma could hear every word.

Norma gave a mysterious half-smile but didn't say a word.

"You mentioned we have some talented first years," Clarice said, looking interested for the first time. "And we've also got our annual elemental skills contest coming up before winter break." Clarice clapped her hands, smiling excitedly. "Who stood out to everyone during entrance exams?"

"Olivia Wright," said Byrne immediately. "Her family's been coming here for several decades. Snooty, but very talented." He grinned. "I saw her absolutely destroy some of the props in the fire building practice room. To be fair, though, she looked pretty worked up about something."

Norma snorted. "Likely didn't get her way. Reminds me of her mother."

"Simon Green is a remarkable water warrior," Clarice said. "Most of the other kids in the exam were just so-so with their pressure and temperature on the strike test. Simon, though..." she chuckled. "His strike would have easily blistered his opponent."

Norma nodded. "I remember him. First-generation student. Shy kid. Wouldn't want to get on his bad side, though."

"What about Sophia Briggs?" Violet put in. "Life elemental. Her dad Walter went to school here—was in my class if I remember correctly. He was fairly talented himself, but Sophia's rapid-climbing vines knocked the socks off the other kids'." Violet paused. "I mean that literally. Her vines knocked the other kids' vines off the walls."

Clarice and Byrne chuckled.

Norma paused. An image of a dark-haired girl gazing at her from the base of Thicket Hall jogged her memory.

"Yes. Sophie." She recalled seeing the flowers in the central garden leaning into Sophie's touch, as well as a stray wind that had blown a leaf from Thicket Hall right onto Sophie's cheek.

What Norma knew, though, was that Thicket Hall *never* dropped its leaves. Not even in the fall and winter.

Norma chewed her lip.

Clarice and Violet exchanged worried glances. Norma *never* chewed her lip.

"She'll be one to watch," Norma said, staring pensively at the wall. "For sure."

She took a deep breath, cleared her head, and stood.

"I think we've accomplished what we needed to here." She nodded at the three professors. "I'll be sending out notices to all faculty and staff to be vigilant and report anything suspicious as soon as possible."

"And we'll be reminding student guides and mentors of the same," Byrne said.

Norma nodded. "Meeting dismissed."

Byrne's protective barrier disappeared under his touch, and the professors went back to their offices and duties.

Norma sat staring at the wall, unable to shake the image of a dark-haired girl pocketing the leaf from Thicket Hall.

How could she have forgotten Sophie so easily?

She *was* getting up there in age. Could it be her mind was starting to deteriorate? She frowned, remembering Byrne's not-so-quiet comment to Violet. For so long, she'd wrapped her mysterious wisdom around herself like a cloak. It had protected her, Thicket Hall, and the town for decades.

But now, with so many variables, so many rumors, so much new talent, and Thicket Hall's blatant gesture of favor to a talented incoming freshman…

She rubbed her temples, heaving an exhausted sigh. She was simply tired from the day. Her mind would not let her rest.

Not now, when so much was at stake.

Because if it failed her now… If *she* failed now…

It could cost them everything.

CHAPTER FIVE

Later that evening, Sophie and her roommates joined the noisy crowd of students filtering toward Thicket Hall for dinner. Sophie's heart beat high with anticipation. She felt for the leaf in her pocket, smiling as she approached the gargantuan double doors of the entrance.

"How does a tree get so big?" Marveled Charlotte, who'd chosen to walk with Sophie instead of her roommates.

"Years and years of patience, sun, and rain," Sophie replied.

They stepped inside, and the chatty teens fell silent. It was as if they'd been swallowed by the tree. Tall walls of worn, polished oak traveled up as far as the eye could see. The circular floor covered an area the size of two football fields. Centuries-old rings adorned the floor, visible through the polished resin flooring that covered it. Sophie lost count of them as she walked. As her eyes traveled the tree's hollow core, she saw several spiral staircases curving up and away, presumably to the classrooms and teacher's offices.

"Wow," she breathed. She wanted more than anything to stop and touch the walls and take in the warm, earthy scent of the hall forever, but the students kept moving toward a cluster of circular wooden tables near the center of the hall.

Along one of the curving walls, to her left, she spotted more plaques like the ones she'd seen in the water building. Instead of professors, these faces belonged to students.

The plaque closest to the entrance sported a young girl with a smug grin, twirling a pinwheel made of water. Sophie tried to get a closer look at the name on the plaque, but the tall young man walking next to her paused in front of it, then stalked away and scowled.

"It should have been you, Marcus!"

Laughter broke out, and the scowling young man stopped in his tracks and whipped furiously toward the voice.

"You were robbed, dude!" Cried another voice. Marcus peered over the crowd, rolling up his sleeves. He whipped off his hood, revealing blond, almost white hair parted so that a dramatic sweep of bangs covered one eye. The other eye, a deep, near-black color, scanned the students' faces, looking for the speaker.

"Say it to my face, loser!" Marcus called. Two spiked wristbands emphasized his angry, clenched fists.

"Just goes to show you death doesn't always win," taunted someone else.

A roar of laughter erupted from the crowd of teens, and Marcus stormed off, brushing past Sophie as he left.

She gasped. Where his arm had brushed hers, soot-like darkness had flared up on her skin. It had already started to fade, but the pain lingered like a bee sting.

"Wonder what that was all about," Janet said, shifting her glasses to look at Sophie's skin. "Sheesh, look what he did!"

Sophie frowned, rubbing her arm. She'd encountered angry death magic before, back at the public school, but this Marcus kid either had a lot of talent or a lot of anger. Or both. "I guess he lost a contest or something. No need to take it out on everyone else, though."

Once she'd gathered herself from that encounter—and stopped gawking at the interior of the hall—Sophie eventually settled at a table with Charlotte, her roommates, and a group of first-year boys. Each place at the table was set with stone dinnerware painted deep hunter-green, with black cloth napkins and silverware.

"It's real silver," Janet said, picking up one of the forks and closing her eyes. "I can feel it."

Sophie took the only spot left, the one between Janet and one of the boys. His sandy blond hair fell in attractive waves around his ears and face, and he smiled politely at her as she pulled out the seat next to his.

"Hi," he said, extending his hand. His bright green eyes twinkled in the warm light of the hall. "My name's Peter."

"I'm Sophie," she said, sitting and shaking his hand. The way his eyes followed her as she shook out her napkin and folded it in her lap made her cheeks warm, but he said nothing else as the food was served and they began to eat.

The dinner was old-fashioned and meant to comfort. Piles of mashed potatoes and fried chicken, a Kentucky classic, filled their plates. They could also choose macaroni and cheese or green beans, and for dessert, it was announced they could choose from Derby Pie or Sweet Pecan Pie.

Sophie lost herself in the delicious meal. It was a traditional meal she was used to but sharing it with her new friends in this beautiful, gargantuan hall filled up something in her heart.

"Are you new, too?" Peter asked Sophie after they'd been served their pie.

"Yeah," she said breathlessly. She cleared her throat and took a deep breath. "So, what's your gift?"

"Earth," he said with a nonchalant eye roll. "Good old dust and rocks."

Sophie giggled, then gestured toward Janet. "She's earth, too."

Janet gave a shy wave, then resumed her conversation with Brianna.

Sophie stared down at her plate, pushing the last bite of pie with her fork. She'd never felt so at a loss for words, but Peter's green eyes wouldn't stop following her every move.

"What's your gift?" he pressed after another silence.

"Life," she replied, then blinked, startled, as something fluttered against her face and landed in her lap. Looking down, a butterfly, one wing crumpled, struggled to crawl up her shirt.

"Poor little dude," Peter said.

Sophie picked up the butterfly, stroking its injured wing. Taking a deep breath, she released it gently over the butterfly's wing. As the butterfly flapped against her breath, the wing's creases smoothed, and the dead spots filled in with color.

She lifted the butterfly in her hand as it moved its wings up and down, both of them now whole.

"Wow," Peter breathed. "That's so cool."

The butterfly flapped, took off into the air, and fluttered away. Sophie met Peter's awed gaze, then blushed.

"You must do that a lot," he said. "It must feel so great to be able to help animals like that."

Sophie nodded.

Peter sighed. "I can't do much of anything except, you know, smash things."

Sophie laughed. "Earth is much more than smashing things. I'm sure you're great at lots of things. Building, carving, that kind of thing. Life needs earth, too. Where would this tree be without it?"

Peter grinned at her.

"I guess you're right. Life and earth do need each other."

Their gazes lingered, and Sophie's face practically burned.

"Um." She stood abruptly and grabbed her glass. "Does anyone need anything from the drink table?"

A chorus of negatives resounded from the teens at the table, and she hurried off, fanning her face. She had to get away, at least for a second, and maybe splash some ice water on her cheeks. No way was she falling for a guy she had just met, no matter how deep his eyes were or how cute his hair was.

She filled her glass with ice and sweet tea, dabbing an ice cube along her cheekbones and patting it dry with a napkin. She couldn't risk messing up her makeup.

Turning to go back to her table, she stuffed more napkins in her pocket, looking down to make sure she didn't jostle her phone.

"Oh!" She bumped hard into a figure, and her tea splashed down the front of a Louis Vuitton patterned dress.

Scattered titters rose from the tables nearest Sophie.

Sophie glanced up at the girl's face, and dread filled her chest.

Olivia glared back at her, shaking with rage. "You again!"

"I'm sorry!" Sophie backed away, then dug out the napkins she'd just stuffed in her pocket. "Here, I'll help—"

"You think it wasn't bad enough I had to take the *stairs* to my dorm because of you? And now this!" Olivia shook the excess liquid off her shirt and snatched the napkins from Sophie. The liquid was evaporating fast—Sophie could see tendrils of smoke coming from Olivia's fingers, face, and hair.

"Um. I can get some more napkins? I'm so sorry—"

Olivia scooped one hand, forming a fireball in her palm. Her dark eyes glowed red, though she shifted her gaze to the security guard near the drink table.

"If you don't get out of my sight," she hissed at Sophie, "*right now—*"

Sophie took the hint. She darted around Olivia and dashed back to her table with her half-empty tea glass.

The entire table was staring at her as she returned.

"You all right, Sophie?" Leslie asked, eyeing her tea glass. "I thought you were getting more tea."

"I did," Sophie said, sliding into her seat and ducking

her head. Might as well keep a low profile so Olivia wouldn't come to hunt her down. "It just ended up all over Olivia's dress."

Charlotte burst out laughing.

"That's twice in one day!" She howled. "Ooh, girl. You are enemy number one in her book."

"Don't remind me," Sophie said, remembering Olivia's fireball. She knew if Olivia ever caught her alone, she'd end up burned. Badly.

"You want me to go get your tea?" Peter offered.

Sophie smiled but shook her head. "No, I'm good."

She didn't know how she kept straying into the path of Olivia's rage. It wasn't like she was trying. And Olivia was honestly just a big bully, throwing a hissy fit because she didn't get her way if Charlotte was to be believed.

But Sophie also wasn't willing to put anyone else in the line of fire. Much less her new crush.

She glanced at Peter, and he looked back at her, giving her an encouraging smile.

At least she'd made more friends than enemies so far, she thought.

CHAPTER SIX

Marcus Jenkins was *not* going to be forgotten because of a lousy third-year water elemental. Not now, and not *ever.*

He stood in the drab, concrete workshop of the death elemental building with his hands pressed firmly against what appeared to be a jet-black crystal, though it reflected very little light. He channeled his anger and destructive gift of death into it, feeding its hungry darkness.

His death spike was nearly finished now. All summer he'd worked on it, giving it form, feeding it death energy from his gift and whatever he could find, even decaying animals and trees he'd found in the forest around his home.

And there was plenty more dead matter to gather strength from here at the school. He'd helped himself to everything rotten he could find from the outskirts of the forest, from the compost pile outside of life's greenhouse to even within the barn, where a female goat had birthed a stillborn kid. He frowned. That one had been gruesome, but he was on a mission.

He paused his work, opening his hands to admire the spike. It barely glinted in the dim glow of dusk filtering through the window. Dark spirals swirled and pulsated through it.

Marcus smiled. They couldn't ignore his talent now. They wouldn't be able to. His spike was finally finished, just in time for the first week of the new year.

He carefully wrapped the spike in a burlap pouch coated with stone. It would keep the spike from inadvertently draining his personal life energy away from him as he carried it.

He looked around the workshop, grumbling until he found the second tool he needed for his task, a simple iron mallet.

Then, shoving the mallet and pouch into the pocket of his hoodie, he pulled up his hood, tucking his platinum blonde hair underneath. Making sure the hallway was clear, he slipped out into the hall, out of the death elemental building, and stole across the lawn toward Thicket Hall.

Dozens of students were heading back to their dorms after dinner as he approached the great tree. He simply ducked in and out of the streams of people, head down, hands tucked in his hoodie pockets, trying to keep casual.

Then, rounding the tree toward the back of the hall, the buzz of their chatter fell away, and he was alone once again.

In the presence of the huge tree, his heart began to race. It was almost as if he could feel the tree's question, feel its fear and unease as he approached one of its gnarled roots.

"Nothing personal, tree," he said, trying not to look up at its magnificent crown of branches and deep green leaves.

Still, he hesitated. A warning seemed to whistle through the branches in a gentle breeze: *Don't do it.*

He gulped, gathering his resolve, and drew the mallet and spike out of his pocket. A few furtive glances left and right told him no one was around.

He acted quickly, ripping the burlap pouch away from the spike and choosing a place in the earth close to where the massive trunk and root met in the soil.

Then, before he could second-guess himself, with a few quick strikes of his mallet, he hammered the spike deep into the ground.

The breeze picked up, then gusted, whipping the hood off Marcus' head.

Startled, he snatched the pouch and mallet from the ground, tugged his hood up, and ran for the boys' dorms.

That spike would do its dark work, poisoning the roots of the tree and stealing the life from it little by little. His work would be evident within a week or so, and then they'd know not to cross him, not to count him out.

He'd never play second fiddle. He refused. And if he had to kill Thicket Hall to make his point clear…

He glanced back at the great tree, a buried sense of shame rising to the surface of his mind. Thicket Hall didn't deserve this.

But anger clouded his heart and burned in his veins as he remembered every taunt and insult he'd endured during his first year at the school.

He looked ahead once more as he ran, refusing to look back.

He'd kill a thousand Thicket Halls if it meant he'd never be ridiculed again. If it meant he got his dignity back.

If it meant victory for death.

CHAPTER SEVEN

Sophie left Thicket Hall with her roommates after dinner, her stomach full and her mind spinning. They joined the chatty throng of students all heading back to the dorms, and Sophie glanced behind to say goodnight to Thicket Hall.

"See you tomorrow," she whispered under her breath.

It had only been her first day, and she'd had so many new adventures already—meeting Roscoe and saving Mincemeat, meeting her new roommates, upsetting Olivia not once but *twice*, and to top it all off, meeting Peter at dinner and gazing into his emerald eyes.

She felt her cheeks blossoming with heat again and tried to put Peter out of her mind.

"So, Sophie," Leslie said, playfully bumping into her arm. "What's the deal with you and Peter?"

"What do you mean?" Sophie cleared her throat.

"I saw you blushing just now. And I saw that butterfly trick you pulled at supper. That's who you were thinking about, wasn't it?"

"No," Sophie lied, letting some of her dark hair fall between her and Leslie.

"Quit bothering her, Les," Brianna said. "I saw you with Vince."

Leslie whirled. "Look, he was just nice, that's all."

"Mmhmm," Janet said, walking in step with Sophie and Leslie. "Right."

"That chicken, though," said Leslie, patting her stomach. "I mean, my mama—bless her heart—my mama doesn't even make chicken that good."

Sophie nodded in agreement, and the other girls murmured their assent.

"I loved the pie," Brianna said. She dug in her purse and pulled out something wrapped in a greasy napkin. "I even saved me a piece."

"Where are you gonna keep that?" Janet asked, eyeing the pie with disgust.

"Who said anything about keeping it?" Brianna unwrapped it and took a bite.

Janet rolled her eyes.

Dusk was falling as they rounded the tree and headed toward the dorms. The girls fell silent. Sophie rubbed her eyes. Brianna had even put away her pie and was now yawning as they walked.

"I don't know about y'all, but I'm beat," Leslie said. "I'm fixin' to take me a shower and hit the sack."

"'Fixin'?'" Janet threw Leslie a confused look. "What on earth—"

"Look, it's a Southern way of saying 'about to,'" Leslie explained.

Janet pushed her glasses up the bridge of her nose. "Interesting."

The elevator ride to the third floor was quiet, and Sophie was grateful, recalling the last time they'd used the elevator. As they approached their room, though, the raucous, shrill laughter from the room next to theirs had them glancing at each other, incredulous.

"You'd think there was a zoo in there," Janet scoffed.

"Let's hope they don't keep that up all night," Brianna said, frowning.

Sophie unlocked their door and headed straight for the bathroom. The laughter from next door echoed more loudly in the bathroom than it had in the hallway. And when she flipped on the switch, she heaved an exasperated sigh.

Makeup palettes, hair dryers, cans of hair spray, and more cotton swabs than she could count littered the countertops of both double sinks on both sides of the bathroom. On one side, the side she'd thought belonged to the room next door, it was clear that Olivia had set up her salon. All of her bags had her initials monogrammed in glittering letters. And she hadn't bothered to clean anything up. Hence the mess from the other girls on what was supposed to be their side of the bathroom.

"Really?!" Janet's eyes bulged as she walked in behind Sophie. Her brows furrowed, and her hands clenched. "Okay. This is not cool." She glanced to the other side of the sink, where Olivia's pink bags sparkled in the light.

Janet, fixating her glare on those monogrammed bags, began to shake. Her clenched fists began to turn gray and harden, and her eyes glowed a warm green.

"Whoa, girl!" Sophie put both hands on Janet's shoulders. She'd never imagined Janet could get so angry. "Look at my eyes, Janet. We can't just—"

"I'm going to put an end to this," Janet growled. She pulled away from Sophie and headed straight for the room next door's entrance to the bathroom.

"Uh, Janet? Janet! Not a great idea!" Sophie ran after her, putting herself between Janet and the door.

"Janet! Babe, calm down!" Brianna rushed in, sending a gust of air swirling around Janet's face. Janet shook her hair, distracted, and the green glow faded.

Leslie came next, and the three girls formed a blockade at the door.

"Let's not forget our fiery friend." Leslie, placing both hands on Janet's face, looked deep into her eyes. "Girl. I know it's maddening, but we gotta chill." Leslie then took Janet's stony hands.

Janet, looking back into her eyes, nodded, and the green glow lessened even more.

Sophie assured Janet she wasn't going to get a fireball to the face, headed to their room's double sink, and started to clear away the mess. Her anger renewed as she threw away what were clearly used cotton balls and swabs, and she wasn't as careful as she normally was when moving eyeshadow palettes around. If one of them broke, she didn't care. They shouldn't have left their stuff on someone else's sinks. She took all the stuff and dumped it on the counter with Olivia's things.

With their counter cleared, her anger began to cool.

Janet wandered over to a sink and washed her face. She'd become quiet, even more so than usual.

"Sorry, Sophie," she muttered as she dried her face off. "I don't know what came over me."

"Righteous anger," Sophie said, patting Janet's shoulder. "It's all right. I think we all feel the same. We just didn't want anything bad to happen."

"For sure," Brianna said, bumping Janet with her hip as she brushed her teeth. "Girl, remind me not to get on your bad side."

Janet chuckled.

The other door to the bathroom opened, and they all turned as one.

"Hey." The girl smiled and waved.

Sophie let out a relieved sigh. It was just Charlotte.

She closed the door quickly behind her. "I was just coming to clean up March and Sheila's stuff."

"Don't worry about it," Sophie said, jerking her head toward the other counter. "We took care of it."

Charlotte glanced over and stifled a snort.

"You sure did."

Sophie suddenly gasped. If Olivia found out… "I'm sorry. I don't want you to get in trouble."

Charlotte raised an eyebrow, folding her arms defiantly.

"Um, you talk like that girl has any sort of power over me." She shook her head. "Most likely, Sheila or March would get yelled at. Olivia barely knows I'm here."

The door opened again, and this time Sophie's stomach filled with dread.

"Why are people talking about me in here?" Olivia glanced at Charlotte dismissively. "I hope you're not gossiping about me."

Charlotte shook her head. "No. Just chatting with our neighbors."

Olivia gave each girl in the room a once-over, stopping when she came to Sophie. Her brow furrowed, and her mouth dropped open.

"I hope this isn't some kind of sick joke," she hissed. "Tell me you're not next door."

Sophie shrugged. "I am." She added under her breath, "Unfortunately."

Olivia crossed her arms, shaking her head.

"No. No, this isn't going to work. Either you have to go, or I'm requesting to be moved." Olivia glanced at the double sink, noticing the piles of makeup on top of her bags. Her hands began to steam. She stormed over and started throwing makeup onto the floor, wiping the colored dust off her pink bags.

"I've told those two to keep their stuff off mine!" She paused, looking at the other side of the bathroom to the girls' cleared-off double sink.

Her eyes narrowed again.

"Which one of you did this?"

"Look, Olivia." Sophie stepped forward, her hands shaking. "We had to make space so we could use the sinks. Maybe you should share your side of the bathroom with the rest of your roommates."

Olivia calmed instantly, stepping slowly toward Sophie with a sickeningly sweet smile.

"And maybe you should learn some respect," she said, snapping her fingers on both hands. Flames engulfed her fingers, and red-orange flecks lit up in her eyes.

Janet ran forward then, to Sophie's shock, and stepped

into the gap between Olivia and Sophie. She formed plates of stone armor on her skin and turned one fist and forearm into a stone hammer.

"Not a chance," she hissed at Olivia.

Leslie and Brianna flanked Sophie, Leslie spinning a vortex of water in the air in front of her, Brianna feeding the vortex with rotating air until it became a formidable waterspout.

Olivia stared at them, taking a step back.

"We don't want any trouble. We just want to be left alone," Sophie said.

"For real though, Olivia," Charlotte put in, "you'll need your beauty sleep for tomorrow."

Olivia threw her a withering glare, but the flames on her fingers went out. She forced a smile.

"Well. That little display entertained me. This time."

She glared at Sophie as the girls released their magic.

"But I'll be asking Headmistress to move one of us. Tomorrow. So don't think I'm letting this go."

Olivia turned and stalked off into her room, slamming the bathroom door behind her.

Charlotte rolled her eyes. "Unbelievable. Like always."

Sophie smiled at her roommates as they each patted her shoulder and gave each other high-fives. They'd done it. They'd fended off the firestorm, at least for tonight.

"Showed her, didn't we?" Janet said.

"Sure did." Leslie's eyes glittered with glee. "I don't think she liked the look of that waternado we made, Bri."

"That was pretty cool," agreed Charlotte. "I was about to find me a hiding spot if crap went down."

The five of them shared a laugh, and as the night wore

on and their tiredness returned, they each found their bed, by now thoroughly exhausted.

Sophie was tired down to her bones, but her mind kept swirling with thoughts, trying to process everything she'd seen, heard, and learned. After several minutes of tossing and turning—and listening to Bri talk to Bluebell in her sleep—she went to the window and sat on the ledge, stroking the plant her mother had sung to that afternoon. It welcomed her touch, climbing hungrily up her fingers.

As she sat, she stared up at the circle of sky overhead that could be seen beyond the treetops, now fully darkened and glittering with stars. She found a few she knew and named them. There was the Summer Triangle, with bright Vega dazzling in its blue-white hue, and Altair and Deneb. Their familiar light soothed her thoughts, and she lost herself in counting all the tiny stars in between that she could never see from her suburban home in Louisville.

Movement on the lawn tore her eyes from the sky and focused her gaze on a tiny moving figure—a cat chasing something across the grass. She smiled. It was likely Mincemeat.

But further on, running toward Roscoe's barn, two figures she didn't recognize crossed the lawn with a bobbing electric lantern. Their flowing cloaks, similar to the one she'd seen Headmistress Case wearing, told her they were professors.

She tilted her head as their silhouettes disappeared over the rise of the hill. What were they doing out so late and in such a hurry? She hoped Roscoe was okay.

Sleep tugged at her eyes, making them heavy, and she resolved to try and check on Roscoe the next day after her classes. For now, while she could finally get her thoughts to calm down, she would curl up under her quilt and drift off to the sound of her roommates' gentle snoring.

Roscoe ushered the two professors into his workshop and shut the door, locking it tightly behind them.

Headmistress Norma Case pulled her hood down.

"Thanks for coming on such short notice, Headmistress," Roscoe said. "You told me to let you know if there was anything fishy going on, and—"

"What is it?" Norma said.

Roscoe rubbed the back of his neck.

"To be honest, ma'am, I'm not entirely sure. All I know is when I was laying down some new mulch around the back part of the Hall, some of it started turning gray or black. And only in one particular spot."

"Did you look under the mulch at the spot?" The other professor, Byrne Murphy, spoke next. "What's it look like?"

"It's strange," Roscoe said. "It almost looks like a molehill or an ant colony, you know, with the dirt all turned up around a small hole. I tried just putting some weed trimmings—you know, they still got a little life in them—and those turned all dusty and black within a minute or two. Just in that one spot."

Norma paced. Never in her wildest dreams would she have imagined someone would pull a stunt like this—whatever this was—on opening day.

"You sure you're not making a mountain out of a molehill? Literally?" Byrne chuckled at his joke, but Norma reprimanded him with a sharp look.

"Tomorrow, we'll have to get to the bottom of this," Norma said, then threw another pointed look at Byrne. "Literally. We'll find the spot and dig. Something's been planted there; I can almost guarantee it. And if we can find whatever it is and remove it, hopefully, we can prevent any damage happening to the tree."

Roscoe nodded. "Yes, ma'am."

Norma returned his nod. "Thank you for letting us know. Please be sure to dig carefully. We don't know what we're going to find, and it could be very dangerous."

She turned to Byrne next. "Now our job will be making sure those who don't need to know continue to remain unaware of what has happened. We need calm and control, not chaos and confusion."

Byrne nodded as well. "Absolutely."

With that, Norma and Byrne donned their hoods once again and traversed the lawn back to their offices.

Norma gazed up at the stars, her chest heavy with dread.

Please, she begged, *don't let this be the beginning of the end.*

CHAPTER EIGHT

The next morning dawned clear and bright, the sun waking Sophie well before her alarm. She rose and hurried to the bathroom for her morning routine, hoping to avoid another confrontation with Olivia.

Sophie breathed a sigh of relief to see that everything was the way they'd left it last night. Either the girls next door hadn't gotten up yet, or March and Sheila had thought better of putting their belongings back on the second counter.

After she and her roommates were ready, it was off to Thicket Hall for breakfast, and after that, their very first class: Elemental History with Professor Violet Rogers.

"I can't wait to learn even more about *everything*." Janet sighed, clutching her books to her chest.

Sophie grinned. For once, she agreed with Janet. She was just as excited to start learning everything she could about her gift.

"It'll be cool," said Sophie.

"Yawn fest," Brianna said, punctuating her words with

an actual yawn. "I want to get to the fun stuff. Combat. Knocking people like Olivia on their butts with a tornado. That kind of stuff."

Leslie bumped Brianna's shoulder.

"Let's not forget, it was a *waternado*."

Sophie got out her interactive map to locate their classroom. "Looks like it's on the west side of the lawn." She pointed at a simple illustration of a wooden building situated across the stone walkway from the greenhouse and the air pavilion.

"Yep. I think I see it there." Leslie pointed up and across the hill after they rounded Thicket Hall. Sophie hadn't remembered seeing it on her first tour, but that's because it was hidden in a close-knit grove of maples.

As they approached the building, students streamed toward it from all across the campus.

"Must be the rest of the first years," Janet said, her shoulders hunched. She glanced warily at the crowd of students. "Didn't realize we'd have such a large class, but I should have known."

"Oh, don't tell me you're afraid of people," Bri chided. "You can't fool me after you went straight up Hulk last night."

Janet's cheeks darkened.

"Listen, that's only when I get angry—"

"Hey, Sophie!" Sophie turned toward the voice to see Peter waving at her. "Happy first day of school!"

"Thanks!" Sophie said, fumbling with her hair, trying to look nonchalant. "You, too."

When they neared the entrance, Sophie noted several wooden signs placed where they'd be impossible to miss.

They all conveyed the same message: *"Absolutely NO elemental magic is to be used while in this building. Violators are subject to suspension and/or expulsion."*

"Wow," Leslie said. "They mean it, don't they?"

"Expulsion," Janet breathed, her eyes wide. "That's horrible."

Sophie wondered how many students had been removed for breaking that rule.

Entering the simple wooden building, Sophie was once again overwhelmed with the earthy scent of the wood-paneled walls. Students filtered in and out of a set of open double doors to Sophie's left, and she glanced at the room number above the doorframe, matching it to the one on her syllabus.

"This is the one," Sophie said. She and her roommates stepped inside a mid-sized auditorium. Here the wooden walls had been painted white, and terraced rows of hunter-green padded chairs with attached desks stretched across and curved around the stage. They entered at the top row farthest back from the stage, where a podium and smart board waited for the presenter to arrive. Another set of double doors, against the far wall, designated where Professor Rogers would likely make her appearance.

"Let's sit closer to the front, shall we?" Janet pulled Sophie's sleeve, leading her toward the stairs that led down to the ground row of seating.

"Suit yourselves," Brianna said, plopping down in the very back row. "I want a good view of everyone. Especially any cute guys. It was hard to scope out the situation in Thicket Hall."

Janet rolled her eyes. "Of course, you would, Bri."

Leslie chose the seat next to Bri, but Janet and Sophie found two seats together in the front row, angled toward the left side.

Sophie couldn't help but glance back to watch for Peter's entrance as she pulled a notebook and pencil from her bag. There were so many kids streaming through the double doors that she couldn't pick him out from the crowd. Slumping her shoulders, she turned back to look at the clock on the wall—8:27. Class would start in three minutes. She wondered when Professor Rogers would arrive.

She decided to look for Peter one more time before she dedicated herself to filling out the title and date of her notebook page.

She glanced back and, startled, found Peter at the top of the stairs, scanning the rows intently. He pulled on his long sleeves, scratching his forearms.

Sophie tilted her head. She'd just noticed Peter's long sleeves. He'd worn a long-sleeved shirt last night, too. It was forecast to be in the eighties today. Wouldn't he get hot?

Peter's eyes found hers. He smiled and gave a little wave.

She grinned and waved back, feeling a weird mix of elation and embarrassment churning in her gut. He'd caught her looking at him.

"Hey, Peter!" A male voice called Peter's name, and Sophie looked to see Vince, toward the middle row, waving Peter over. Peter glanced between Vince and Sophie just as another girl took the seat next to Sophie's.

"You mind if I sit here?"

Peter headed toward Vince, giving Sophie an apologetic smile.

Sophie turned around in her seat, forcing herself to smile politely at the girl. Only then did she realize it was Charlotte.

She laughed, both to shake off Peter's gaze and the irritation she'd almost unleashed on her new friend. "No, not at all."

Charlotte settled in, greeting Janet, as the smart board suddenly whirred to life and the lights dimmed. The chatter quieted, and Sophie focused on a figure stepping into the room through the double doors to the left.

"Good morning, class," said a rich, deeper female voice. "Welcome to Elemental History." She stepped into the light from the interactive display. Her steely gray eyes glittered as she scanned the rows of students, and her auburn hair smoothed neatly into a no-frills bun, added to the hardness of her demeanor. "My name is Professor Violet Rogers. I've been teaching here for nearly two decades. Longer than you've been alive," she added, shooting a glare off to the right where someone had snickered. "So, it would be in your best interests not to try me or my patience."

Sweeping one last glare across the auditorium and seeming satisfied with the dead silence, Professor Rogers strode to the podium and shuffled a stack of papers together. "Today will be an introduction to elemental history. An overview, if you will. We'll look at when the first elementals were recorded in ancient texts, what they did, and how they were treated in various societies around the world. We'll also touch briefly on the most famous—or infamous—events in history that have had more to do with elementals than you may have originally thought." A hint of a smile crossed her lips. "Give me just a moment to open my presentation, and we'll begin."

Janet gazed at Professor Rogers like a wide-eyed child. Sophie glanced at Janet's notebook page, already titled in decorative, multi-colored letters.

"I can't wait," Janet mouthed to Sophie.

Sophie smiled back. She could already tell this class was going to be good.

The smart board flipped to Professor Rogers' computer screen, displaying a slideshow titled *Introduction to Elemental History.*

"Now. We will proceed from the past to the present. The first recorded instance of elementals, as you all may be aware, was in the hieroglyphs of ancient Egypt." A click from her remote brought up a photo of a limestone wall covered in symbols and pictograms. "For many years, historians and sociologists believed that these depicted the powers of the Egyptian gods, passed down through divine right to the rulers, the pharaohs and queens." She highlighted a pictogram of a human figure with a distinct royal headdress, with what seemed to be water flowing from its hands into a river. "But what we now realize is that there's an alternate theory. Perhaps the ancient Egyptians, instead of ostracizing and erasing elementals, decided to explain their existence by deifying them, or make them into demigods, blessed by the gods and given special powers."

Janet raised her hand, visibly quaking with excitement.

Professor Rogers nodded. "Yes?"

"That sounds a lot like what happened in Ancient Greece, with the gods and demigods of Olympus."

Professor Rogers smiled approvingly.

"You're onto something there." She returned to the slideshow, clicking ahead to the next slide. "As our quick friend has just pointed out, many cultures have deified elementals or given them demigod status, most famously the ancient Greeks. Even among the cultures that elevated elementals and their abilities, there were some taboos and gifts that were not tolerated."

She clicked again, showing a photo of a famine-stricken field. "Although their gift is of utmost importance to the cycle of life, those with the death element were often seen as witches, sent to curse and destroy. And because of this negative association and the psychological strain placed on them, many of the most famous death elementals, unfortunately, became the villains they were made out to be." The next image, a haunting portrait of a figure in a plague mask, drove the point home.

She clicked again, and the next image was of a fortune teller, smirking wickedly at the camera while her hands caressed a crystal ball.

"Similarly, there was once another gift, another type of magic altogether. They were also often seen as witches and sorcerers, but most often today, we would call them psychics or mediums. They were known as psionics. Because so little was known about this gift, and because it was so rare, those with the gift had no training and were also tormented by the psychological and emotional maladies that accompany such abilities. Those abilities include reading thoughts and emotions, seeing past and present emotional or physical states, and knowing the history of objects, living things, animals, or people by touch." Professor Rogers swept her gaze across the rows, her eyes pausing as they met Sophie's gaze.

Sophie's mind swirled. Something in that list had struck a nerve. Knowing emotional states in animals? Wasn't that what had happened with Mincemeat? When she'd sensed his fear and gone running to help him?

Or had it simply been a fluke?

Charlotte touched Sophie's arm, and Sophie saw the question in her eyes. She was thinking the same thing.

Sophie shrugged, just barely, though her thoughts wouldn't stay silent.

Professor Rogers went on. "Though this type of gift is still possible and in existence today, it is extremely hard to verify its veracity. Much harder than a typical elemental gift, which can be verified by a simple examination. I trust each of you recalls your exam?"

Quiet chuckles rose from the students.

Sophie was frowning. Thinking. She doodled the word "psionics" in big letters across her page, shading in the letters as she pondered.

What had happened with Mincemeat and the raccoon was something she'd never experienced before. And it happened to fit perfectly into this new type of magic, something she'd never heard of before. Was it possible there was some sort of psionic magic in her? Something she'd never known about?

Or was it all just coincidence?

What was happening to her?

CHAPTER NINE

Sophie's mind spun with questions she couldn't answer long after Professor Rogers had moved on and even after class was over. Charlotte bumping Sophie's shoulder on the sidewalk finally broke her reverie.

"Hey, Soph. You okay?"

Sophie tried to pull all the swirling trains of thoughts back into line.

"Yeah." She smiled at Charlotte, tucking her hair behind her ear. "Just thinking."

"There was a lot in that lesson, right?" Charlotte pointed to her schedule. "I'm assuming you have Life Elemental Fundamentals next, just like me."

Sophie dug her schedule out of her backpack, confirming Charlotte's guess.

"Yep." That helped draw her into the present. She'd been looking forward to exploring the greenhouse since she'd seen it up on top of the hill the day before.

They headed off together across the cobbled sidewalk. As they walked, Sophie noticed a plain, concrete building she hadn't seen before, over the other side of the hill from Roscoe's barn and the greenhouse.

"What's that?" Sophie pointed. At first glance, it looked like there were vines and ivy climbing up the concrete walls. As they got closer, though, Sophie realized they were painted on.

"You think they did that because nothing can grow around it?" Sophie wondered.

"Yeah," Charlotte said with a short, humorless chuckle. "Probably why it's just a concrete box, too."

Sophie frowned. She remembered Professor Rogers' exhortation that death elementals had a very important place in society.

She couldn't imagine being such an outcast or being seen as cursed or unnatural. It wasn't fair.

But as she watched the students filtering into the death elemental building, most of them similarly withdrawn, wearing dark clothes and extravagant, garish makeup, she shuddered.

It wasn't just that her gift of life, and theirs of death, as a rule, were natural opposites. Their appearance, the way they chose to present themselves, seemed opposed to humanity, as if they were trying their hardest to appear alien.

Maybe it was *because* they were shunned that they chose to appear that way. Maybe they took pride in being different.

A ringing bell jerked her attention back to the present.

"Come on, Sophie!" Charlotte pulled her arm. "We'll be late!"

Sophie pulled her gaze from the death elementals and ran into the greenhouse.

Once inside, she forgot everything else and simply gawked.

Plants of all varieties spanned the walls and sprouted up from beds of soil on the ground and the standing beds, adjusted to be waist high.

A woman with curly red hair and a hunter-green apron bustled toward them, a stern look on her face.

"I trust you won't be late again in the future," she said, leading the two girls to a stainless-steel counter that edged the walls of the greenhouse. Under the counter were two metal stools, which she pulled out and gestured for them to sit.

"No, ma'am," Sophie replied. "We won't be late again."

The woman gave them another hard look and then hurried away.

In front of the girls, on the counter, stood a mesh cage. Within, Sophie saw several little hairy worms, most of them eating their fill from a yellow disc near the bottom of the cage.

"Caterpillars!" Charlotte clapped her hands together. "Look how cute they are!"

Sophie grinned. She didn't know about cute, but she supposed they were charming in their little creepy-crawly way.

"Welcome, class!" The red-haired woman called, and the excited chatter died down. She climbed up onto a platform so she could be seen above the leaves of the plants all around. "Welcome to Life Fundamentals. I'm Professor Hannah

Garver. Today, we'll be doing some practice with acceleration." She smiled. "Would you believe me if I said that before you leave today, we'll have a greenhouse full of butterflies?"

Some chuckles and excited whispers broke out.

"Well, believe it. I'm going to show you how to channel all that luscious life energy so we can see these little guys go through metamorphosis in well under an hour. Talk about instant gratification," she added, earning more laughter. She bent down, retrieving a mesh cage identical to the ones dotted throughout the class. "You'll find between four and six larvae in your habitats. There's enough for each of you to practice with at least two larvae, so if something goes wrong and your caterpillar—" she drew a finger across her throat and stuck her tongue out, "you know, it goes kaput, or gets too big and explodes—that's happened in the past—then you'll have a backup."

"Oh, gross," Charlotte said. Sophie giggled.

"Obviously, the goal is not to speed things up so much that you end up with a dead butterfly. The goal is to accelerate metamorphosis without upsetting the natural balance of chemicals needed to bring the larvae successfully through to the adult stage. That can be hard to gauge, but I and my assistants," she gestured to several older students, who waved from around the greenhouse, "will show you what to do." She clapped her hands together excitedly. "So, let's get started!"

Sophie let Charlotte reach into the habitat and pull out two caterpillars.

"I'll give you this one," Charlotte said, placing the smallest one in Sophie's hand. "Since you like to be such a showoff. Let's see how big you can get it."

Sophie snorted, then laughed as the little creature's tiny hairs tickled her palm. It crawled around, frantically searching for the food it was just eating.

"Now, you know my thing is trees," Sophie said. "I probably won't be as good with bugs as I am with plants."

"Yeah, yeah." Charlotte petted her caterpillar. "I just don't want to explode mine."

"Yeah, ew," Sophie said, grimacing. "I'd rather not do that, either."

"Hi, there!" A tall young man with dark skin and a bright smile greeted them. "I'll be helping you out today. My name is Reggie. I'm a second-year, but I've got a lot of experience with this." He chuckled. "Insects are my specialty."

"That's awesome," said Charlotte, and Sophie noticed her widened smile and star-struck eyes. "I'm Charlotte."

"And I'm Sophie."

Reggie shook both their hands, then stood in between them, taking an extra caterpillar from their habitat.

"I'll demonstrate on this one since it looks like you girls have plenty." He held the caterpillar cupped in his palm, then reached in and brought out the food disk, holding it in his other hand. "Remember that any insect needs energy to go through metamorphosis. That's why caterpillars eat so much food. They need all of that energy in order for their bodies to create the chrysalis. So, what you'll need to do is channel the energy they would have received from the food, into the caterpillar. And you just take that energy right from the food."

He nodded toward the food disk in his hand, then closed his eyes, breathing deep. As they watched, the food disk seemed to start dissolving, forming a yellow-green glowing ring on Reggie's hand. After a moment or so of this, he opened his eyes, then put the food disk down, showing them the green glow on his palm. "There it is. All the energy from the food is now here in my hand."

"So, it's kind of like predigesting the food for them?" Charlotte asked, intrigued.

Reggie laughed. "That's a good way to think about it." He put the caterpillar into his glowing hand. It naturally went for the center of the glow, bobbing its little head up and down hungrily.

"It's like it knows what's there," Sophie said.

"Yep," Reggie said. Then he smiled and gestured at the girls. "Now it's your turn. I'll watch and give some guidance as you try it."

Sophie gulped. It felt like exams all over again.

Charlotte went first. The food disk formed the same green glow on her palm, but her brow was furrowed, and it seemed to be taking much longer than Reggie's process had.

He put a gentle hand on her shoulder. "Try to relax. It'll make everything flow better."

Charlotte took a deep breath, relaxing her brow, and the green glow brightened.

Reggie beamed. "Great job."

Charlotte smiled shyly.

Sophie went next. She closed her eyes, focusing on the food, picturing it as energy waiting to be channeled. The energy began to flow quite fast, and the disk practically melted in her hand.

"Whoa, Sophie. Slow down."

Sophie pulled back, restricting the flow as if she were turning a faucet.

"That's better. I think you've got enough, though."

She opened her eyes, horrified to find half the disk was gone.

Charlotte rolled her eyes. "Yeah, Sophie. Tell me again how you're not gonna be good at this."

Reggie chuckled. "The next step is to give this energy to the caterpillar, but you don't want to do it all at once. Especially if your gift is on the strong side," he glanced at Sophie, "you'll want to hold it back and channel it down 'til it's just…" Reggie searched for the right word. "I don't want to say 'channel' again. Like a stream instead of a river, or a string instead of a rope."

"Okay. That makes sense," Sophie said.

"This is where if you do it wrong, it'll explode. Am I right?" Charlotte asked. She stuck her tongue out at Sophie, who laughed out loud.

"Now you're hoping I'll explode my caterpillar," Sophie shot back.

Reggie laughed again. "Your caterpillar will absolutely burst if you do too much, too fast. That's the primary reason you don't want to overdo it." He then closed his eyes again, and the green glow in his palm lit up. The caterpillar, too, began to glow, and its tiny body began to slowly grow, much like Sophie had seen her ivy grow when she took her exam. Soon the caterpillar was full size, and the glow stopped.

"Your turn," he said, nodding to them again.

Once again, the girls tried their best. Charlotte's energy

flowed much better this time, her caterpillar fattening up nicely.

Sophie struggled hard to keep the flow of energy even and slow, and several times Reggie had to remind her to breathe and release tension. Soon, she had a nice plump caterpillar as well.

"Now, here's the hard part," Reggie said, pulling a piece of flexible wire from within the mesh cage. "You'll have to get them to hang onto this so they can form their chrysalis. I mean, if they don't hang onto it, it's not the end of the world. You can always tape their chrysalis to the hanger, but it's not ideal. And this," he said, struggling to get the caterpillar to even recognize the presence of the wire, "has nothing to do with life magic and everything to do with patience."

"So, how long do you wait for them to grab it?" Sophie asked, chasing her caterpillar's face with the wire.

Reggie shrugged as his caterpillar finally latched on, and he lifted it above his palm. "Don't spend more than five minutes, or if you're starting to get frustrated, just move on. Feeling frustrated will interfere with the rest of the process. Now you'll just push them over the edge and gently nudge the chrysalis process faster."

For the third time, Reggie closed his eyes, the glow coming back to his palm. This time the caterpillar dangled above, and as they watched, it slowly took the shape of a J and began to split the chrysalis.

"You know, they turn into goo when they're inside their chrysalis," Sophie said. "At least, that's what I've heard."

"Ew," Charlotte said. They watched the chrysalis become more and more transparent, turning into a chrysalis right before their eyes. Then Reggie took the wire and hung it at the top of the habitat.

"I've gotten it right to the point before it hatches," Reggie said. "You know you're there when you can feel that the butterfly is fully formed, but it's still in a resting state. It can be tricky to find that spot, but if they start hatching in your hand, it's not a super huge deal."

Charlotte went first. Hers took a moment longer than Reggie's to form its chrysalis, though once it did, she smiled, and her energy flowed faster. Soon her chrysalis was hanging from the habitat next to Reggie's.

"Nicely done," he said, giving her a high five.

She grinned back at him, and Sophie noticed their gaze lingered longer this time.

Smiling to herself at Charlotte's new crush, she took her turn. Prodding the caterpillar to form its chrysalis was easy enough but being patient while the creature liquified and reformed within its chrysalis made her queasy.

As soon as the caterpillar was no longer a larva but a full adult, Sophie attempted to clamp down on the flow of energy, stopping it too late.

"Oh, a little too much. But it's alive, so there's that."

Sophie opened her eyes to see the orange and blue butterfly struggling out of the chrysalis and onto her palm.

"Look!" Charlotte pointed to the habitat. "Ours are hatching now, too!"

Sophie smiled at her newborn butterfly, watching the other two butterflies emerge into the habitat. From all around the greenhouse, she could hear similar expressions of delight and more than a few squeals of disgust—from exploding larvae, she guessed.

"Well done, ladies!" Professor Garver stopped at their station to admire their butterflies. "Reg here always does a great job teaching."

Reggie smiled as she shook his shoulder in approval, then frowned as he glanced at a spot on her cheek.

"Um, Professor?"

"I've still got caterpillar guts on my face, don't I?" She yanked a handkerchief from her apron pocket and bustled off, grumbling to herself.

They laughed, and Sophie's butterfly walked up to her fingertips, flexing its brand-new wings. Looking up, she could see several other butterflies already fluttering overhead, the results of her fellow students' projects.

She sighed in satisfaction. Her dad had been right. This was going to be a place full of good memories. She could already tell.

A few moments later, Professor Garver called for a break. Sophie wandered outside, chatting happily with Charlotte. Reggie's butterfly had taken a liking to Charlotte and was perched in her cornrow braids.

"Do you think he likes me?" Charlotte asked.

"The butterfly? I mean, obviously," Sophie replied. "Though I can't really tell if it's a girl or a boy."

"No." Charlotte punched her arm playfully. "I mean Reggie."

Sophie chuckled. "I mean, you only just met him, but if he's helping Professor Garver, chances are you'll bump into him again. Why don't you just give it some time?"

"Yeah. You're right." Charlotte let the butterfly crawl onto her finger, smiling as it fluttered off on the breeze. "If it's meant to happen, it'll happen."

Sophie followed the butterfly with her gaze as it flew across the lawn toward Thicket Hall.

But her eyes latched onto something else—a large, burly figure also headed toward Thicket Hall. She peered closer, recognizing the dark, messy hair and stocky frame. It was Roscoe. He glanced back at his workshop, and his deep blue eyes were frantic, scared, even.

Sophie's stomach dropped. Her mind brought back a similar image of professors running toward Roscoe's barn last night.

Now Roscoe was doing the same thing.

What was going on?

CHAPTER TEN

After her Life Fundamentals class, Charlotte and Sophie met up with Leslie, Bri, and Janet for lunch in Thicket Hall. Their fare consisted of a delicious veggie soup in a bread bowl, with a salad with lots of late summer berries sprinkled on top. And of course, more sweet tea. Sophie was relieved to see that Olivia and her friends hadn't made it to lunch, hopeful she'd avoid her this time.

"How were classes for you guys?" Sophie asked her friends.

"Well, they had us trying to blow pinwheels," Brianna scoffed. "Not like we'd never done that before."

"You're not telling them the whole story, Bri," Janet pressed.

Bri sighed. "Fine. We had to blow them in a particular order. And not move any of the others." She shoved a giant hunk of bread in her mouth.

"Let me guess. She didn't do so hot," Leslie said.

Brianna glared at her while Janet nodded.

"I had to compress stones to make quartz." Janet

produced a tiny, rose-colored gem from her pocket. "It's very rough, but I think I did an okay job."

"That's cool," Sophie said, turning the gem over in the light and watching it sparkle. She passed it to Leslie, who grinned as she turned it over.

"We made caterpillars turn into butterflies," Sophie said.

"And we didn't make them explode," Charlotte added.

The other three girls grimaced.

"That sounds horrifying," Janet said.

"Yeah, the professor walked by with caterpillar guts on her face," Charlotte said.

"Well, we did some mist work today," Leslie said, changing the subject as they all stared at their food with distaste. "Had to break water up as fine as we could, like an aerosol, and try to form a geometric shape out of it. Our professor said something about using them in elemental mosaics down the road."

"That sounds cool!" Sophie said. "A whole picture made with all the different elements."

"I wonder how death fits into that picture. Literally."

The girls chuckled, though Sophie grabbed her glass to avoid joining them. She didn't feel right about teasing the death elementals, not after what she'd thought about today.

As Sophie took a sip of her tea, she noticed a short, plump woman hurrying toward their table.

"Sorry, darlings. I don't mean to interrupt your lunch, but I'm looking for a young lady named Sophia Briggs."

Sophie stared at the woman. "That's me."

"Ah!" The woman beamed. "Excellent. I've been informed by our caretaker Roscoe that you've quite the talent for healing. I was wondering if you'd like to have a part-time job with me. I'm Nurse Bonnie, by the way." She took Sophie's hand and shook it excitedly.

"Only your second day, and the nurse wants you to work for her," Charlotte snarked, elbowing Sophie in the ribs. "I don't want to hear any more about how you're not good at this."

Sophie gave Nurse Bonnie a nervous half-smile. "Um. I don't know. What'll the hours be like? And the pay?" And what would she even use the pay for? She hadn't seen a single vending machine or shop on campus yet.

"I'd only work you a few hours a week, maybe one hour each day? And it'd be minimum wage. Sorry it can't be more, but you know." She leaned in and whispered to Sophie, "Not really supposed to have young'uns working, you know."

"You should do it, Soph," Leslie said. "You'd learn a lot about healing!"

"Yeah!" Janet added. "It'll be like an internship."

Sophie chewed her lip. On the one hand, it would be nice just knowing she had extra money she'd earned herself. And the on-the-job experience she'd get might lead her to some other cool places. Maybe even working with Roscoe to take care of the tree. That possibility made her smile.

Besides, it was only an hour a day. She'd still have all the rest of her time to study and hang out with her friends.

"Ok," she said.

"Good!" Nurse Bonnie shook her hand again. "If you want to come by sometime today when you have a break, I can fill you in with a little training. Paid, of course." She winked.

"Well…" Sophie pulled her schedule out of her bag. "I don't have another class for a couple of hours."

"Even better," Nurse Bonnie said, clapping her hands together. "You can come now if you'd like." She gestured to Sophie's food. "I mean, once you're done here, of course." She fished in her pocket and pulled out a map. "If you go around Thicket Hall on the left side, I'm in a cozy-looking building that looks like a house with a big front porch. Just walk right in."

Sophie took the map, noting the house symbol with a red plus sign above it.

"All right. I'll be there after lunch."

"Looking forward to it, Miss Sophia." Nurse Bonnie bustled away, and Sophie faced the girls, all of them gazing at her with some mix of awe and jealousy.

"Man. I wish I could get a part-time job handed to me like that," Brianna said, shoving a forkful of chocolate lava cake into her mouth.

"And you'd probably eat all your money buying snacks," Janet retorted.

Sophie laughed with the rest of the girls, then finished up her lunch and headed off to the nurse's office.

Nurse Bonnie's office looked like a cozy Southern home, complete with two porch swings on a covered patio and potted flowering plants everywhere. Sophie smiled as she walked up the porch steps, noting the honeybees milling around the lavender asters and fiery pink dahlias growing in box planters along the railing.

As she walked into the foyer, a charming bell jingled

above her head, and the aroma of vanilla and sugar overwhelmed her nose. Subtle blue floral wallpaper covered the walls, and to one side stood a light oak-wood desk.

"Sophia, is that you, darling?" Nurse Bonnie appeared from the staircase against the far wall and waved happily as she approached. "Good to see you didn't get lost."

Sophie chuckled. "This place is hard to miss."

Nurse Bonnie laughed, patting Sophie's shoulder.

"I like you already."

Nurse Bonnie led Sophie to the desk. "This is where everyone checks in. You'll be checking the sign-in list," she tapped on a clipboard, "and making sure I get to everyone, as well as helping along the way with some patients, of course. You'll also screen some kids to see if they're actually sick or not." Nurse Bonnie sighed and rolled her eyes. "Especially around mid-term exam time, we'll see tons of kids in here with tummy issues and headaches, and those can be solved with a pack of painkillers or some antacid tablets, which we keep here." She took a key from her neck and unlocked a drawer in the desk, filled to the brim with single-serve packets of over-the-counter medications. "Not something we have time to deal with in here, so you'll be in charge of that."

Sophie nodded. It all seemed simple enough. She'd learned how to check her plants for signs of disease at a very early age, and the same process worked for humans. She should know. She'd been able to call out Millie for staying home "sick" several times.

Nurse Bonnie then led her to an adjacent room, a large, open space with cots stacked up against the wall. "This is the infirmary, where we'll serve the patients who get past you. It's actually fairly unusual to have a lot of kids at once who get injured or whatnot, but sometimes we'll see a spike right after combat training or the Elemental Skills Contest."

"A contest?" Sophie pressed. She hadn't heard anything about a contest, but hadn't that Marcus kid lost a contest? Maybe that was the one. Or maybe it was a different one.

"Oh, yeah. It's an annual thing. We always have it right before winter break. It's not quite a mid-term, but more of just a friendly competition. Whoever wins gets their picture in Thicket Hall with a plaque, and it stays up until the next contest."

That had to have been the one Marcus lost. Sophie could understand a little better why that might have been upsetting, especially if he'd been fairly confident in his ability to win.

Still, all that anger over a photo in Thicket Hall? Sophie rubbed her arm, remembering what his accidental touch had done. Marcus was incredibly powerful. Whoever he lost to must have been even more so.

"You were robbed, dude!"

It suddenly started to click in Sophie's mind. Marcus was a death elemental. Maybe he lost because...because the judges favored the water elemental girl over him and his powers of death, despite Marcus' obvious superior ability. Maybe they were scared of glorifying death.

Maybe Marcus had a right to be angry.

Sophie shook her head, dispersing those thoughts. She had no idea what had happened. She couldn't attribute discriminatory motives to judges she didn't even know.

And besides, that didn't help Marcus now, even if it were true.

She turned her attention back to Nurse Bonnie, who was happily chatting away despite Sophie's lack of response.

"You know they've been talking about Thicket Hall and the School a lot this year, more than any year since I've been here, at least," she was saying. "Everybody always worries about something going wrong here at the school. I mean, when you concentrate all this magic in one place—and especially with all the young, untrained elementals (no offense, Sophia)—something is bound to go wrong. I don't know. Just seems the rumors are flying like fall leaves this year."

Sophie shuddered. She hoped it was merely a coincidence and not an omen that so many people were worried about the school.

"What do you think?" She asked Nurse Bonnie. "Do you think we should be worried?"

Nurse Bonnie shrugged. "To be honest, I really don't know. You just never *can* know. That's why I always say, be alert, not anxious. It never helps to worry about things you can't control."

Sophie nodded. That made sense. She glanced at the clipboard in her hand, noting there was a list of appointments.

"So, you regularly see patients for ongoing conditions?" She asked, absentmindedly scanning the list.

"Yes. Sometimes they need a specific treatment or therapy on a regular basis while they're here."

Sophie caught a glimpse of a familiar name—*Peter*

Travis, age 15, first-year. Her heart leapt, then sank. What was wrong with Peter?

"What does Peter come in for?" Sophie asked.

Nurse Bonnie shook her head, taking the clipboard from Sophie.

"Can't discuss student medical history unless it's pertinent to get them treatment." She eyed Sophie again, noting her red cheeks. "Seems you've got a crush already."

Sophie folded her arms. "I wouldn't say that. Peter's just a friend. I just wondered if he was okay."

Nurse Bonnie patted her arm. "Don't worry, Sophia. You're secret's safe with me. And while I can't talk medical stuff, I can tell you Peter's just fine."

The bell jingled in the foyer, and Nurse Bonnie hurried away, leaving Sophie to her thoughts.

CHAPTER ELEVEN

After her orientation with Nurse Bonnie, Sophie found herself with an hour to kill before her next class. She remembered Roscoe running across the lawn earlier that morning. Hadn't she resolved to go see him as soon as she could?

She set off across the lawn toward the stone pathway up to Roscoe's workshop. She'd forgotten all about him in the day's hustle and bustle, but she had to make sure he was okay.

As the stone path began to ascend toward the hill, though, movement from the left toward Thicket Hall caught her attention.

At first glance, she didn't see anything unusual. Her dorm building, covered with river stones, shone in the afternoon sunlight. The pond rippled merrily under a clear blue sky. And Thicket Hall itself stood magnificent and breathtaking above it all.

A breeze stirred its branches and rushed toward Sophie. Another dark leaf swirled through the air and around Sophie, fluttering and spinning wildly. As it fell into her hand, she smiled. The tree was trying to say something to her, just like it had when she'd first arrived.

But as she looked more closely at the leaf, her heart dropped into her stomach.

Right in the center, spreading from the little veins, a small, dark spot, like soot, stained its surface.

She touched the spot, then quickly drew her finger back. A sting, like the one she'd felt when Marcus brushed past her, pricked her finger.

Whatever was happening to the tree, it was because of death magic. She was sure of that.

Another sharp movement jerked her gaze back toward Thicket Hall. Along the path leading behind it, the path leading to the dorms, a puddle she hadn't noticed before was stretched across the stones.

She furrowed her brow, taking a few steps closer to examine it. The water didn't move, not even as another breeze swept down the path toward Sophie.

The hairs on the back of Sophie's neck stood up. Peering at it closer, she could see it didn't reflect the foliage or the sunlight, either.

She paused, fear seizing in her gut. Whatever this was, it wasn't natural.

"Sophie!" Roscoe's booming voice echoed across the lawn. "Step back!"

Sophie did as she was told. The puddle pulled in its edges and sprang up into a vaguely humanoid shape.

Sophie gasped. Was this some kind of water trick? But Roscoe didn't have a gift. Not that she could remember, anyway.

The water creature turned toward her, then rushed at her.

Sophie yelped and turned to run, but a massive gust hit the creature and clipped Sophie, knocking her on her behind. The creature doubled back on itself and flattened into a puddle once again.

She stared at it, fear now coursing fully through her. What was going on?

"Sophie," said a female voice. She turned to see Headmistress Case jogging up the path. "Get out of here."

Sophie started to get to her feet, but the path beneath her began to quake. She screamed as the rocky path built upon itself, becoming a towering figure holding Sophie on its shoulder.

"Oh, no. Put me down!" Sophie shrieked. "I hate heights!" She put her hand against the rocky figure and, putting every bit of energy she had into it, sent a shock-wave of life through it.

Plants, flowers, and vines began to sprout from every crack and crevice in the creature. It groaned, batting at the flora until the plants overtook the creature and it collapsed into a pile of stones.

Sophie, using the collapsing rock as a slide, landed awkwardly on her backside.

"Ow." She stood and rubbed her hips, then glanced at the rocky creature. "What *is* that?"

Headmistress Case gawked at her.

Sophie noted more movement across the path from where they stood. Something bright, like a flame or a flash of sunlight, passed by the fire elemental building.

"Um, Headmistress?" Sophie pointed. "I think there might be more. And I think these ones are fire."

Headmistress Case turned, then nodded. Lifting her hands, she positioned herself beside the puddled water creature.

"Sophie. Do you think you could weave a basket? Something airtight?"

Sophie frowned. "I don't know, but I'll try." She knelt on the grass and placed her hands on the ground, focusing on the small shoots of grass. Just like she'd done to rescue Mincemeat, she told herself. The grass began to elongate all around her, sprouting until she was lost in a close-knit forest of green blades. She parted the curtain of grass to see Roscoe running up the path, shearing scissors in hand.

"Got you covered, Sophie," he said, trimming the grass quickly while she pulled the pieces together into her lap.

Once all the grass had been cut, she put her hands on the blades, envisioning a large basket without any holes.

The grass began to shiver, then move, awkwardly at first, then with purpose as Sophie's vision became clearer. As the grass wove itself, she added more length, more sprouts, filling holes and patching gaps until the basket she'd imagined sat ready in her lap.

Headmistress Case nodded her approval. "That'll do nicely."

Roscoe took the basket while Headmistress Case began to move her arms and hands in a careful choreography. The wind began to rush in, converging on the puddle. Sophie watched as the water creature resisted the steady gust, but only for a moment. Soon it became enmeshed with the swirling wind, and Sophie smiled as she thought of Leslie and Brianna. Here was their waternado, only amplified and directed by a master.

"Now, Roscoe," Headmistress Case said. "Take Sophie's basket. When I give the signal, trap them."

Headmistress Case then led the raging waterspout up the path, slowly at first.

The fire creatures seemed to realize what was going on. They darted behind trees, their flaming hands leaving scorch marks on the bark.

"Oh, no, you don't," muttered Headmistress Case. She set her sights on the first creature, who'd leapt out from behind its tree and was taunting the other.

The waternado moved like a flash.

The fire creature turned, its glowing eyes widening as the waterspout sucked it in. Its spinning glow blazed up once, but soon the waterspout began smoking, and the glow died down to black.

"Yes!" Cheered Roscoe.

"Don't celebrate yet," Headmistress Case said. Sophie gasped as the second creature escaped across the lawn, straight up the hill toward Roscoe's barn.

"Aw, heck no!" Roscoe spat, taking off after it. "Not my animals, you—"

"Roscoe!"

He fell silent at the headmistress' sharp rebuke, though he kept running.

Headmistress Case followed Roscoe, pushing her waterspout ahead of her, and Sophie was right on her heels. The older woman looked back at her briefly.

"Sophie, you really shouldn't be here."

"I want to help," Sophie insisted, panting as she jogged

to keep up. "Besides, what if something happens to that basket? I'm the only one that can fix it."

The headmistress took a long moment to respond, but when she did, it was to discreetly beckon Sophie to keep following.

Sophie smiled.

As they reached the top of the hill, they found nothing but an overturned metal trough, with scorched hay scattered everywhere.

"Where is it?" Roscoe huffed, trying to catch his breath.

Headmistress Case approached the trough, pushing the waterspout close enough to it that a few drops of water fell on it. The drops sizzled as they touched the metal.

"It's using the trough as a shield," she said.

Sophie's heart raced with an idea.

"I got this," she said. Then, bending down to touch the ground, she sent a wave of energy into the grass around the trough, sending it further into the ground, awakening anything sleeping or waiting for its season. Flora sprung up around the trough, though she was careful not to send them under it. If her plan went well, no plants would lose their lives today.

Sophie then directed the grass to intertwine and the flowers to join forces until there were ropes of grass and flower stalks, thickening and growing all around the basin.

Finally, she moved her fingers, spreading them in an outward-and-up motion, and the plant ropes obeyed her command. Their thickened vines snaked beneath the hot metal, pushing up with all the strength Sophie could give them.

Slowly but surely, an opening formed.

Headmistress Case wasted no time. As soon as the gap widened enough, she slammed her waterspout under the trough.

The fire creature scraped at the earth as the spout pulled it in, yanking at Sophie's vines. The trough fell back down over it, but steam was already escaping from under its makeshift shield.

"We might not need the basket after all," remarked Headmistress Case. "It chose its own coffin. Fire and water cancel one another, and without air, fire cannot survive." She smiled. "Sophie, can you flip the trough with those vines? Let's examine our handiwork, shall we?"

Sophie frowned. It had taken most of her strength to do it the first time. And her vines were losing life already, scorched by the fire creature or crushed under the trough.

"I'll try," she said.

Headmistress Case put a hand on Sophie's shoulder. She felt strength and energy returning to her. She stared at the headmistress, awed.

Headmistress Case merely nodded and smiled.

"Go ahead, Sophie."

Sophie focused again, summoning life both from the headmistress' energy and the trees and plants around her. The vines slowly snaked their way up, then plunged down and under the trough. Sophie struggled not to clench her fists with the effort, instead clenching her teeth and pushing up with her open palms.

The vines, though trembling, pushed the trough past its tipping point and turned it over on its side. Billowing steam escaped and rose rapidly into the air.

Sophie let the vines go, gasping for air. They collapsed

into a graying pile, and Sophie frowned again. So much for not killing them.

"Well," Roscoe said as the steam cleared, "there's nothing left of 'em."

Sophie suddenly remembered the rock creature. "What about the other one?"

Headmistress Case patted her shoulder. "You took care of that one just fine. It won't be able to put itself back together. Nor will it want to. Once defeated, most pure elementals will retreat. Somewhat like animals."

Sophie's mind raced with thoughts.

"Pure elementals? So that's what those were. I had no idea that kind of thing even existed."

"That's the way I'd like to keep it," Headmistress Case said, her hard demeanor returning. She put both hands on Sophie's shoulders and looked into her eyes. "You must keep everything that happened here to yourself. This never happened. Do you understand?"

Sophie opened her mouth, then furrowed her brows in confusion.

"But why?"

"You will have to take me at my word that if the wrong people find out that pure elementals were running wild on campus and something was wrong with Thicket Hall, it will endanger the entire school. Promise me you won't tell a soul."

Sophie shivered, remembering the diseased leaf. She'd been right. Something was going on with the tree. And that's why she'd seen so many professors—and Roscoe—rushing around campus, looking frantic.

"What's wrong with Thicket Hall?" Sophie asked.

Headmistress Case heaved an aggravated sigh.

"You leave that to me. For your part... Don't. Tell. A. Soul."

Sophie nodded reluctantly.

Headmistress Case nodded, then let go of her shoulders. "It's time for you to get ready for class," she said, checking her watch. "Go and remember what I said. Tell no one."

Sophie nodded and headed down the path toward the dorms.

Norma watched Sophie go, following the girl with her eyes until she disappeared down the path toward the dorms. Sophie had surprised her—really surprised her—with her ability. True, the girl had no idea how to manage her energy, so she'd used up a good deal of it on what should have been fairly simple tasks for someone with a powerful life gift. The raw power behind Sophie's command of the plant life around her...was impressive.

Norma chewed her lip. She really shouldn't have let Sophie help. A first-year, fooling around with pure elementals? It used to be unthinkable. Her fellow professors would probably scold her when they found out.

Norma had to admit she wanted to test Sophie. She wanted to see what the girl was capable of. It was evident Sophie cared for Thicket Hall and the tree for her as well. She'd seen that diseased leaf Sophie had received.

Was Thicket Hall trying to tell Sophie something? Was it trying to tell her something?

Norma shook her head and turned to Roscoe. There were more important things to worry about.

"We need to go check out that tree before anything else goes wrong."

Roscoe nodded. "Lead the way, Headmistress."

Sophie had every intention of doing as she'd been told, but halfway to the dorms, she ducked behind a tree. One of the same trees the fire elementals had hidden behind if the jagged scorch marks were anything to judge by.

If there was something wrong with Thicket Hall, she wanted to know what it was. From her hiding place, she watched Roscoe and Headmistress Case hurrying down the path toward the tree like she'd suspected they would.

As they passed her, Sophie edged closer to Thicket Hall, darting behind the other trees that lined the path. She watched them examine the back of the tree. Focusing on a particular spot that looked like a large hole near one of the tree's massive roots. They then split up, Roscoe going around one end of the tree and Headmistress Case examining the other, running their hands along the bark. Every once in a while, Headmistress Case would scribble something in a small notebook. They then met back at the hole, both looking exhausted and frustrated.

Sophie crept as close as she dared, desperate to hear their conversation.

"Doesn't seem like much else is affected," Roscoe was saying. He rubbed the back of his neck like he always did when he was nervous, Sophie noticed. "And we still haven't gotten to the bottom of this weird hole."

"Keep your eyes peeled," Headmistress Case said. "It seems whatever is down there is only sickening it. Any weakness, and...well." She gestured tiredly. "You've seen."

"Yes, ma'am." Roscoe gave a casual salute.

"And let me know the moment you find out what's down there."

"Of course."

Headmistress Case nodded and rounded Thicket Hall, presumably to go back to her office, while Roscoe headed up the walk toward the barn.

Once she was sure they were both gone, she approached the great tree, pulling the leaf with the dark spot out of her pocket. An inexplicable sadness washed over her. She'd just been introduced to this behemoth of a tree, and yet the fact that something was wrong with it squeezed her heart.

Without thinking, she opened her arms and pressed herself against the trunk, the bark rough against her cheek and fragrant.

"I wish I could help you," she whispered. She pressed her palms against the trunk, using the technique she'd learned to diagnose her plants whenever they'd get droopy.

Sophie gasped as a wall of pain washed through her. Startled, she drew back, looking up at the mighty crown of branches high above her head.

"You're really hurting, aren't you?" She took deep breaths, steadying herself, then leaned in against the tree once more. The same wave of pain struck her again, but she pushed it back, holding it at arm's length, examining it.

The immensity of the pain, she realized, wasn't so much because the cause of the pain was massive. It was because the tree itself, and its ancient voice, were massive, rooted in centuries of experience.

Sophie breathed out, somewhat relieved. Still, feeling so much of the tree's pain had shaken her.

But there was something else—a glimmer of an image. Sophie's brow furrowed. She'd never experienced such a complex level of communication from any of her plants before, not even from any of the trees she'd helped grow and heal. Maybe it was because they'd been much younger. Maybe plants, she realized, were a lot like humans, having stages of life. Learning more complex responses to things and eventually expressing themselves in a way that matched the complexity of their understanding.

Pushing her pondering aside, she focused on the image the tree was giving her. As she watched it develop, she realized it was more like a video, or a playback of a memory. The fuzzy mind picture clarified—the tree, sending Sophie a leaf on the breeze. Thicket Hall, feeling full and warm with a cafeteria full of kids. Sophie smiled, her heart swelling. The tree had an almost motherly affection for the students that gathered within it. Then, that night, calm, peace. And a young man with his hood up, staring at the tree with determination in his eyes.

Then a sharp pain, like being pricked by a thorn, only amplified, spreading, throbbing, like a wasp sting.

The image faded, and Sophie was left with the tree, in the present moment, showing her the pain had faded but wasn't gone. Whatever poison had struck the tree had traveled into its root system and was blocking access to nutrients in a very particular part of the tree.

"Where?" Sophie asked.

The tree showed her the large root near the hole in the ground. Sophie sprinted over, stopping just at the edge of the hole. She could feel an unease radiating from it as if whatever was inside was toxic to her.

Curious, she looked at the leaf in her hand, then placed it at the edge of the hole.

It immediately shriveled and turned black. Sophie jumped back, clamping a hand over her mouth.

Whatever death magic was in that hole was powerful. Very powerful.

But how did it get there? Who put it there?

And how could she help the tree when even Headmistress Case and Roscoe were at a loss?

A bell trilled out in the distance. Sophie gasped.

"My next class." She looked longingly back at the tree. "Sorry. I'll come back."

The branches seemed to wave at her, and she broke into a run, joining the stream of students now traveling along the stone path.

Sophie's next class was Elemental Science with Professor Clarice Nelson. She chose a spot near the front, with Janet again, but struggled to focus. Her mind kept drifting back to the tree, to that creepy death hole near its root.

A drift of air brushed past her face, and she looked up to see Professor Nelson staring at her expectantly.

"Sophie, I asked you a question," she said, tapping her foot.

"I'm sorry," Sophie said. "What did you ask?"

"What are the two elements that can never mix?"

Sophie thought for a moment before the answer came to her, straight from her childhood memory.

"Life and death," she said.

"Good," Professor Nelson said. "And what happens when they mix?"

"Disease," Sophie replied. "Life can push back death, and death can overcome life, but they can't work on the same thing at the same time. So, if they do, you get disease."

Professor Nelson nodded, her eyebrows raised. "Nicely said."

Sophie smiled shyly. "My dad told me that."

As Professor Nelson moved on to the next question, Janet, the next student elbowed Sophie.

"Nice," she whispered.

Sophie grinned, but it soon faded as her thoughts turned back to Thicket Hall.

How could she get the death out? She'd just said life could push out death...but that death magic was powerful. She knew, somewhere within herself, that it was too much for her gift to push back.

But what if she had help? Or what if she simply gave the tree an extra push of life energy? Would it be enough?

A sense of dread in her stomach warned her not to get too optimistic. If Headmistress Case, an absolute master of her gift, hadn't come to that conclusion already, it was probably not a logical option.

That sense of dread stayed with Sophie throughout her

class and into dinnertime. She was glad to go back to Thicket Hall with her friends. Maybe a good meal would help her anxiety. And being within the beautiful giant itself always soothed a special place in her heart.

As she met up with her roommates, though, muttering rumors abounded in the students milling around them.

"Did you hear about Thicket Hall? Something's going on with it."

"Yeah, what's that hole doing by that root? Are they looking for buried treasure?"

"More like looking for tree poison."

When Sophie tried to make eye contact with a few of the students, some of them laughed or turned away and whispered something to the person beside them.

"What's going on?" she asked Leslie.

Leslie shrugged. "I'm not sure. I guess there's something going on with the tree?"

"Yeah, there is," cackled a familiar voice. "It's got a girlfriend. A precious little tree hugger."

Laughter erupted, and Sophie rolled her eyes as Olivia, March, and Sheila appeared in the crowd.

"That's right, we saw you!" Olivia teased.

"I was trying to figure out what was wrong!" Sophie shot back.

"It's okay. You don't have to be embarrassed," Olivia cooed. "I even took some commemorative photos." She flashed her phone in front of Sophie's face. Sophie caught a zoomed-in glimpse of herself, arms wrapped around the tree, face turned toward the camera, and eyes closed.

Sophie batted the phone away. "Look, Olivia, this is serious!"

"I know, it really is getting serious! Just make sure you don't get any splinters."

Sheila and March hooted with laughter, and many of the surrounding students followed suit.

Sophie glowered while Olivia waved sweetly as she continued into the hall.

"You little—" Sophie began.

"Sophie." Janet clutched Sophie's hand. "Remember what you told me."

Sophie drew in several deep breaths, taking comfort in Janet's iron grip on her hand. She wasn't going to do or say anything stupid. Olivia wasn't worth it.

Together, she and her roommates got settled at their table, followed shortly by the guys.

"So, what *is* going on with the tree?" Bri asked.

Sophie squirmed in her seat. She couldn't say a word. She'd promised Headmistress Case.

"I don't know, but someone was saying they saw some kinda fiery thing going up the path earlier today," Vince said. "And there were scorch marks on a lot of the trees."

"I just love baked potatoes, don't you?" Sophie said, shoving a bite into her mouth.

Her remark was mostly ignored, except for Janet, who gave her the side-eye.

"I heard something got up into the barn," Simon said, stirring his tea until the liquid formed an image of a barn. "We did hear something banging around while we were in the life greenhouse, 'misting' the plants." He bent his fingers into quotations.

"What do you mean, 'misting?'" Janet asked, mimicking him.

Simon chuckled. "Well, we were supposed to be making a fine mist. A lot of us ended up super-soaking some tomatoes, though."

"We heard it, too, over in earth's place," Peter said, pulling at his sleeves. "I also saw a bunch of rocks and vines scattered off the path when I came to dinner." He glanced at Sophie, those emerald eyes boring into hers as if he knew the secret she was hiding. "Did you hear anything?"

Sophie shook her head too forcefully, then coughed.

"Uh, no. I mean, I saw the scorch marks on the trees, like Vince said." She gestured at Vince, then busied herself with her meal.

"What *were* you doing hugging the tree?" Peter asked her, then chuckled. "Olivia's picture was pretty funny, not gonna lie."

Sophie looked at him, but it must have been a glare because Peter cut off his laughter and cleared his throat.

"I mean, sorry. You don't have to answer that."

"Like I said," Sophie said, "I was trying to figure out what was wrong. I was listening to it."

Leslie squinted at her. "Listening?"

Sophie sighed, putting her fork down on her plate. The loud clank made everyone jump.

"Yes, listening. I don't know how else to explain it. Like how I can tell if a plant is sick or not. That kind of thing, but it was talking back to me, too." Sophie's voice trailed off as everyone stared at her.

They all gave a nod of confused comprehension, though Bri and Simon still looked incredulous.

"I got you, girl," Charlotte said, pulling up a seat at the table. "So…what did you find out?"

"Well," Sophie sighed, "it's in pain, and there's death magic working on it. It even showed me where the magic was, but that's all I know."

"You should tell Headmistress," Janet said. "That might be valuable information."

Sophie snorted. "I get the feeling she probably figured that out way before I did."

"Well," said Peter, "hopefully, Headmistress knows how to fix it. Or maybe she just needs the right kind of help." He gave her one of those knowing stares again, pulling on his long sleeves.

Sophie looked at his sleeves, wondering how much he knew...and wondering why he always wore those long sleeves.

Peter cleared his throat. "I'm going to go get more tea. Anybody want some?"

Sophie shook her head with everybody else, but she watched him leave the table. He tucked his arms around him as he walked. It was odd, she thought. He was certainly not a shy person. At least, he didn't seem to be, but his body language—hugging himself, pulling his sleeves down constantly—suggested otherwise.

Dinner went on as usual, and the conversation turned to other things, for which Sophie was grateful. She was willing to disclose her discoveries about the tree, but though she wanted to, she couldn't tell anyone about the elementals she'd helped battle that afternoon.

She could see why it might not be a great idea. Her friends would be terrified of encountering one of those strange creatures. Or they might try to go out and battle one themselves for the social brownie points. None of that was safe.

Sophie herself didn't relish the fact she'd helped fight them, though she was glad to have impressed Headmistress Case and glad to have listened to Thicket Hall. She'd just stumbled into the fight and had somehow—probably by chance—come out victorious.

As they meandered from the Hall toward the dorms, a deep, low hum caught Sophie's attention immediately. She glanced up, thinking maybe it was an airplane, but she didn't hear the telltale variations in pitch that accompanied aircraft flying overhead. The hum was steady and almost overwhelmingly loud.

"What is that?" Sophie said, peering all around campus.

"What do you mean?" Leslie said. "Do you see something?"

"No. I hear something. It's this loud hum, almost like an airplane or a diesel engine idling." As they walked farther from the tree, the hum decreased in volume. "I think it's the tree."

"What are you talking about, Soph?" Bri asked. "All I hear are crickets and frogs at the pond."

Sophie glanced at Janet. "Do you hear it?"

Janet shook her head, then put her hand on Sophie's shoulder. "Are you okay? Maybe you should get your ears checked out. My sister had early hearing loss. That was her only symptom, hearing this loud ringing that no one else could hear."

Sophie shook her head. She could still hear all the ambient sounds, but the tree's hum filled all the spaces in between.

"I don't think that's it." She glanced up the hill toward Roscoe's barn. "But if anyone could help me figure out what this is, it's probably Roscoe. He works with the tree all the time."

"Yeah, go talk to him," Leslie said. "Maybe it's a 'life' thing or something?"

Sophie smiled. "I'll catch up with you guys later."

They waved, and Sophie took off up the path to Roscoe's workshop.

She found Roscoe busily flipping through books and adding ingredients to a small saucepan.

"What are you making?" she asked.

"Whoa!" Roscoe jumped, then turned and threw her a glare. "Knock next time!"

"Sorry." Sophie rubbed her arm.

"If you must know," Roscoe said, "I'm making some pasta sauce."

Sophie raised an eyebrow. "For the tree?"

"No. For my dinner."

"Oh."

Mincemeat mewed happily and ran across the room to rub Sophie's leg. As his little furry body touched her, Sophie saw an image flash in front of her mind's eye—a can of cat food, open, and Roscoe pouring it into a bowl.

"I, um…" Sophie said with wide eyes. "I think Mincemeat wants you to feed him."

"Oh, shoot! I totally forgot his lunch." Roscoe opened a cabinet and pulled out a can exactly like the one Sophie had seen. Mincemeat hurried over excitedly and started pawing Roscoe's pant leg.

Roscoe peeled open the can, then paused, looking at Sophie suspiciously. "Wait. How did you know?"

Sophie took in a deep breath. "That's kinda why I'm here. I wanted to ask you about something."

Roscoe dumped the food into Mincemeat's bowl, then ladled his pasta sauce on top of a heaping bowl of spaghetti noodles and gestured to a chair.

"Go on, sit down. I'll eat and listen. You talk."

Sophie sat down and told Roscoe all that had happened after their adventure with the elementals—listening to the tree, feeling its pain, and figuring out that the magic within the hole was death magic.

"I know you and Headmistress probably already knew what kind of magic was hurting the tree," Sophie said. "It's just...so weird. I also, just tonight after dinner, started hearing this hum from the tree. I've never heard it before, and none of my friends say they can hear it. Just this deep, low hum..." Her voice trailed off.

Roscoe, who had finished his pasta, put down his bowl and rubbed his scratchy chin.

"That's a real interesting story you got there," he said. "Seems to me I once heard of a rare type of magical ability where they could do that kind of stuff, like you said—hearing the tree, hearing Mincemeat, communicating with animals and plants and other people through touch or thought alone. Some of them could even see the future or be able to tell who had lived in a house just by touching it—that kind of thing. From what I know, those don't exist anymore, if they ever did. You know, all those fakes at carnivals and wack-a-doodle people who think they're dog whisperers." Roscoe snorted.

Sophie shivered, remembering Professor Rogers' talk about psionics.

"Then again, I don't know much about the life gift," Roscoe went on. "All this could just be an offshoot of your gift. You got a pretty strong one, you know." Roscoe leaned forward, keeping his voice low. "Headmistress Case doesn't let students get involved in truly dangerous stuff, like what happened today. Especially not first years."

Sophie felt a thrill of pride race through her, followed by a sinking feeling of dread.

If Headmistress Case was willing to let Sophie get involved, if she felt it was important to have Sophie's help, even though Sophie was an amateur and Headmistress was a pro…

What were they up against?

Marcus tossed angrily in his bed. He couldn't keep the raging thoughts out of his head long enough to fall asleep.

There were very few signs that his death spike had worked. Sure, rumors were flying, and some weirdo girl had hugged the tree because it was in pain. Marcus snorted. Life elementals were such crybabies.

He tossed for a little longer, waiting until all the lights were out and his roommates' snores filled the air.

Then, he slipped on his hoodie and snuck out of his room. He had to go find out what was happening with Thicket Hall.

He kept to the shadows of the trees as he crossed the lawn and the stone pathway leading to Thicket Hall. He glared up at its branches, still sturdy and strong. They waved gently in the breeze as if mocking him.

Gritting his teeth, he quickened his pace, finally arriving at the spot where his death spike had been hammered into the ground.

There was, of course, a hole that had been dug around the spot. When he reached into the hole, he found that the death energy still pulsed deep below the ground. It had burrowed its way further into the root system, just like he'd wanted.

He glared at the root nearest the hole. It still dripped with sweet life energy; he could feel it. Deep down, he could feel his death energy creeping, lurking in the shadows, sickening but not killing.

Marcus growled, then kicked the root. Nothing was dead about this tree. Nothing except one blackened leaf that lay near the edge of the hole.

Was that all he could do? Had he overestimated the strength of his gift?

Or had he underestimated the life force of Thicket Hall?

He halfheartedly kicked the tree one more time, then sprinted back to his dorm.

CHAPTER TWELVE

"All right, class!" Professor Ann Schuyler called. She snapped her bedecked fingers, her metal bangles clinking against each other as she moved. "Today is the first day of Elemental Art. We'll be starting to learn how to turn our wonderful gifts into magnificent mosaics. Who's excited?"

Leslie and Janet, who'd chosen seats next to Sophie, raised their hands enthusiastically, along with several other students.

"Wonderful!" The professor peered across the class through half-moon glasses. "We'll have a volunteer from each gift, shall we?"

Janet raised her hand again, and a few other students shyly raised theirs as well.

"Let's have you. What's your gift?" She pointed at someone toward the back.

"Air," said a familiar voice, and Sophie saw it was Bri who'd volunteered.

"And what about you, young lady?"

"I'm water." Sheila, with her curly red hair, came

bouncing to the front of the room.

As Professor Schuyler picked the rest of the volunteers, Sophie opened her notebook, right to the page where she'd doodled the word "psionics." She added notes about what Roscoe had told her the night before, hearing plants and animals and seeing their memories and thoughts.

Could she be one of them? Professor Rogers seemed to imply they still existed, though they were rare. Roscoe, on the other hand, felt more skeptical. He wasn't sure if they existed or if they ever had.

Sophie wondered if that gift ran in families or if people just had it randomly. She wrote a note to do some research on that, though her hopes were low that that particular aspect of psionics had been studied.

"Now that everyone's gathered, let's have earth go first. You'll create the 'ground' of the piece if you'll pardon the expression." Professor Schuyler's tinkling laugh rang through the classroom.

Sophie put down her pencil. She supposed she really should be paying attention. There was an exhibition of some sort at the end of the year, and she didn't want to fail it.

Janet—because of course, she'd volunteered—closed her eyes, then opened them. Sophie recognized the green glow from their confrontation with Olivia in the bathroom and watched in interest as Janet wove a rough foundation, turning the unfinished stones and gems on the lab table into a patterned, climbing terrace.

"Good work."

Janet beamed with pride.

"Now, let's have fire. That will 'seal' the foundation and

purify the gems and rocks."

Vince stepped up next, looking nervous. He closed his eyes and took deep breaths.

When he opened his glowing eyes, a brief tingling sensation wash through Sophie. She shuddered.

Leslie glanced at her sharply. "Did you feel that? Like an electric current."

Sophie nodded, her eyes wide. "What was that?"

Screams suddenly erupted. The empty seat where Janet had been sitting burst into flame. Leslie practically jumped into Sophie's lap, screeching, and shot a burst of water at it.

"Sorry! I'm so sorry!" Vince had clenched his hands to his chest, his eyes still glowing as he looked at Leslie apologetically. "I can't make it stop! I don't know what's happening!"

Flames began to spread. Sophie dragged Leslie to the side of the room, and Janet quickly joined them.

"My book bag! My book bag is on fire!" She wept on Leslie's shoulder.

"Seriously?" Leslie shook her shoulders. "That could have been *you*! And you're crying about your *book bag?*"

"Calm down, everyone!" Professor Schuyler blew a whistle, and several hunter-green-clad staff members rushed in. "Up the sides of the class, through the exit doors. Everyone!"

Sophie and Leslie joined the stampede of students trying to escape the flash fire. Sophie glanced behind her to see a few of the staff members step forward, their eyes glowing aquamarine. Jets of water burst from their hands as they drenched Janet's seat and flaming book bag.

Smoke was rapidly filling their mouths and noses, and

Sophie ran for the exit with her friends. They escaped to the fresh air outside, many of the students coughing and red-faced.

"All my notes were in there," Janet said as soon as she could talk. "What am I gonna do now?"

"Janet. Babe." Bri threw her arm around Janet's shoulders. "We've only been in class, what, two days? We'll buy you a new book bag, okay? And you can copy my notes."

"But you don't take notes!" Janet started crying again.

Sophie glanced around, noting that whispers were starting up, about Vince, about that strange feeling right before the fire broke out.

"Did you two feel that weird current?" Sophie asked Janet and Bri.

"Yeah," Bri said, shivering. "That was weird. I wonder if that had anything to do with Vince's powers going haywire."

"Probably," Janet pouted. "But that doesn't get my book bag back."

"Janet!" All three girls chorused.

Janet cowered. "Sorry. I'll shut up."

Norma Case ushered the three professors into her office a mere forty-eight hours after their first meeting. This time, Clarice Nelson sat rigid on the loveseat, Violet Rogers twisted a tissue in her hands until it began to tear, and Byrne Murphy's soundproof wall layered twice as thick as usual.

"We're in deep trouble," Clarice said. "Deep."

"It's only the second day of classes, and the tree is sick, kids are causing flash fires..." Violet Rogers' hands shook. "Ann's studio went up in smoke in that fiasco."

"On the way over, I saw water coming out of a window in the water building like a volcano erupting," Byrne said, his fists clenched. "Headmistress, what's going on with the tree?"

Norma took in a slow, steady breath. She had to stay calm and logical for their sakes as much as her own.

"That isn't all," Norma said. "I'm sure you heard about the ruckus yesterday afternoon."

"Is it true?" Violet leaned forward, pieces of tissue falling off her slacks. "Were there elementals?"

Norma nodded. The three professors exchanged wary, nervous glances.

"That's not good," Clarice said. "The only reason elementals would be here is if..."

"If history is repeating itself. If we're reliving what happened in 1896." Violet snatched another tissue from the box on Norma's desk and started to twist it. "But how?"

"We think we have a pretty good idea," Norma said. "It's death magic, just like in 1896. Someone has injured the tree, and it can't contain the channels as well. Not everything is the same. It's not mismatching powers to gifts like it did the first time, but things are getting out of control."

"So, what do we do?" Byrne asked. "We can't just cancel classes and send everyone home, but we still have to protect the students."

"Agree," said Norma. "We're getting close to the source of the death magic. If we can find it and somehow remove it, the tree won't sicken anymore and will start to heal slowly. Then Roscoe, Nurse Bonnie, and any other talented life elemental professors we can find can help the tree reverse the damage. That means replacing dead soil, cutting off dead roots, as well as pushing the death sickness out of the roots with life energy."

"But whoever sickened the tree must be very strong," Clarice said. "If we're already seeing elementals because its buffer is weakened…"

"That's all true," Norma said. "But at this point, we don't know how strong it is, and we'll assume it's something we can handle if we can get enough people to help."

"We also don't have that many life professors. Nurse Bonnie, Garver, maybe one other that's slipping my mind right now," Byrne said.

"There are other talents we could pull from," Norma said mysteriously. "If the need arose."

"You mean students?" Violet said. "Norma, that's crazy."

"Perhaps," Norma said. "But probably not as much as you think. You see, I had help fighting back the elementals. More help than just Roscoe."

The three professors stared at her incredulously.

"Headmistress," Byrne said, straining to keep his voice respectful, "You know that's against our code."

"The code is there to protect us in ordinary times," Norma said sharply. "I should know. I was there to see it ratified."

Clarice barely masked a scoff.

"But these are not ordinary times," Norma continued, ignoring her. "We will need both students and staff to contribute to protecting the tree if we're going to survive this crisis. And need I remind you how much new talent we have? The student that successfully helped me ward off the elementals was only a first-year. And yet, she showed more raw talent and power than most of the senior class combined."

"Who was it?" Clarice asked, now curious.

"It doesn't particularly matter who," said Norma. "Though I'll tell you she has the life gift. I watched her single-handedly take down an earth elemental that was ready to throw her across the lawn."

"Whoa," Byrne said, smiling. "That's some skill."

"True, she wore herself out quite quickly. With the right training and a good mentor, she—and any others who are very talented—can learn to control their gift and their energy and join us in the fight."

"So, we're definitely not canceling classes," Violet asked apprehensively. "Even though students were severely burned today?"

"Correct," Norma said. "We will have to take many more ordinary precautions. Burn-proof gear, face shields, and goggles, that kind of thing. Much more of that. We mustn't let go of the talent that could help us get through this crisis with the tree—and the school's legacy—intact."

"What about the Elemental Safety and Containment Board?" Byrne asked.

"You leave that to me," Norma said. "If I play my cards right, they will never know and never need to know."

"This is risky," Violet said. "Are you sure we don't need outside help?"

"If I call the ESCB, they will gladly jump on any opportunity to shut down this school and send everyone home. Forever." An angry breeze began to blow around Norma's desk. "Do you know what they would do with Thicket Hall? What unlimited resources they would have with the ley lines in their possession? What bureaucracy and utter malarky…" She took a deep breath, and the winds, which had begun whipping papers into a frenzy, dispersed.

The professors, who'd been covering their heads, slowly looked up, their eyes wide.

"We will not call upon their…*services*…unless it's absolutely necessary. A last resort, if you will."

The three professors nodded.

"I'll need you three to compile a list of all the talent you see, especially any outliers. Really push for them to be put through their paces. Fast track their mentors. Then, as we progress with getting rid of whatever is wounding the tree, we'll know which students to pull if needed."

"Will do," said Byrne, echoed quickly by the two ladies.

As the professors gathered themselves to leave and Byrne pulled down his stone barrier, Violet turned to Norma.

"I hope you know what you're doing," she said quietly, so the others couldn't hear. "Don't let pride get in the way of protecting what matters."

Norma stared pensively at her desk but said nothing, even after Violet and the others had gone and shut the door behind them.

She couldn't fail. She absolutely couldn't. Thicket Hall could *not* fall into the wrong hands, especially not hands at the ECSB that had caused so much suffering to so many magicals through the decades. And if it meant bringing students into the fight…

Norma sighed. "So be it."

CHAPTER THIRTEEN

That afternoon, Sophie, Charlotte, and Sophie's roommates traipsed up the path toward the open arena for gym class. They'd been told to dress in athletic wear, or at least shorts and short-sleeved t-shirts.

Sophie had gone through the motions of her morning classes, though she did notice that Reggie made a point of helping Charlotte in Life Fundamentals. And, of course, there had been the bizarre fire in art class. Janet had been a mess ever since, even when the girls had pooled together their extra supplies to give Janet a new set.

But her thoughts were still preoccupied with Thicket Hall and what might be wrong with it, and whether that had anything to do with the strange sensation they'd all felt. She'd heard its humming all night and still heard it now. If anything, it seemed to be getting louder, never quite blending into the background no matter how long she had been hearing it.

"You still have that weird ringing in your ears?" Leslie asked as they walked.

Sophie nodded. The open arena was farther away from the tree, and Sophie was somewhat glad of it. It lessened the buzzing in her ears and made her feel like maybe she was normal after all and not a weird, semi-non-existent psionic.

At least, that was her best guess. No one else in her family had ever experienced anything like she was, or if they had, they'd never told her.

"I really do think you should go see an ear doctor," Janet said, her eyes bloodshot. "Hearing loss is nothing to mess around with."

"But I can hear everything else just fine," Sophie protested. "I don't think it's my hearing. It has something to do with Thicket Hall because how loud it is depends on how close I am to it."

Janet shrugged her shoulders. "It's worth getting checked out, in my opinion."

"That is interesting, though," said Charlotte. "I've never been able to 'hear' things like that. I wonder if your life gift is just super strong, and that's why."

Sophie sighed. "I don't know, but I wish I could figure it out."

They filtered into the arena, where several different stations had been set up around the perimeter.

"Hey!" Sophie glanced up to see Peter and his roommates waving at them. She and Leslie waved back. Peter tugged at his sleeves—still long despite the syllabus' dress code—and when Sophie made eye contact, he looked away.

That was odd. Did it have anything to do with the reason he had appointments with Nurse Bonnie, Sophie wondered?

She didn't have time to think much about it, though, before Olivia, Sheila, and March walked past them, snickering and whispering. Sophie's stomach dropped when she watched them go to the dodge ball station—the same one she and her friends were supposed to go to.

"Oh, great," said Bri, biting into an oatmeal cream cookie. "Just what we need."

"Seriously, where do you keep those things?" Janet snarked.

"Why? You want one?" Bri asked with her mouth full.

For once, Janet nodded and took one from Bri, devouring it instantly.

"Dude," Bri said, her eyes wide.

Janet looked back at her. "I've had a rough morning, okay?"

They reluctantly made their way over to the dodgeball court.

"Hey, look, it's the tree hugger!" Olivia said while Sheila and March cackled. "Hey, Charlotte! Get over here."

Charlotte begrudgingly shuffled over across the center line to join Olivia.

"We need two more on each side over here!" Shouted a well-built, though short, man. "How about you?"

Sophie saw a group of four boys pause. The tallest one, his hood drawn up, frowned.

"Coach Hughes, do we have to?"

"Just one game, fellas," Coach Hughes said, ushering them over. "Remember, all the normal rules apply, except you can only use your powers to move the ball."

The tall one and a dark-skinned boy with happy amber

eyes shuffled toward Sophie. The taller one looked at his phone and grumbled under his breath.

"Hi," said the other boy. "My name's Geoff."

"Hey." Sophie gave him a polite smile. "I'm Sophie."

She glanced expectantly at the tall boy, but he didn't register her existence.

"Eh, don't mind Marcus," Geoff said, then leaned in and whispered, "He's a sourpuss."

Sophie started and glanced at the tall boy again. Just under his hood, she could see a glimmer of bright white hair.

He glanced sideways at her, his brow furrowed angrily. "What are you looking at?"

"Nothing." Sophie folded her hands in front of her. "Just wondering how you're gonna play with that hoodie on."

Marcus clicked his phone to turn the screen off, then tucked it in his pocket and stepped closer to her, straightening to his full height.

Sophie had to admit that he was intimidating, especially because she'd accidentally experienced his gift firsthand. Still, she didn't cower.

"I'm not playing this game. That's how," Marcus growled.

"Well," she said, crossing her arms, "if you're on this team, I'm not picking up your slack."

Marcus stared at her, his dark eyes widening. Then he shrugged nonchalantly, shoved his hands in his pockets, and turned away from her.

"Suits me just fine. I'd rather be out anyway."

Sophie sighed in exasperation.

"Don't worry about it, Sophie," Bri said. She was

jogging in place and punching the air with more energy than Sophie had ever seen her exert. "I'm a whiz at dodgeball. I'll carry this team solo if I have to."

Sophie laughed and rolled her eyes. "Good to know, Bri."

"Hey, wait a second." Marcus pulled down his hood, suddenly smirking at Sophie. "Aren't you the one that was hugging Thicket Hall? Yeah, Sophie. I remember now."

Olivia's tinkling laugh sounded across the court. "That's right! You want to see my pictures?"

Marcus laughed. "Nah. I believe it. You're just like every other little life princess I've ever met, crying over dead things. Well, guess what? Death happens. And some of us are really good at making it happen. Despite people like you." He rolled up his sleeves and gave a dismissive snort, walking to the other side of the court. He jerked his head, and one of the boys ran over to Sophie's side, taking his place. "Looks like you did win on something, though, cause now I'm in the mood to knock you dead."

"Yeah!" Olivia walked over and high-fived Marcus, who glanced down her figure appreciatively before taking his place against the stone half-wall.

Sophie wished she was more quick-witted, but the only response she could come up with was to heave a frustrated growl and stomp back to her team's wall.

"What a jerk!" Leslie scowled at Marcus, who sneered at her. "Don't worry, Soph. He's just bitter and jealous."

"Bitter, yes," said the boy who'd taken his place. He was fitting his glasses into a sports band. "Jealous, no. The guy is a narcissist. Thinks he's the greatest death elemental of all time."

Sophie snorted. There was no denying he had talent, but the best? At *death,* of all things? Who in their right mind would take pride in that?

Professor Rogers' lecture came back to her full force, and she clamped down on those thoughts. The guy *could* take pride in his abilities, she supposed.

Marcus flashed her a smug grin from across the court as the players lined up and prepared to grab their balls from the center line.

Her blood ran hot. He didn't have to be such a jerk about it, though.

"Three, two, one, dodgeball!" Cried Coach Hughes.

Sophie scrambled to the center line, remembering at the last second that she had to use her powers. Summoning whatever flora she could find below the packed dirt, she hurled the ball at the stone half-wall behind her. Bri let it bounce and caught Sophie's ball, then spun a vortex that whirled the ball before spitting it toward the other team.

Sophie ran back, noting Olivia's focused gaze was on her—and Olivia had a ball. Sophie hurriedly formed a netting of grassy vines in front of her just as Olivia blasted the ball toward her.

But instead of hitting Sophie, Olivia's flaming ball crashed into the boy with glasses. Despite the sports band, his glasses were still knocked askew as he shuffled himself out.

Sophie picked up the ball Olivia had thrown and gave her a grin.

"Right back at you!" she yelled, using her vine netting—and her anger—to flick the ball at Olivia.

The ball soared over the center line, walloping March

in the stomach. She curled over herself, and Sophie felt a sudden rush of guilt.

But before she could apologize, another ball hurtled toward her, carried on a trail of toxic, oily smoke.

"Take that, princess!" Marcus snarled. Sophie caught the ball just in time, though the sickening smell of Marcus's death magic made her eyes water. Her hands began to sting, and looking down at them, she saw the same sooty darkness spread over her palms and fingers.

"Ugh," she said, grimacing as the bee-sting sensation overtook her hands. Thinking quickly, she fashioned a slingshot out of a few new vines and aimed it directly at Marcus' shiny blond head.

"Yah!" she cried, imagining herself as a warrior as she released the springy vines and let the ball sail across the court.

Elation erupted in her chest as the ball made contact with Marcus' face. Triumphantly, she grabbed another ball, intent on getting Olivia this time.

Coach Hughes blew a whistle, calling a pause. Sophie glanced at him, then at her teammates.

Dread sunk in her stomach. They were all out, even Bri, who looked to be nursing a swollen eye.

And across the court, similarly alone, stood Olivia, panting and glaring at Sophie.

Sophie's guilt returned when she noticed March crying in the corner, Sheila's arm around her shoulder.

"Looks like we have a showdown!" Coach said. "Man, y'all really played rough today!" He scratched his head. "Either y'all got really talented all of a sudden or very spirited."

Sophie wondered for a moment if everyone's increased energy—and their balls going awry—had anything to do with the elementals and the tree being damaged. She looked at March and Marcus' bruised cheek and sighed, dropping her ball.

"Coach, it's okay. I don't want a showdown." She gestured at the injured kids. "We need to get these kids to the nurse."

Olivia threw her ball at Sophie. "You're just scared I'm going to beat you!"

"No," Sophie said, gesturing at March. "Look, people got hurt. I work with Nurse Bonnie, so I'll help."

March stopped sniffling for a few seconds, peering at Sophie suspiciously.

Coach scratched his chin. "That'll be a loss for your team, Sophie."

"It's fine. Olivia's team can have the win."

Olivia huffed before storming off the court. "Whatever."

As Sophie led the injured kids down the path, Marcus called, "Hey, princess! You totally just lost, and you know it. Copped out because you couldn't face Olivia on your own."

"Shut up, Marcus!" Sophie snapped. "There are more important things in life than winning."

Marcus merely cackled in response, but Sophie headed down the hill, walking so fast that Bri had to ask her to slow down.

"Hey. What was that all about?" Bri asked. "You could have beaten Olivia. It would have been okay. March was just being a brat."

Sophie gently touched Bri's black eye, channeling

energy so the broken blood vessels closed and her eye didn't look as puffy.

"It was my fault everyone got hurt," Sophie said. "It didn't feel right trying to take Olivia out, knowing that."

Bri patted her eye. "Hey! That's neat. It doesn't hurt as bad anymore."

Sophie smiled sadly. "Good. It shouldn't have happened."

None of it should have happened, Sophie thought.

As she shepherded her classmates through Nurse Bonnie's door, the nurse peeked in from the other room.

"Well, hello... Oh, dear." Nurse Bonnie glanced at Sophie. "That's a lot of patients. What happened?"

"Our dodgeball game got...rough." Sophie looked at anything but Nurse Bonnie's questioning gaze.

"Well, my goodness. I've seen some doozies, but..." She tutted, then walked up and down the line of students, touching each arm. "Second-degree burn, a black eye, and...my goodness! Bruised ribs!" She stopped at March, taking her face in her hands. "Poor dear."

Sophie gulped back guilty tears. March *hadn't* been faking it.

"How did all this happen?"

Sophie cleared her throat. "Well, like I said. The game got intense." She kneaded her hands. "How can I help?"

Sophie let herself get lost in helping and healing, bringing ice for Bri's black eye, ointment for the boy with the glasses who'd been beaned by Olivia's ball, and bandages for March's abdomen.

She held the tape in place as Nurse Bonnie wrapped it gingerly around March's ribs.

After Nurse Bonnie had moved on to the next patient, Sophie handed March a water bottle, then ripped open a pack of ibuprofen and held it out to her.

"Here. It'll help with the pain."

March took it, her gaze focused angrily on Sophie.

"I know. It was my fault. And I'm sorry."

March remained silent, though she swallowed the pills, cringing as she tried to breathe deeply.

"It probably doesn't help that I was trying to hit Olivia."

March snorted. "I wish you'd pegged her, honestly." She rolled her pretty blue eyes. "Makes my life torture."

Sophie couldn't hide a grin. Seized with an idea, she placed her hand gently over March's abdomen.

March drew back. "What are you doing?"

"I wanted to try and reduce your pain," Sophie said. "I have the life gift. My specialty is plants, but I was able to get Bri's swelling down on the way over." She jerked her head toward her friend, who was sitting on the next cot. Bri waved with her fingers, smiling grimly. One hand held the ice pack to her face.

March glanced at Sophie worriedly. "What if it doesn't work?"

Sophie shrugged. "Well, it's not going to *hurt* if it doesn't work."

March weighed her options, pursing her lips as she thought.

"Okay."

Sophie closed her eyes, seeking March's energy as she had with the tree. A pulsating ache that coincided with the rhythm of March's breathing trickled into Sophie's mind. She pressed further, trying to find the source. As she narrowed in, she moved her hand up, then slightly to the back.

"Ow!" March sucked in a breath as Sophie touched the injured spot.

"Sorry." Sophie then began filtering her energy, targeting the sore rib, calming the rush of blood to the area, and strengthening weakened muscle and tendon fibers. Humans were more complex than plants, it was true. It seemed to work the same, though.

"Oh. Wow." March took a deep breath, and Sophie noted that while there was still some discomfort, it had lessened significantly. "That already feels better."

Sophie smiled and began slowing the trickle of her energy. When she was fully present in her mind and body again, she swayed on her knees and almost fell.

"Whoa!" March reached down and steadied Sophie with a hand on her shoulder. "You okay?"

Sophie sat on the ground, the room spinning. "Must have used more energy than I thought." She pressed a hand to her forehead. It was clammy and slick with sweat.

"Nurse Bonnie!" Bri jerked her head toward Sophie. "Think she needs some help."

Nurse Bonnie hurried over, took one look at Sophie's face, and tutted.

"Pushed yourself too far, young lady." She disappeared into the other room, then came back with an electrolyte drink and a banana. "You'll have to replace the energy and nutrients you used up."

"This never happened with plants," Sophie said, leaning her head back against March's cot.

"Yes, well, plants are much simpler and not nearly as

needy as human beings," Nurse Bonnie scoffed. She examined March's rib, and her eyebrows rose. "I must say, Miss Sophia, you did an excellent job." She smiled proudly at Sophie. "You've got the makings of a great healer in you. Just don't overdo it." She waggled her finger at Sophie, then patted her head before hurrying off to help someone else.

Sophie took a huge swig of the drink.

March smiled at her. "Thanks, Sophie."

Despite the swirling room, Sophie's heart was full.

She'd helped make it right.

Marcus had laughed at Sophie, insulted her, and called her a coward.

But as he watched her and the hurt kids disappear down the path, he frowned.

"There are more important things in life than winning."

His father had once told him the same thing but had always turned it into a joke.

"There are more important things in life than winning, Marcus. Though I can't think of any right now."

He and his father would laugh together every time. Watching Sophie give up winning to help her friends had stirred something in Marcus he relentlessly tried to push down.

He tried hard to be the best at everything. He insulted everyone else, deeming them inferior. He worked his *butt* off to get where he wanted to go. He'd even worked hard to get into this school, the very school he was now trying to destroy to bolster his ego.

To watch someone like Sophie, who'd been so alive with antagonism and disdain for him and Olivia, simply drop the ball and walk away? It didn't make sense to him.

But it made sense to the thing he kept pushing down.

He crossed his arms, still staring at the path.

He wouldn't admit it took more courage to lose than to win. He refused to acknowledge that Sophie had something he didn't and would never have—the ability to walk away from a fight for the sake of people she cared about.

He couldn't stop himself from hurting Thicket Hall, even when he'd looked up at those gigantic branches and felt pity rising in his throat.

He'd been taught never to lose, and he didn't intend to. Not to Thicket Hall, and not to Sophie.

Not to anyone.

CHAPTER FOURTEEN

The next afternoon, Sophie jogged down the path to Thicket Hall, holding her backpack over her head to shield her from the late summer rain shower pelting the grounds. Nurse Bonnie had kept her late, and she was late for the first years' meeting.

As she approached the hall, the humming in her ears grew louder. Yesterday, she'd been so busy she hardly noticed it buzzing in the background of her mind. Today, she'd noted a significant reduction in the volume of its hum. She hoped that meant Headmistress Case and Roscoe were making progress toward healing it.

She blew a stray piece of hair out of her face as the rainy wind tossed it around. She couldn't help but feel resentful at how busy her classes were keeping her. What she wanted to be doing was helping heal the tree, not learn fifteen ways to crisscross vines for a mosaic or learn even more about how her gift of life had been revered historically and how castigated the death gift had been.

She frowned, recalling the ugly dodgeball game with Olivia and Marcus. She had enough to feel guilty about.

As she approached the entrance to Thicket Hall, she saw Headmistress Case standing under the awning. The imposing woman nodded as Sophie ducked inside, then shook her backpack off in the foyer.

Sophie found a seat next to her roommates and hastily pulled her long, damp hair into a ponytail. Olivia's straight black hair was as shiny and perfect as ever. She frowned. How did anyone have a good hair day in *this* weather?

"Where were you, Soph?" Leslie asked.

"Yeah. We were worried." Bri threw a blast of air toward Sophie. It dried her clothes and hair.

Sophie patted her hair, frowning as she felt tendrils of frizz.

"Thanks, Bri." She sighed. "I was helping Nurse Bonnie and lost track of time."

"Quiet, everyone!" Professor Violet Rogers strode into the hall, hands outstretched. "Quiet!"

"Looks like you were just in time," Janet whispered, elbowing Sophie.

"Today, we'll be forming the teams for the annual student project," Professor Rogers continued. "Each team will contain six members, one from each gift. The goal is to work together *as a team* to complete the project. This means no riding coattails for those of you who like to sit back and not participate."

Her piercing gaze swept the hall. "Everyone is expected to contribute something of worth. No work, no grade, and you will repeat this experience in your second year. You can ask our current second-year participants how they feel about this arrangement." She gestured at a grim-looking group of students that were sitting at a table by themselves.

Mutters and stifled laughter broke out. Sophie cringed, watching the second years frown at the table, mortified.

"Harsh," Bri said.

"This project will take the full year to complete and will add around two hours a week to your current workload, so plan accordingly. It will also account for twenty-five percent of your final grade. It is *not* skippable."

Bitter groans rose around Sophie. She couldn't help heaving a sigh. She was already starting to feel swamped, and it was only day three of school.

"Now for the groups."

Sophie listened halfheartedly as Professor Rogers began calling names, arranging students into groups, and giving them their assignments. One by one, each of her friends was sorted into a different team, and Sophie's heart sank. She'd hoped they'd at least be able to stay together.

"Group number nine will include Sophia Briggs for life," Professor Rogers began.

Sophie's ears perked.

"Peter Travis for earth."

Sophie glanced at Peter, who gave her a broad smile and a thumbs-up. She grinned back. At least there was one friend in her group.

"Sheila Matthews for water."

Sophie tried to hide a grimace.

"Luke Barron for air."

Luke, seated next to Peter at their table, pumped his fist and high-fived Peter.

"Genevieve Summers for death."

Sophie glanced at the second-year table. A willowy red-headed girl in black jeans rolled her eyes as the table hissed with quiet laughter.

"And Olivia Wright for fire. Team members, please pick a spot and gather."

Professor Rogers handed Sophie a sealed manila envelope and moved on to the next group, leaving Sophie gaping.

Olivia? On her team?

This project was *so* doomed.

One by one, her teammates found their way to the table. Peter and Luke were the only friendly faces. Their smiles almost counterbalanced the sneers and glowering coming at Sophie from the three girls. Almost.

"Let me see the packet," Olivia demanded, snatching it from Sophie's hands.

Sophie opened her mouth to protest but decided that battling Olivia for a flammable object wasn't the best idea. Especially since so much of their first-year grade depended on doing whatever was *on* that paper.

Olivia yanked a paper from the envelope and skimmed it, her brows furrowing as she read. Sheila looked over her shoulder, but she couldn't read as fast as Olivia.

"You've got to be kidding me." Olivia tossed the paper on the table. Sophie grabbed it and shared it with the boys and Genevieve, who crowded around her to read it.

Group Nine First-Year Project: Plant and grow a maple from seed to a five-foot young tree by end of the year.

All six elemental gifts must be used in the process and fully documented for credit, using the log pages in the envelope. Each of you will take a log and keep it with you each time you work on your project together.

Plan a consistent time that works for the six of you to meet and work on the project. Working on it alone is not acceptable. This is a team *effort.*

You will also find your maple seed starter in the envelope.

"Well, this should be cake," Luke said, gesturing at Sophie. "That's, like, your whole thing, right?"

"You heard what Professor Rogers said," Sophie said. "It has to be *all* of us when we work on this. You can't just show up and get credit."

"This is totally not fair," Olivia said. "What does fire have to do with growing things?"

"Or death," Genevieve said, her voice high and musical. She tossed her curly red hair over her shoulder.

Sophie took a deep breath. "I'm sure there are ways you can contribute to this project. There has to be. Otherwise, Professor Rogers wouldn't have assigned this to us."

"That's probably what we're supposed to learn," Peter said. "All the different ways our gifts work together."

"Easy for you to say, dirt boy," Olivia said. "Earth is very relevant to growing things."

"So is water!" Sheila said shrilly, raising her hand.

Olivia shot her a glare, and she withered.

Peter frowned, crossing his arms. "Look. We're not going to get anywhere calling each other names."

Olivia rolled her eyes but didn't say anything else.

"Let's figure out when we're going to meet, I guess," Sophie said. "Do you all have your schedules handy?"

For a moment, the sound of rustling papers filled the

air. Sophie pulled out her schedule, circling a couple of blocks of free time each day. Her heart sank as she glanced once more at her already-packed schedule. When was she going to visit Roscoe again and ask about the tree?

After a few moments of back and forth, Sophie and her team settled on Saturday afternoon before dinner.

"We should probably come in clothes we don't mind getting dirty," Sophie added.

Olivia scoffed, examining her nails. "I don't own anything like that."

"Maybe you could borrow from someone," Luke suggested. He closed his mouth when Olivia glared at him.

"Wearing other people's clothes? Ew."

"Was just a suggestion," Luke mumbled.

"What about gym clothes?" Sophie asked. "Like the ones you wore to dodgeball?"

"That was five-hundred-dollar name-brand athleticwear!" Olivia hissed. Her eyes began to glow, but as she glanced at the second-year table, she closed her eyes and took deep breaths. "I guess that'll work," she growled, defeated.

"Good." Sophie nodded, then made brief eye contact with everyone. "We'll meet this Saturday. I'll keep the seed with me so it can get a head start."

As they dispersed, she could hear Olivia mocking her. "I'll keep the seed with me 'cause I'm Miss Miracle Grow."

Sheila cackled and glanced at Sophie. She laughed harder when she saw Sophie's glare.

Sophie harrumphed, crossing her arms.

"Ignore her," Peter said, handing her the envelope. "She's just mad that it's not gonna be easy for her."

Sophie's gut twisted. What if their project had been something else, like building a miniature volcano or turning coal into diamonds? What if it had been something outside Sophie's comfort zone, like growing a tree was for Olivia?

Wouldn't she feel the same about Olivia as Olivia felt about her right now?

She had to admit, although she couldn't stand Olivia, the girl had a right to be frustrated.

Of course, it didn't help that Olivia didn't like Sophie.

"I mean, it *is* unfair," Sophie said. "When you think about it."

Peter snorted in disdain. "Just karma coming for her, in my opinion," he said, glancing at Olivia with an uncharacteristic hardness in his green eyes. "She's done plenty of unfair things to you."

Sophie looked at him, surprised, and he softened. "I mean, I get it. And I admire that you can be so...gentle toward other people." He picked at his long sleeves. "I wish I could be that way."

Without thinking about it, Sophie put her hand over his. He stopped picking at his sleeve, startled.

"You've been nothing but kind to me," Sophie said. "This is the first time I've ever seen you be harsh toward someone else. I can't imagine you any other way."

Peter smiled, though he kept his gaze on the ground. Sophie realized she was still touching his hand and blushed. From deep within Peter, where her fingers touched his, she felt an odd, faded ache.

Sophie furrowed her brows, trying to understand the sensation. It evaded her probing, staying just out of reach.

"Peter," Sophie asked. "Were you ever…hurt? Are you hurt now?"

Peter glanced down at her hand, then back at her, confused. The aching sensation vanished as suddenly as it had appeared.

"Um. No. I mean, of course, I've gotten hurt in the past, but..." His voice trailed off. "Why?"

Sophie shook her head, withdrawing her hand quickly.

"Nothing. I just wondered." She laughed nervously and shrugged. "Sometimes my life gift picks up on weird things, and it's hard to sort it out."

"Huh." Peter rubbed his hand where she'd touched it, then firmly tugged his sleeves down. He glanced up at her, his eyes probing. Now she was the one hiding something. "Interesting."

The hum of the big tree didn't invade her mind nearly as much that night. She tried for several minutes to go to sleep, but questions nagged at her mind, keeping her awake.

Finally, she slipped out of bed, quietly dressed, and tiptoed out of the dorms, heading toward Roscoe's workshop.

As she headed up the path behind Thicket Hall, she thought she heard some rustling nearby and stood stock still, her heart thumping.

Another figure darted out of the shadow of Thicket Hall and headed toward the boys' dorms.

Sophie let out her breath as soon as the figure was out

of earshot. Another kid out past curfew? It was probably more common than she thought. Still, she didn't like the creepiness of walking alone in the dark.

Mincemeat started mewing when Sophie was still a few dozen yards from the workshop. She was close enough for the tabby to recognize her from the window.

Sophie didn't even have to knock. She simply waited until Roscoe had had enough of Mincemeat's incessant crying at the door.

"All right, ya mangy cat. Move out of the way, will you?" Roscoe opened the door, his eyes widening when he saw Sophie.

"What are you doing here?" He glanced behind her. "It's after curfew."

"I know," Sophie said, nervously twisting her hair. "I just...wanted to know about Thicket Hall. I haven't heard that weird humming much today. Have you and Headmistress made any progress?"

Roscoe sighed, rolling his eyes. "Would you not blab in the doorway? Here, come in. Quick."

He ushered Sophie through the door, then shut it behind her.

Sophie reeled. Oily darkness covered her mind.

"What...what is that?" Sophie shook her head.

"Oh, you feel it," Roscoe said. He pointed at the far side of his workshop, where something small and pointed sat on a wooden table. "It's death magic."

Mincemeat rubbed Sophie's legs ferociously, and she could feel the same darkness crowding the poor cat's energy.

"Hey, um, Roscoe? You might want to let your cat out. He doesn't like that thing." She grimaced. "Neither do I."

Roscoe let Mincemeat out the door, then handed Sophie a heavy vest-like garment with a flat rock sewn onto the front.

"Here, put this on."

Sophie struggled into it. The oily darkness receded, and she was able to approach the table without gagging.

The small dark spike swirled with the smoky blackness that had stained her hands during the dodgeball game when Marcus had tried to knock her out.

"Don't touch it. Don't reckon you'd want to, anyway."

"What is it?" It barely glinted in the light, looking more like a spike-shaped hole in the table than an actual object.

"It's a spike of pure death energy," Roscoe explained. He grabbed a handful of healthy leaves and scattered them around the spike. Each one shriveled and turned to black, sooty material instantly.

Sophie gasped, remembering the hole by Thicket Hall. Everything about that encounter now made sense, from the throbbing pain localized in one root to the tree showing her where it had been hurt.

"This is what hurt the tree, isn't it?"

"From what I can tell," Roscoe agreed, rubbing the back of his neck. "The problem is, I don't know how to reverse it."

Sophie glanced at him, alarmed.

"A lot has seeped into the roots, you see? It's not doing anything right now, but it could, given enough time."

Sophie's heart constricted. "How can I help?"

Roscoe studied her, then grabbed a book from the bookshelf. He flipped rapidly until he reached the page he wanted, then shook his head and shut the book sharply with one hand.

"Nah. I can't let a first-year get involved." He shelved the book. "What if you get hurt? Then I get fired, the ESCB gets involved..."

"I can handle myself," Sophie retorted. "You saw how I handled those elementals. Headmistress Case wouldn't have let me help if she thought I wasn't strong enough."

Roscoe stared at her, a mysterious smile on his face.

"Besides," Sophie went on, pacing, "what if Thicket Hall doesn't survive this? Then what?"

Roscoe's smile faded. His deep-set eyes glistened, and Sophie sensed she'd hit a nerve. Thicket Hall was important—no, vital—and especially dear to Roscoe, who'd taken care of it for years.

He reached for another book and skimmed the pages.

"I suppose..." He flipped a page and read more, then shut the book with a resigned sigh. "I suppose that'll be fine, but just a couple of experiments, okay?" He waggled his finger at her. "We're not talking save-the-tree stuff, just testing some possibilities on some smaller plants to see if they work."

Sophie beamed. "Yes!"

Roscoe couldn't help but smile.

"Now, you'd better go back to bed. I'll let you know when I want you to come for the experiments, okay? But no more breaking the rules."

"Okay, Roscoe." Sophie took off the stone vest, stumbling as the death energy pummeled her again. "I'm gonna go before this thing tries to kill me."

Roscoe chuckled, watching as Sophie ran across the lawn, excitement fueling her steps.

CHAPTER FIFTEEN

Sophie found herself going through the motions of her classes the next day, vigilantly keeping an eye out for Roscoe in case he decided he needed her help with the tree. She'd been ecstatic when Roscoe had agreed to let her help with a few experiments. Maybe she could help get them one step closer to healing the tree…or maybe even contribute to its healing herself.

The afternoon hours found her in Nurse Bonnie's office. It was a slower day, and Sophie sat behind the check-in desk, munching on a bag of chips Bri had given her.

"Can't have you fainting on the job anymore," Bri had told her, stuffing the chips in Sophie's bag with a wink.

Sophie smiled. She and her roommates were so close already. She couldn't wait to see how their friendships would blossom even more throughout the year.

A jingling bell announced someone's arrival through the door.

"Coming!" Called Nurse Bonnie from upstairs.

Sophie glanced up, shocked to see Peter standing in the foyer. Checking her clipboard, she realized she shouldn't have been so shocked. He was right on time for his 3:30 appointment.

Peter made eye contact with her, but instead of smiling, his eyes went wide.

"Oh, um. Sophie. What are you doing here?" He glanced around furtively for the nurse.

"I work here," Sophie said with a laugh. "I never told you?"

"Uh, no. I don't guess so." Peter chuckled nervously, rubbing his neck and backing toward the door. "I guess Nurse Bonnie is busy right now, so I'll just go—"

"Here I am!" Nurse Bonnie bustled down the stairs, beaming at Peter. "On time, as usual, Sir Peter."

Peter gave a nervous smile, his cheeks darkening, then glanced back at Sophie, dread in his eyes.

Sophie smiled back, gesturing toward Nurse Bonnie. The nurse ushered Peter into the next room, pulling the door behind her until it was just cracked.

Sophie wanted to respect Peter's privacy. Still, she couldn't help but wonder to herself what his ailment might be. And what it might have to do with the fact that he was always tugging those long sleeves down.

Some time passed, and all was quiet. Sophie finished off her chips, then pulled her Elemental Science notebook from her book bag and tried to focus on studying her notes. Professor Nelson had said something about a pop quiz.

But all she could focus on was the ticking of the clock on the wall, loud in the silent room, and the soft rustling of activity from the other room.

"Thanks, Nurse Bonnie!" Sophie looked up as Peter re-entered the room, followed closely by the nurse. Peter nodded and waved at Sophie, seeming much more like his usual self, but his other hand was clenched around an object Sophie couldn't see.

"Slow day today, huh?" Nurse Bonnie leaned against the check-in table as they both watched Peter leave. "After all the activity in recent days, it feels kinda weird."

"Yeah," said Sophie absentmindedly, still focused on Peter's form and the object in his hand as he traipsed down the porch steps and across the lawn.

"You know, those rumors have been picking up again. This time, people are starting to talk about rough types." Nurse Bonnie lowered her voice, leaning closer to Sophie. "You know. Thugs and hooligans."

Sophie stirred to attention. "Here? In Bardstown?"

"I know! It's absolutely mind-blowing. Such a small, friendly little town, and now people are starting to get nervous. Car windows are being smashed, random fires have been started... It's awful."

Sophie's mind spun. Random fires? She'd seen what a wild fire elemental could do just by touching a tree. Was it possible they were escaping Headmistress Case's notice and traveling into town?

"I would expect that in a big city like Louisville, but not here," Sophie said. "What do you think those types are doing here?"

Nurse Bonnie was practically in Sophie's face.

"You know, I've heard some stories. Some say they're here because of what's happening with Thicket Hall. Not all people with an elemental gift are friendly, you know. Some want to see the school fall into disgrace. Some want what they think is unlimited power provided by such an ancient tree."

Sophie nodded. It made sense. If the tree was a source of elemental power, it would make sense that damaging it would mess up the balance of things, releasing wild elementals and causing havoc with their gifts. Hadn't Vince just burned Professor Schuyler's studio to a crisp?

And what about that weird, electric-feeling current they'd all experienced?

There were too many links for it to all be a big coincidence.

"But I don't know about the tree being some power source," Nurse Bonnie laughed, backing up and heading into the next room. She gestured for Sophie to follow. "It's just a big old tree. A big sweetheart of a tree, I'm sure," she said, glancing out the window toward Thicket Hall. "But just a tree all the same."

Sophie followed the nurse. She, too, glanced out at Thicket Hall. The tree's familiar hum sounded gentler today, but something about it tugged at her. There was a dissonance there that hadn't been there before, and when Sophie closed her eyes and focused on it, there was a hint of the same oily blackness that had swirled in the death spike Roscoe had found.

She frowned, her heart sinking. Roscoe was right; the

poison was spreading. She had to help him find a cure for Thicket Hall and fast.

Otherwise, the school, the tree, her friends, and the community of Bardstown would all have to face the consequences.

CHAPTER SIXTEEN

"Seriously?" Olivia stomped off the small white bus. "I can't believe we're growing something *again.*"

Sophie repressed a snort as she and her roommates got off the bus. Their Community Service Class, a once-a-month Friday afternoon class, had broken the first years into smaller groups. Blessedly, Sophie had been paired with her roommates, but the teachers had kept it simple and grouped next-door rooms, two boys' rooms, two girls' rooms, four rooms to a lot.

The nice thing was, they'd been paired with Peter and his roommates on the same lot, as well as another group of boys that Peter and his friends seemed amiable with.

But they have also stuck with Olivia and Sheila again. March had grown considerably warmer toward Sophie, though she tried to stay neutral when Olivia was around. Sophie couldn't say she blamed her.

They walked out into a large, grassy lot covered with weeds, rotting logs, and other assorted flora growing rampant. A couple of old oak trees towered near the back of the lot, dropping leaves and acorns. Two older buildings flanked the lot, and ivy crawled up their faded brick walls.

"This place is a dump," Bri said, crunching on a corn tortilla chip.

"Your diet is a dump," Janet retorted, though she, too, surveyed the grounds with a grimace.

"How are we gonna grow anything with all this stuff in the way?" Leslie asked, kicking over a log. She recoiled in disgust as worms and grubs crawled out from under it.

"We need some way to clear it," Sophie said. She glanced at Bri. "Do you think—"

"Uh-uh." Bri shook her head, rolling her bag of chips closed and stuffing them in her backpack. "I'm not about to make a bugnado. Gross."

"Hmm." Sophie looked at the damp, rich soil beneath the log Leslie had kicked over. "I mean, maybe we could work with it. The nice thing about all this yucky stuff is that it's great for the soil."

She bent down and touched the ground, feeling her way beneath the soil. Life pulsed there, eager in her presence. There were young seedlings, bulbs of flowers now dormant, and tons of weeds.

Pushing in with her energy, she awoke some of the dormant bulbs and coaxed their shoots to the surface. The tangled roots from weeds kept slowing it down, and Sophie found she was exerting way more energy than she needed to. Why was it so hard all of a sudden?

Finally, after several moments, the head of a daffodil poked out above the soil, its stalk still half-buried and constricted by weeds.

"Wow," said Bri. "Um. I somehow thought I was going to be impressed by that."

Sophie stood, wiping sweat from her brow, and brushed off her hands with a frustrated sigh. "There's a lot already here. So even though there's a lot of life, there's just too much going on. This daffodil kept getting snagged by everything under the surface. If we're gonna have nutrient-rich soil for our vegetables, we're gonna have to purge it somehow once we dig it up."

Leslie sighed. "None of us are great at that. We're a dream team for making things grow. Destroying things? Not so much."

"Maybe I could help," Vince said, smoothing back his dark hair as he walked over. He glanced at Janet. "And uh, hey, sorry about your backpack." He looked at Leslie last, his blue eyes shining apologetically. "And almost burning you."

Leslie raised her brows, smiling disbelievingly at the ground. "My dude. You gotta be more careful."

"Understood, ma'am." Vince gave her a salute and a charming smile, and Leslie eventually relented, smiling back.

"Now listen," Vince said, turning to Janet. "You and Pete could maybe dig up the dirt, and then I could hit it with some fire to get rid of all that stuff Sophie was talking about."

"It's not gonna hurt the soil?" Sophie asked.

"Heck no!" Vince said. "My parents own a farm, and they use fire all the time. Helps break down everything and get it back into the dirt. We use fire on our compost pile for the same reason."

Understanding began to dawn in Sophie's mind. That was how death and fire fit into their growing assignments. That was how they fit into society. They offered the ashes from which new life could grow—literally.

"Kind of makes you want to appreciate me more, huh?" Olivia snarked from several yards away.

Sophie looked at her incredulously. Olivia just smirked and went back to talking with her roommates.

How was she always able to hear their conversations? First with Marcus and now with Vince. The girl had superhuman hearing or something.

Sophie shook her head. They had work to do.

After the boys had helped move the wooden boxes for the garden out of the bus's trailer, Janet and Peter set to work moving the soil. Janet used her arms, turning them to stone as she dug. Peter opted instead to turn his hands in a tilling motion until the dirt was softened and mixed, then scoop the dirt into the boxes with a shovel.

Sophie couldn't help but admire how Peter's eye color didn't change as he used his gift. It intensified and brightened. She picked up a shovel and helped Peter move the dirt, and he smiled at her with his glowing eyes.

Sophie felt her heart skip a beat but focused hard on what she was doing so she wouldn't blush.

Once the soil had been moved, Vince pushed his fingers into the soil, his eyes glowing red-orange like they had in art class.

Sophie took an unconscious step backward. Vince laughed, and the soil began to smoke and steam.

"No worries, okay? It's all under control this time." He beckoned with his head to Bri and Leslie. "I'm gonna need y'all here in just a second. You'll help keep the fire going," he said to Bri, "and then you'll rehydrate the soil," he told Leslie, winking at her. "You can also stand by just in case things get out of control."

Sophie thought she saw Leslie's cheeks darken. She smiled. Everything was working well, and everyone had a part.

She glanced at the other boys, noticing one sitting on the steps of an adjacent building. His emo clothes and shaggy hair gave him away as a death elemental. He was amusing himself by shriveling the weeds that had grown up through the cracks in the concrete.

Sophie wondered why he wasn't helping. When she glanced at Olivia, she also saw March looking at the boy. Concern sparkled in her blue eyes.

Without thinking, she focused on March, following a nagging feeling pushing her to do so. There was a kind of electric hum around her, much like the one she heard from Thicket Hall, only with a different frequency. She found it and let it wash over her, closing her eyes.

Vincent looks so lonely.

Sophie opened her eyes, startled. Had she just…

She pressed forward again, her heart racing.

Snippets of emotions flowed into her mind—worry, a growing attraction, shame, and guilt. A flash of a memory —March, sitting with the boy named Vincent behind a tree, hiding from Olivia so she could talk to him. The boy finally laughed at one of March's goofy jokes and looked into her eyes.

Sophie heard Olivia snap at March, and the memory faded, falling apart like scattered dandelion seeds on the wind. The connection was broken, March noticed Sophie looking at her and smiled gently back before getting back to their garden.

Sophie, wide-eyed, shook herself, then pressed her hands against her forehead, her mind reeling.

"Hey, Soph. You're up, girl."

Sophie whirled toward Leslie, almost losing her balance. Leslie took one look at her face and gaped.

"Girl. You're white as a sheet. Come sit down."

Sophie, realizing she was dizzy, let Leslie lead her to their garden box and lower her gently to the ground, Peter helping as well. Sophie leaned against the box, staring blankly up at the sky, willing it to stop spinning.

Bri heaved a sigh and handed Sophie her corn chips. "I think you did it again. That daffodil put up one heck of a fight, I guess."

Sophie's hands shook as she took the corn chips. She didn't know how to explain what had just happened, so she said nothing, silently munching on Bri's chips until the roaring in her ears died down.

"Your color's coming back," Janet remarked after a moment, sitting next to Sophie. Their shoulders touched, and Sophie felt a surge of energy rush through her.

Janet glanced sidelong at Sophie. "You feel that?"

"Yeah," Sophie said. "I think you helped me."

Janet raised her eyebrows. "I hope it's not that weird current thing again." She looked suspiciously at Vince, who shook his head.

"I didn't feel anything that time."

Peter looked at Sophie thoughtfully, then sat down on

her other side so that their shoulders touched. Another burst of energy rushed through Sophie, and she smiled.

"No, guys. This is really cool. I can feel, like, your energy coming through me."

Janet and Peter exchanged curious glances.

"Does it work with other elements?" Leslie reached down and put a hand on Sophie's shoulder. Yet another channel of energy opened, though it felt different from Janet and Peter's.

"Yep," Sophie confirmed. Soon everyone followed suit, and Sophie's mind practically buzzed with the rush and chaos of all their gifts.

"Okay, guys, stop." She pushed herself up, letting their energy fall away. She could stand without getting dizzy and felt better than if she'd eaten a full meal.

They all looked at her, wonder in their eyes.

"You're practically glowing, Soph," said Leslie.

"What did you do to drain yourself like that, though?" Peter asked.

Sophie looked away, though he continued to look at her questioningly.

"It's. Um. Hard to explain." She shook her head. "Don't worry about it, okay?"

Peter frowned for a moment, but his expression cleared, and he nodded.

"All right. I'm just glad you're okay now."

Sophie smiled, then approached their garden box, rolling up her sleeves.

"Let's get growing, shall we?"

CHAPTER SEVENTEEN

Several weeks passed, and late summer splendor began to fade into the gentle orange glow of autumn. Thicket Hall made a spectacle of itself as always, its leaves remaining a deep emerald green as the rest of the trees on campus gave way to the march of time, their leaves gilding, then burning scarlet, then drying to brown and carpeting the lawn.

Sophie found herself busier than ever as the weeks went by. Saturdays with her service project team were always exhausting. It was taking way more out of everyone than they had anticipated coaxing their seedling into a tree. Even with Sophie's impressive ability to grow trees, their sapling stood only a measly seven inches tall at the end of the first five weeks. There was just so much packed within that tiny seed, and Sophie was having a hard time giving it all the energy it craved without draining herself in the process.

The hum from Thicket Hall had faded but had been replaced with something more sinister, a more disjunct and volatile sound that was amplified some days and muted others. Sophie knew it was the death sickness creeping further into the tree's roots. She also knew Headmistress and Roscoe were doing what they could. She'd seen the gigantic machinery sitting behind Thicket Hall, near the root that had been poisoned with the spike, presumably to dig up the diseased parts.

What was more worrisome was that Roscoe hadn't yet called on her for the experiments he'd promised to let her help with. She was getting impatient with his lack of communication, though she knew he might be using all his free time to try and save Thicket Hall at this point.

She felt torn between wanting to help and wanting to let the professionals do all they could. They would know better than her what to do to save the tree. After all, she was only a lowly first-year, who apparently couldn't even grow a tree after she'd saved herself from a pure earth elemental.

The first week of October found Sophie, tired and dejected, waiting in Thicket Hall with several other first years to have their mentors assigned to them. Sophie felt vaguely hopeful that her mentor could teach her something new, some missing piece of the puzzle so Sophie could make progress with her more advanced projects.

At the moment, with rain pelting the windows of the hall and Olivia snickering a couple of tables away, all she really wanted was a glass of iced tea and a mindless day to do nothing in particular.

Sophie listened as Professor Rogers began calling names. She was quick to be called, as the list was in alphabetical order.

"Sophia Briggs, first-year life, will be paired with Kelly Jentry, third-year life."

Sophie glanced up and saw a friendly-looking girl with glasses giving her a kind smile and a wave. Her yellow glasses were round, and her dark, curly hair was cut short at the shoulders.

Sophie smiled back, and Kelly made her way over to Sophie's table.

"Hi, Sophia!" Kelly extended her hand. "I'm Kelly. I'm excited to mentor you! I hear your skills are growing."

Sophie gave a shy smile. "You can call me Sophie. And I don't know if my gift is growing or not." She heaved a tired sigh. "I can't even seem to make my class project's tree grow. And everything is just making me so tired."

"Hey, I remember my first-year project," Kelly said. "It was really difficult! But a lot of it came down to my techniques. There was a lot I didn't know. Heck, there's a lot I still don't know. We'll probably learn from each other." She gave Sophie an encouraging smile. "Why don't we go find us some flowers or something, and I'll show you some things that might help."

Sophie brightened. "I've got an African violet in my room. I doubt we'd want to spend all day out in that." She jerked her head toward the rain-streaked window.

Kelly laughed. "For sure." She glanced down at her watch. "Rogers gave us an hour to work with you guys today. You want to lead the way?"

Sophie nodded, slinging her backpack over her shoulder. Kelly was growing on her already.

The girls made their way through the soaking rain, Kelly sharing her umbrella with Sophie.

"Here it is," Sophie said as they traipsed down the third-floor hall and stopped at her door. She unlocked the door and let Kelly in.

"I remember this room," Kelly said slowly. "I might have had this room as a first-year."

Sophie smiled. "Hey, cool." She led Kelly to her desk, where the violet was overflowing its pot. She needed to remember to ask Roscoe for a bigger pot the next time she saw him.

"Oh, it's beautiful!" Kelly touched the violet, and it brightened happily. "You obviously take great care of it."

"Thanks," Sophie said. She touched the plant as well, reassured that the leaves brushed her fingers and not Kelly's. It still knew she was its caretaker.

Feeling jealous about her plant liking someone else seemed ridiculous when she thought about it.

"Okay." Kelly set her umbrella aside and rolled up her sleeves. "I want you to show me how you normally channel your energy, like if you were going to perk up your violet here." She put her hand on Sophie's shoulder, then gently held a leaf between two fingers on her other hand. "That'll help me feel what's going on so I can guide you."

Sophie noted that what Kelly was doing was a lot like completing a circuit in her old science classes at the public high school. Filing that information away, she closed her eyes, took a deep breath, and began to send energy into her violet. The stalks and leaves began to tremble and then grow up her fingers, slowly at first and then faster as Sophie let more of her energy go.

"All right, taper off now."

Sophie did as she was told, clamping down on the flow

of energy like a brake on a car.

"You do have a lot of energy, and it's very potent," Kelly said. "But you're using way more of it than you need to. It's kind of like when you're trying to lift something you think is going to be heavy, but when you pick it up..." Kelly demonstrated with an empty water bottle on Sophie's desk. She lifted the bottle with so much force that it flew out of her hand.

Sophie giggled. Kelly smiled.

"I know that was a silly example, but it was the first thing that came to mind. The work we're doing here is light, but you're using *all* your 'muscle,' so to speak. A lot of it could just be that your gift is really strong. You're like a muscle man trying to lift a feather."

"Okay," Sophie said, nodding. "So how do I...not do that?"

Kelly laughed. "You kind of have to reduce the scope of your object—the thing you're trying to make grow—and let your energy *drip* instead of flowing full force like a river. Now, there are times you *want* that river when you need a lot of power all at once, but this simple task shouldn't take much energy. And you know how you had to really rein in that energy? Like, you felt like you were stopping a locomotive instead of turning off a faucet?"

Sophie nodded. She'd exhausted herself so many times doing exactly that, wondering why it had become such a chore to simply stop her energy.

"If you start with a very small object, a very focused drip of energy, you won't have to use nearly as much effort to stop it." Kelly gestured at the violet. "Now, let's try again."

Kelly replaced her hand on Sophie's shoulder and the plant, and Sophie closed her eyes, focusing this time on the leaf she was touching instead of the entire violet. Then, as she began to release her energy, she let it go in small pockets, thinking of raindrops in a puddle, dripping one by one.

The leaves began to curl around her fingers once again, more slowly and steadily, and instead of the heavy pull she'd felt practically her whole life, the sensation of her energy leaving in droplets allowed her to open her eyes, take a deep breath, and see her work in real-time.

To her shock, the leaves were still growing at a reasonably rapid pace.

"Good! Now taper off."

Sophie barely had to exert any focus to simply stop the next droplet from leaving her. The stalks quit growing immediately, their length now trailing on the floor.

"Wow!" Sophie exclaimed. "It's never felt so easy before."

"And girl, you were still growing those a mile a minute!" Kelly laughed exuberantly. "Talk about power. When I do that, it grows maybe half that rate. And I've been doing this for two years now!"

Sophie smiled, glancing out her window. The hum from Thicket Hall had just dropped in pitch, and she tilted her head, concerned.

"Um, Kelly?"

"Yeah?" The older girl looked at her expectantly.

"There's a weird hum coming from Thicket Hall." Sophie glanced at Kelly, hoping to see recognition in her eyes.

Instead, Kelly frowned in confusion.

"What do you mean?"

Sophie sighed. Not even a third-year life student could hear it. "Well, it's just…ever since word got out that there's something wrong with the tree, I've been hearing this buzzing or humming sound. I know it's from Thicket Hall because it gets softer when I'm far away from it. And it's been changing lately. It's not steady anymore. Sometimes it gets louder or softer, too."

Kelly looked more concerned than confused now.

"Have you talked to Nurse Bonnie? She's very talented with her gift. She might be able to tell if there's something going on with your ears or with your gift." Kelly shrugged. "It's possible you might just have a sensitivity to living things that are hurt. Especially something as big as Thicket Hall, and with the level of power you have…" Kelly pushed her round glasses up the bridge of her nose. "It's worth asking about."

Sophie sighed and smiled kindly at Kelly. She knew her mentor was just trying to be helpful. It boggled Sophie's mind that no one else—not Nurse Bonnie, not Charlotte, and not even Kelly—could hear the tree.

Was she just a psionic weirdo? Or was her life gift just super powerful?

Either way, all Sophie wanted was an answer.

Despite the disappointment of finding out she was still alone in hearing the tree, Sophie had learned a lot from Kelly in their short time together that morning. She took that new knowledge with her to her Life Fundamentals class, where they were busily creating—and accelerating—new and exotic breeds of florals to decorate the campus for homecoming. Professor Garver seemed especially pleased with Sophie's new restraint. Just the week before, Sophie had caused the hibiscus flowers to sprout prematurely and die within a minute.

"It's a good thing I'd ordered extra!" Professor Garver had scolded Sophie, much to her chagrin.

At dinner, Sophie noticed how much lighter she felt. She hadn't expended all her energy, and she wasn't as hungry for the well-seasoned meatloaf and roasted vegetables they were having that night, though she still enjoyed her meal.

"Rogers is killing us right now," moaned Bri. She was busy shoveling food into her mouth with one hand while the other skimmed through the hastily scrawled words in her notebook. "I haven't had to study like this since my honors classes back in middle school."

"Well, you knew midterms were coming," Janet scolded. "And what did you do all those weeks? You FaceTimed Bluebell instead of studying."

Bri glowered at Janet. "I love my dog, okay? She's like a child to me."

"How is the tree going?" Leslie asked Sophie. "Has Olivia killed it with fire yet?"

Sophie snorted. "No. She really wouldn't have to, with as little progress as we've been making."

"Really?" Charlotte asked. "I would have expected Miss Miracle Grow to have it all done already."

Sophie shoved Charlotte playfully. "Oh, shush."

"Hey, at least you didn't kill a hibiscus today," Charlotte shot back.

Sophie rolled her eyes. "That's true."

"How're the homecoming flowers going?" Simon asked. "The greenhouse looks chock full already. I can't imagine you have much more to do?"

"Garver says we've got a whole truckload of roses still to come in," Charlotte said.

"And speaking of homecoming," Bri said slyly. "Guess who's already got a date?"

"No way. You already got a date?" Janet squeaked.

"No, not me," Bri said, dropping crumbs onto her notebook. She jerked her head, glancing at a table near the large window. "Miss March."

Sophie glanced over, and her heart ached with joy. March and Vincent sat together at a table by themselves, happily chatting as they ate. March had started going with a more subdued, casual wardrobe instead of the high fashion she'd worn around Olivia.

"Well, that's precious," Leslie said with a happy sigh. "Glad to see Olivia's dominion broken, that's for sure."

"Yeah," Bri said. "I definitely wouldn't date a death elemental, but if it makes her happy..." she shrugged.

"Olivia's going with Marcus, I heard," Vince whispered. "Talk about chaos."

"That's like a volcano dating a plague," Bri said. "It won't last long. He'll get sick of Her Royal Highness soon enough."

Sophie couldn't help but chuckle. They both had huge egos, and eventually, one would dominate the other...or their relationship would self-destruct.

"What about you, Char?" She bumped Charlotte's shoulder. "Has Reggie asked you yet?"

Charlotte blushed, tucking a long braid behind her shoulder. "Actually, he did last week. You didn't see because…well, the hibiscus thing."

Sophie beamed. "I knew it would happen eventually."

"I'm taking Janet," Simon announced suddenly. Janet looked up sharply, confusion in her eyes. He smiled at her. "We'll go as friends, okay?"

"What, because you think I can't get a date?" Janet shot back. Her cheeks reddened.

"No, of course not!" Simon said, clearing his throat. He looked sheepishly at her. "It was mostly because I didn't want to be left out."

Janet glared at him. "You *would* pull something like that." Still, she smiled. "I guess that's fine. Then I won't have to worry about gussying myself up."

"Sure. Just come in jeans. I like you the way you are, anyway." Simon stood up as if he'd said too much and hurried off to refill his glass.

Bri smirked as Janet gaped after Simon.

"He likes you. He's just too chicken to say so."

"Of all the…" Janet tried to be angry, but Sophie could see the half-smile in her eyes. "Ugh. Boys."

"Well. So that leaves me, Leslie and Vince, Sophie and Peter, and Luke." Bri shrugged, though mischief lurked in her gray eyes. "We'll be the lonely ones, I guess."

"Yeah." Sophie chuckled, but her cheeks began to burn. Bri had been intentional with how she'd paired the names, and everyone at the table knew it.

Dinner continued, but no one dared bring up homecoming again. Sophie noticed Peter tugging at his sleeves more than usual, and he'd fallen rather quiet.

After dinner, Sophie left with her friends, but the stars were out and twinkling, and she lingered in the front garden as they walked ahead, listening quietly to the hum of the tree and counting the bright stars in Queen Cassiopeia's W shape overhead.

"Hey, Sophie!" Sophie turned to see Peter heading toward her. The rest had gone on ahead to the dorms.

"Hey." She looked at the sky again, feeling awkward. She'd only talked to Peter in a group setting, or with others nearby. It felt weird to be alone with a guy.

"That's Cassiopeia," he said, pointing up as he stood beside her. "I remember she's shaped like—"

"Like a W. Yeah. My mom taught me that." Sophie smiled.

"I taught myself," Peter said quietly. Sophie sensed turbulence under his words but didn't pry.

"If we had a darker sky, we'd see the Milky Way," Peter went on with a sigh.

"I'm sure, if there weren't so many lights, we'd see it every night," Sophie said. "I could never see so many stars back at home. In Louisville."

"I should have brought my binoculars," Peter said, chiding himself. "It's straight overhead, and when you look through those binoculars, it just comes to life, even with all this light around." He gestured at the lights near the entrance to Thicket Hall. "Oh well. Maybe some other night."

"That would be fun," Sophie said. Peter smiled, giving

her one of his signature piercing green gazes. He then looked at the ground.

"Listen, Sophie. I'm sorry. About earlier."

"What do you mean?" Sophie asked.

"When everyone was talking about homecoming, and then Simon just up and asks Janet." Peter began to pace. "I mean, he'd told us he was going to, but I didn't know it was going to be tonight. If I'd known that..."

Sophie put a hand on his shoulder, stopping his pacing.

"What are you saying? You wanted to ask Janet?"

"No!" Peter sighed. "I wanted to ask... I mean," he said, taking her hands. "I mean, I *am* asking. You. I'm asking you." His hands were shaky and slick with sweat, but he managed to look into her eyes and draw a deep breath. "Will you go to Homecoming with me?"

Sophie's stomach filled with butterflies, and she found herself laughing with joy.

Peter's hopeful gaze turned worried.

"Yes. Yes, of course, I'll go with you," she said. "Don't look so concerned."

His expression eased, and he started laughing, too.

"Awesome."

Their laughter died down, and Peter must have realized he was still holding Sophie's hands because he let go suddenly and cleared his throat.

"Great. Well. Um, I guess I'll head back. It's almost curfew, you know."

"Right." Sophie felt a sudden rush, and before she could second guess herself, she leaned forward and kissed Peter's cheek. "Thanks for asking me. I've been waiting."

Peter's eyes widened, and he touched his cheek, then

smiled.

"Sure thing, Sophie."

"Night." Sophie smiled and headed down the path, her heart racing. That had been the craziest and most fun thing she'd ever done.

"Night." He mumbled dreamily after her.

When Sophie got back to her dorm, her roommates suddenly stopped talking.

Sophie raised an eyebrow.

"Were you all talking about me?"

"No," Janet said, but the squeak in her voice gave her away.

Sophie sighed with a smile. "Peter just asked me to homecoming."

The girls chorused a squeal of excitement. Leslie jumped off her bed, followed quickly by Bri and Janet.

"I knew it!" Janet said.

"Tell. Us. Everything," Leslie demanded.

"Did you kiss?" Bri asked.

"Slow down, slow down!" Sophie laughed. "Well, he asked me in the front garden, under the stars."

"Aww!"

"How adorable!" Janet sighed.

"And no, we didn't kiss, but I did kiss him on the cheek." Sophie's eyes widened as she remembered how bold she'd felt. "I think I surprised myself as much as I surprised him."

The girls laughed.

"That's so sweet!" Bri said, flopping back onto her bed. "Now, if Vince would just ask Leslie."

"Hey!" Leslie said, though her smile and blush told everyone that was exactly what she wanted.

Sophie smiled and worked absentmindedly through her evening routine, her thoughts on Peter, on the stars, and the dreamy look in his eyes as he'd told her goodnight.

It had been a good day.

Sophie couldn't quite get her mind to calm down as she lay in bed that night. The full moon peeked its head above the trees, brightening the curtains covering the windows.

Sophie sat up in bed. The humming of the tree had intensified just now, coinciding with the moon's light on the window. She wiggled her feet into her shoes and threw a light jacket on over her pajamas, tucking her phone in her pocket.

Then, as quietly as she could, she snuck out of her room for the second time and ran down the path to Thicket Hall.

The hum grew louder, little by little, as she approached. The large machinery Roscoe had been using to dig up the diseased roots was no longer there. Sophie glanced around, noting the stillness around her. Nothing moved in the branches, and nothing made a sound except a distant owl and the frogs at the pond.

Sighing peacefully, she crept up to the tree and wrapped her arms around it. The hum in her head increased in volume, but at this point, the noise didn't bother her.

"Sorry it took me so long to come back," she whispered.

In response, the tree's hum dropped to a much more comfortable pitch for Sophie's ears and head as if it were inviting her in.

She pushed toward the hum with her mind as she had with March.

Concepts and emotions filtered into her mind. They weren't as concrete or visual as March's had been, but Sophie realized she was listening to a plant rather than a human. An ancient, powerful plant, but a plant nonetheless.

A feeling of majesty and power began to grow within her. Sophie parsed out some of her life energy, like Kelly had taught her, and pushed it into the tree, trying to understand what it was telling her.

More emotions came then—growth, towering growth, through seasons, decades, centuries. And then pain. A dull, faraway pain that didn't seem fully in the present.

Sophie gasped. The hum was changing, and instead of emotions, she began to see images and hear words and phrases.

Long ago. Pain. Like now, but different. Images of cruel faces sneering at the tree flooded Sophie's mind. *Happening again?*

Sophie's eyes widened.

"Are you...are you *talking?*"

Yes. You understand?

Sophie nodded wordlessly.

Good. Sapling, you are? Young. Not grown. The tree radiated intense warmth. *Power is strong. Older, I thought.*

Sophie smiled, feeling proud despite herself.

Must not be like them. The tree's warmth intensified, and Sophie recognized that it was angry. *Steal, burn, destroy for own gain. Caring, they do not.*

Sophie's smile fell. Whoever had hurt the tree was very

selfish.

"I won't do that," she said firmly. "I want to help you."

The warmth faded, and a light breeze ruffled Sophie's hair.

Know, I do. Came here with power and courage, you did. Sophie saw herself from a bird's eye view on the lawn on her first day. Buoyant joy overwhelmed her, and she watched the leaf from Thicket Hall leave its branch and flutter toward her. *Show you I saw you. Gave leaf.*

"'I still have it," Sophie said with a smile.

You help, could. Sent leaf again. This time, a rivulet of fear sliced through Sophie as she watched the memory of the second leaf, the diseased one, flying toward her. *Pain grow fast. Not kill. Other trees help.* Sophie saw an image of roots, growing long and wild beneath the ground, glowing with yellow-green streams of energy, nutrients, and water, carrying dark packets of the deadly sickness away. *Help others, near and far, I did. Many seasons. They help me now. Know, they do, what happens when sickness with me.*

Sophie's stomach sank with dread as the tree showed her, through a dark green haze, scenes of chaos, fires, floods, destroyed buildings, and people lying motionless on the lawn she now recognized as the campus.

"So...so, when you are sick..." She remembered the pure elementals, the strange current of energy they'd felt before Vince's flash fire.

Yes, sapling. Things happen very bad. Chaos. Wild beings, no control. Power, as you have, is changed to different. Fire is wind, ground is water. Life is death.

Sophie shuddered. "Why?"

The tree's hum quieted for a moment. Then, an image

brightened in her mind. Bright, silver channels criss-crossing miles beneath the tree. Then, the tree showed Sophie, but only a silhouette, with the same silver color threaded throughout her form like the veins on leaves.

Power flows in rivers underneath me. A soft feeling reached Sophie. *Keep it, I do. Safe, so nothing gets out.*

It all clicked in Sophie's mind, and her jaw dropped.

"And when you get sick, you can't keep everything in. It's happened before." She grimaced, remembering the tree showing her human bodies lying on the grass.

Yes, sapling. Need your help, I do.

Sophie stifled the tears rising in her throat. No wonder Headmistress didn't want her telling anyone what was going on. She'd been correct in her assumption that the chaos they'd seen so far had to do with the tree's sickness, but this was worse than anything she could have imagined.

Whoever had hurt Thicket Hall must have either been a complete idiot or was purposefully trying to unleash another catastrophe.

"How?" Sophie whispered. "I'm just a first-year. I don't know what I'm doing."

The tree buzzed warmly, and another breeze dried the tear on her cheek.

The answer will come. Speak Roscoe. Speak Norma. Try much, you do.

Sophie looked hopelessly up at the sky. Cassiopeia had given way to bright Capella, and she suddenly realized she'd been here for hours.

"Oh, no." She squeezed the tree once more. "I'll come back soon. I'll do what I can, I promise."

The leaves gently rustled in response, and when Sophie

released her energy and came fully back to her own body, her knee joints ached in protest. Stretching her sore muscles, she headed back to the dorm, her mind storming with worry.

She had to help. She had to go talk to Roscoe.

No matter what, they couldn't let the tree fail.

Roscoe massaged his aching joints and headed back to his workshop. He'd settled in behind another tree, keeping an eye on Sophie as she'd leaned against Thicket Hall once more. The girl had been talking to it; he was sure of that.

He was certain it had spoken to her. How else would she have concluded that Thicket Hall was "keeping everything in" and that it "had happened before?"

Roscoe scratched his chin as he walked. Sophie *did* have a psionic ability. He'd never seen the likes of it in all his years at the school.

However, he'd often noted that extraordinary talent came at the most extraordinary times, when they needed it most.

He entered the workshop and collapsed into his recliner, scratching Mincemeat behind the ears. He frowned at the stone vest he'd covered the death spike on the table with.

One thing was certain, he thought. They needed that extraordinary talent now if the tree was to survive and Norma was going to keep the ESCB away from their school.

He hoped it would be enough.

CHAPTER EIGHTEEN

Sophie found time to go see Roscoe the next day on her lunch break, but he couldn't seem to find the time for her in return. He bustled around his workshop, frantically flipping through books, then shoving them back onto the shelves.

"I haven't got time right now, Sophie," Roscoe told her as he scanned an oak fertilizer recipe book. "You really need to go. I'll let you know when you can come help."

"But the tree told me I need to talk to you!" Sophie tried to protest.

Roscoe paused, his eyes narrowed.

"Yeah, I reckon it did, but we're trying our best right now, and we don't have much time. If that's what you're coming to tell me, we already know, trust me." He ushered her through the door. "I've got to get cooking now. Wait for me to send for you. Promise."

Sophie heaved a frustrated sigh. "I promise."

"Good." Patting her awkwardly on her head, Roscoe

smiled, then hurried inside the workshop and locked the door behind him.

Sophie struggled through the rest of her classes, then decided she'd take Peter up on his offer to bring his binoculars and stargaze. She had to get her mind off the tree. Its urgency and fear still tugged at her, but if she didn't find a way to keep herself busy, she'd only mess things up. When she told her roommates, they all wanted to come, so Sophie set them all up with an impromptu tour of the night sky.

"This is the coolest thing!" Janet sighed. Sophie and her roommates lay on their backs on the lawn, gazing up at the sky late that evening. Sophie had found them a clear patch up on the hill behind the greenhouse, where the view of the stars was unobstructed by trees.

They were out just past curfew, but they'd had to wait until the sky was completely dark, Peter had said. Otherwise, they wouldn't have a chance to see the Milky Way or any other deep sky objects.

Peter was going to bring his binoculars, but the girls had arrived early, and Sophie took the opportunity to point out the constellations and stars that she knew.

"There's Cepheus the King, right next to that W of Cassiopeia," Sophie said, pointing to a pentagon-shaped constellation. "And on the other side of the W, there's their daughter, Princess Andromeda."

"Is that where the Andromeda galaxy is?" Leslie asked, batting a firefly away from her face.

"I think so," Sophie said. She saw something bright from the corner of her eye. "Hey Bri, turn your phone screen off. It'll ruin your night vision."

"I don't have my phone out," Bri said. All four girls looked toward her, but Sophie couldn't see the light anymore.

"Weird," Sophie said. "Maybe Roscoe's out with his lantern or something."

"You think he'll get us in trouble?" Janet asked, her voice trembling.

"Nah," Sophie said. "If anything, he'd just tell us to go back to bed. He wouldn't snitch."

"What's that bright star there?" Janet pointed down toward the tree-studded horizon.

"Capella," Sophie said. "Part of the Winter Hexagon, which we'll see a lot better closer to Christmas since it'll be overhead."

"Um. Why is it moving?" Leslie sat up and pointed at the forest, directly under the sky where Janet had pointed to Capella. "Wait. What is that?"

Sophie looked too. A pinpoint of light was moving toward them from the edge of the forest beyond the school's grounds. It moved like a snake, ducking to one side and then the other as if it were searching for something.

Sophie's hackles rose. "Guys. Stay quiet." There was something unnatural about its movement, and yet something familiar as well. The four girls huddled together, watching it slowly move closer.

Sophie lifted her hand, only to feel a damp sensation on her palm. Strange. The ground hadn't been wet. She gingerly lowered her hand to the lawn once more, stifling a gasp as her hand submerged in a puddle.

Her heart raced as she pulled her hand back. "Guys," she whispered. "I think we're in big trouble."

"What do you mean?" Janet stammered.

The dancing light stilled, and the girls held their breath.

A second later, an explosion of flames erupted from the light, taking on a humanoid form. Its eyes, black holes in the inferno of its face, narrowed.

"What is that thing?" Bri shrieked.

Just as swiftly, the puddle Sophie had stuck her hand into sprang into an upright position, reflecting the flames from the fire creature.

"Oh, sugar honey iced tea!" Leslie said. The girls stood back-to-back as the creatures advanced.

"These are pure elementals," Sophie explained in a rush. "I've seen them before, but I didn't think they would come back."

"You've seen these before?" echoed Janet shrilly. "And you didn't say anything?"

"Headmistress told me not to!" Sophie said. "But since you can see them yourselves, I suppose it's all right to tell you."

"You suppose, huh?" Leslie asked.

The fire creature lunged at them. Janet's eyes glowed and her body became a stone shield, repelling the flames. Leslie shot water at it, but her jet missed and was absorbed by the water creature, who grew taller. It gurgled at them, the noise like a menacing chuckle.

"Yah!" Bri swept her arms in broad circles, attempting to pull the water creature into the fire, but her winds weren't quite strong enough to do the trick. Instead, she pulled the water creature's arm into the fire, causing both to emit piercing shrieks.

"I think you just made them angrier!" Janet yelled.

"That's weird," Sophie said. "Headmistress says that usually once you show you'll fight them, they'll back off. These aren't doing that."

"No kidding!" Bri said, barely dodging a flaming swipe.

Sophie knelt on the ground that had been dampened by the water creature and summoned all the life she could find. If she could make a basket again, she might be able to trap them under it and let them cancel one another out. Grass shot out of the ground, and Sophie yanked the stalks up and began to weave.

"What are you doing?" Bri shouted at her.

"Making a basket," Sophie said matter-of-factly. She checked as she wove that each section was as airtight as she could make it, and within a minute or two, she had a large, wide basket.

"If we can get them both under here, Leslie and Bri, do you think you could use that waternado trick to get the fire thing?"

"Maybe," Bri said, nodding at Leslie. They pooled their powers, and the vortex began to spin. Sophie could tell it wasn't going to be powerful enough to subdue the fire elemental, though. She tucked her basket under her arm and put her hands on their shoulders. She let her energy drip into them, helping the vortex spin faster and grow wider.

The fire creature shrieked at it, but Janet got behind it, her skin covered in a deep-onyx stone shield. She pushed it toward the vortex, and Leslie and Bri moved their waterspout until the two met. Flames began to spin into the cyclone, and the fire creature fought and struggled against it, then broke free.

"Uh-oh," Sophie said.

The fire elemental produced even larger flames, and the girls were forced to back away from the intense heat.

"Get back, you screaming devil!" a male voice cried. Sophie saw Peter, arms raised and brow furrowed, running toward the fire.

"Don't do that!" Janet cried.

"Peter! You'll be hurt!" Sophie shouted.

He charged at it anyway, and the girls watched in shock as he sparred with the fire elemental, using his stone arm to block each fiery strike and land some of his own.

"Hang on, Pete!" Bri and Janet rushed to Peter's side, and Sophie waited with her basket. Janet and Peter formed a blockade, and Bri whipped a gust of wind at the flames, Sophie and Leslie helping with hands on her shoulder to give her more energy.

The wind tore at the flames, making them smaller, shrinking the creature until finally, Leslie shot a jet of water at it, and Sophie dropped her basket on top of the shrieking, sputtering creature. Smoke poured out from under the basket, and the shrieks died into silence.

"Yes!" They high-fived each other, but a sudden wall of water crashed into Peter and Sophie, knocking them to the ground.

Sophie gasped for breath, her nose and throat stinging. Peter, already on his feet, offered her a hand and pulled her to her feet.

"You okay?" he asked. Sophie nodded, and his eyes

began to glow green again. "Good." He charged off after the water elemental, Sophie close on his heels, still coughing up water.

The water creature, realizing it was being pursued, collapsed into a puddle, and Sophie and Peter almost ran right into it. Peter plunged his stone hands into the ground, lifting a pile of dirt bigger than himself, then hurled it at the puddle with a loud battle cry.

The soil smothered the water creature, and he continued to pile more dirt on top of it. Sophie joined in, summoning the grass, flowers, and trees all around to absorb the water as quickly as they could.

Soon, there was nothing left of the creature except a viscous pool of mud.

Peter stood panting at the edge of it as the glow in his eyes slowly faded. He looked at Sophie, only the whites of his eyes showing now that they were in the dark again.

"I'm tired," he said, then fell forward onto his knees.

"Peter!" Sophie knelt beside him, putting her arm around his shoulders. Her roommates hurried over, quick to put their hands on his back or arms and replenish his lost energy. Janet pulled out her phone and turned on the flashlight so they could all see one another.

"Dude," Bri said with a note of admiration, "That was really dumb. Brave, and really cool, but also dumb."

"Mostly dumb," Janet corrected.

Peter laughed. He was leaning on Sophie's shoulder. "I don't know what I was thinking."

"You were thinking about your damsel in distress," Leslie said slyly.

Sophie blushed, and Peter chuckled.

"I guess so."

"Hey, Pete!" Vince's drawl carried across the lawn. "You out here?"

"Yeah." Peter straightened, though Sophie could sense his energy wasn't back yet.

"Your roomie just fought off a fire elemental," Leslie said.

"You girls out here too?" Vince, Luke, and Simon appeared over the hill and joined them. "What is this, a secret nightclub?"

Everyone laughed.

"It was supposed to be an astronomy club of sorts," Sophie said. "But we ran into some elemental creatures."

Luke frowned. "You mean, like, the ones in the stories? Like, pure flame things and stuff like that?"

Sophie nodded.

Vince, Simon, and Luke looked at the rest, but no one contradicted Sophie. Simon's eyes widened.

"Man. Why do I miss all the fun?" He patted Peter on the shoulder. "And you fought it off. Lucky dog. Got all the ladies looking after you now."

They all laughed again.

"How did you fight it off?" Janet asked. "I could only shield with my gift. At least, that's all I've been taught to do. You were striking at it somehow."

"Well," Peter said, "I kind of was angry. So, I used the same technique as you, but I just went after it instead of simply blocking or shielding. I guess earth has kind of a dampening effect on fire because it was working."

"Nice," Bri said.

Sophie touched Peter's long-sleeved arm as he

continued telling his hero's tale, searching with her life energy, looking for injuries. She found a couple of burns on his forearm and one near his elbow.

Alongside the burns, she felt something else—a pattern of painful squares along his arm from wrist to elbow. Confused, she tried to match it to an injury Nurse Bonnie had taught her about, but the only other information she could gather was that the pain was old, and it ached, and had likely been there for a long time.

Understanding dawned. This was why he wore long sleeves all the time. This ailment was why he came to see Nurse Bonnie every week. It was chronic, and he was embarrassed about it.

"Yeah, it was pretty cool," Peter was saying to his roommates. "I went all berserk on the water thing, too. Smothered it with a bunch of dirt."

Sophie glanced at him, making sure his attention was fully on the conversation. She then began to gently channel her life energy, dripping slowly, healing the burns first, then reducing the pain of whatever the patchwork ailment was. She kept her eyes open, focused on Peter, thankful Kelly had taught her this less-draining way to use her gift.

Peter suddenly glanced at her, then at his arm. He looked back at her again, but fear had widened his eyes. He pulled his arm away, rubbing it angrily.

Sophie let go, warmth rushing into her face. She'd pushed too far.

"I'm sorry," she whispered. "I was just trying to help you."

"What's going on, Pete?" Bri asked. "Your girl heal the battle scars you wanted to keep or something?"

Peter sighed. Sophie didn't dare look up. She'd breached his privacy, and he had every right to be angry with her.

But Peter touched her cheek gently and looked at her. "Sophie, you're such a sweetheart."

A chorus of "Aws" rang out.

"Guys, I should have told you about this. I've just been too embarrassed." Peter took a deep breath, then rolled up his sleeves.

Sophie touched her chest in sympathy. Squares of dark stone lined his arms, the skin around each square pink and raw, though Sophie could tell her healing work had had some benefit. The burns were still pink but looked several weeks old instead of brand new.

"I have stone skin," Peter said, his voice rough. "Some earth people get it, and it's hereditary. Makes me have a permanent covering of rock on my arms. Hurts like heck, so I go to the nurse every week. Sophie was just…" He glanced at her and smiled apologetically. "She was trying to heal my burns, and she found out by accident." He took her hand. "I should have realized you wouldn't judge me when you were halfway through reducing the swelling from it."

Sophie giggled.

"Dude." Luke reached out a finger and gingerly touched Peter's arm. "That's cool."

"Very cool, bro," Vince agreed. "You're, like, a human brick wall."

They all laughed, and Sophie squeezed Peter's hand.

"You're as brave as they come," she told him. "Thanks for coming to our rescue. And for sharing with us."

He smiled at her, releasing a shaky breath. Glancing

around, everyone was still going on about how he'd rushed into battle and how they'd all worked together to fight off the elementals. It was clear that no one cared very much about the way his arms looked.

Least of all Sophie, who smiled back at him encouragingly, relishing the happy glow in his green eyes.

CHAPTER NINETEEN

Several days later, Sophie trudged up the hill to the open arena once again. It was one of those strange October days when the morning air felt damp and frigid, but the afternoon heat demanded an entire change of wardrobe. Sophie pulled off her hoodie as she walked, dabbing at the sweat around her nose.

"Golly," said Leslie, fanning herself with a notebook. "These Southern falls are, like, not even fall. I thought it would be better here in Kentucky, but it sure ain't."

Sophie snorted. "Yeah. You can always count on Kentucky to give you the exact opposite weather of the season you want. Springtime? Ha. There'll be tornadoes one day and snow the next. At least once. And all those poor tulips that thought it was time to sprout just get sucker punched with a snowstorm in March."

The girls laughed.

"Well, up in Michigan, it's just pretty much snow for half the year," Janet said. "We live by the lakes, so...yeah."

Bri shuddered. "We get snow, too, sometimes, but mostly just cold rain."

As they entered the arena, Sophie gazed around in awe. Several different centers had been set up, with obstacles and challenges tailored to each element. She watched a woman at the fire center creating a tiny, thin blue flame that burned its way slowly and carefully through a maze of paper.

Further on, a student pulled together two opposing walls of water, forming the turret of a tower on a sandcastle. The falling water melted part of the sandcastle, and an air horn was blown. The student stomped away in frustration.

"Look at that!" Bri pointed toward a field of paper pinwheels and groaned. "I knew that would come back to bite me." A boy was inside the maze of pinwheels, waving his arms desperately as he tried to get the pinwheels to spin the way he wanted them to.

As they walked on, a tall column of vines began to rise near the edge of the forest. Intrigued, Sophie watched as the vines intersected, forming a beautiful pattern. On the very top of the column, several feet in the air, a glass bowl filled with water was nestled in a viny basket. Floating on the water, Sophie could see a tiny flame.

The vines continued to rise into the air, but one of the vines suddenly snapped, and the bowl of water came toppling down, smashing onto the packed dirt below.

"Oh, so close!" Someone called, and she could hear muted applause.

"All right, ladies!" Professor Ian Markel, an angular but

well-muscled man with silver hair, waved at them and handed them each a piece of paper. "Take your places at your element's station. Whoever gets the highest score from each element will have a battle." He grinned mischievously.

Sophie groaned. Why did there always have to be a battle? She glanced down the paper, noting that the viny towers everyone was trying to grow had to be thirty feet high—and that life's station was shared by death, whose job was to slowly kill the vines the life student had just raised with the goal of getting the bowl of water back to the ground safely.

As the afternoon wore on, Sophie watched bowl after bowl of water fall from walls of foliage. Her fellow life students could either keep the bowl level *or* get their tower of vines to thirty feet, but not both. The death students had just as big of a challenge. Most of them wanted to kill the vines too quickly, so the bowls kept raining down. Sophie wondered if they had bought a truckload of glass bowls for this event.

"Sophia Briggs!" called Professor Garver from the starting point. Sophie took deep breaths as she stepped up to take her turn.

"You know what to do," Garver said, patting Sophie's shoulder. She set a glass bowl filled with water, with a lit candle in the center, on the ground in front of Sophie.

Remembering what Kelly had taught her, Sophie focused on making her energy drip, not flow, and began to feel for the vines beneath the dirt.

The wiry green stalks pushed through the ground at her touch. She carefully wove a small net around the bottom of the bowl before directing the vines to grow up slowly and carefully.

The vines lifted the bowl from the ground, and Sophie told herself to breathe. It wouldn't do any good to hold her breath as she watched the bowl. Her power would get away from her, and she'd have to use all her energy to stop it. Instead, she focused on providing a strong framework for her tower, crisscrossing the vines until they were ten feet high and going strong.

She continued, weaving, plaiting, and crisscrossing as she went, careful to keep the bowl level as the tower gained height.

Reggie stood on a metal platform ladder at the thirty-foot mark, his hand extended as Sophie's vines approached.

Her heart raced with glee. She was going to do it!

That glee zipped through the vines, pushing them the last few inches the tower needed but dipping the bowl in the process.

Sophie cut off her energy and froze. The vines held, only one droplet of water falling to the ground. The candle flame burned steadily.

"You've done it, Sophie!" Professor Garver high-fived Sophie and shook her shoulders. "Your tower was the tallest and the *only* one not to lose its bowl."

Sophie smiled, though her insides writhed at the thought of another competition. Maybe if it was one-on-one, she wouldn't end up sending a truckload of kids to the nurse's office again.

Had the paper said when this competition was going to be held?

Sophie had a sudden revelation and gasped. What if they were being sorted out for the elemental skills contest, the one Marcus had lost? Was he going to compete again? She glanced around, noting that only the first years were in the arena today. It was possible that the whole school competed, but the contestants from each grade were selected separately.

Sophie fumed. She hadn't signed up for this contest. None of them had. Hadn't they proven enough by taking the exam to get in? She'd assumed the different centers were for training each element, getting in extra practice, and refining skills, not another ego-boosting—or squashing—battle.

Sophie huffed and crossed her arms. She needed to take a walk and wrap her mind around this. She was likely going to be a competitor, as she'd proven her growing skills just now. Maybe she could pretend to be sick on the day of the contest. Or maybe Headmistress Case would just let her opt out entirely. Surely, they would consider the second-place contestant if Sophie refused to compete.

The problem wasn't that Sophie didn't want to compete. She'd loved the thrill of knocking Marcus in the head with that dodgeball weeks ago and being marveled at for her powerful talent satisfied something in her and pushed her to get even better.

But she couldn't shake the image of all those kids—Bri with her black eye, March with her ribs—hurt because of her. She didn't know how this contest was going to be set up. She didn't know if she'd face one person or a whole team, like in dodgeball. She had no idea what the tasks would be, either.

She slowly released the tension in her arms as she walked, watching the other elements perform their obstacle courses. Maybe she could get some more information out of Roscoe or one of her professors. If she could get an idea of what the contest was like, she'd have a better understanding of whether or not she should compete.

At the fire center, she paused. Olivia had stepped up to the starting line and was preparing to take her turn.

She watched as Professor Rogers put a hand on Olivia's shoulder and whispered something in her ear. Olivia nodded but saw Sophie out of the corner of her eye and pinned her with a glare.

Sophie froze.

Professor Rogers let go of Olivia's shoulder and her eyes began to glow, still fixed on Sophie. A flame in her hand became a fireball.

"Olivia? What are you doing?" Sophie heard the warning in Professor Rogers' voice.

Olivia threw the fireball at Sophie, her face contorted with anger.

Sophie stepped to the side, dodging it easily. She glowered at Olivia. What was her problem? Not bothering to bend to the ground, she felt for life under Olivia's feet and brought vines up around her ankles. With a quick swipe of her fingers, the vines swept Olivia off her feet and onto her face on the dirt.

The rest of the fire students watched eagerly, forming a circle around the two girls. Students from earth and water crowded around, too.

Olivia got to her feet and stormed toward Sophie.

"You'll pay for that!"

Sophie let her anger grow with the vines she pulled out of the ground in front of Olivia, forming a thorny wall that tore at the girl's skin and clothes. She was sick of Olivia's attitude, sick of her girl-boss sleaziness, of her holding so much power and control over her and her friends.

She was sick of being afraid of her. Who did Olivia think she was, anyway? No better than the rest of them. Sophie didn't care if she came from old money or not. Her family had always taught her that people deserve respect, regardless of their wealth or status.

Olivia shot a blast of fire at Sophie's wall of thorns. Sophie ducked and rolled as the flames flew past her, though she had to pat out a lock of her hair.

"Look at my clothes, you twit!" Olivia shouted, advancing on Sophie. She shook her ragged and torn Gucci t-shirt at Sophie. "You'll pay for this, too!"

"Why don't you just run back home to your parents?" Sophie snarled back. "Maybe they let you have your way all the time, but that's not gonna happen here. We don't care if you're rich or pretty or talented. If you're a gigantic jerk—" Sophie dodged another fireball aimed at her head, "that's what you'll get in return."

"I'm not gonna stand here and let you lecture me, Miss Miracle Grow," growled Olivia. "What did you do to March during dodgeball, huh?" She blasted the ground at Sophie's feet, and Sophie leapt backward with each strike, panting. "What do you call that?"

Sophie curled her fingers and raised her hand. A vine shot out of the ground, and she used it like a whip against Olivia's arms. Olivia yelped, then incinerated the vines.

"Like you ever cared about March! I said I was sorry,

and I helped heal her. I realized when it had gone too far." Sophie punctuated each sentence by gripping each of Olivia's limbs with a thick, ropy vine. Olivia struggled against the vines, but even as her steaming skin tried to burn them away, Sophie made them tighten until Olivia's fingers and sandaled toes were blue.

Sophie stepped in front of Olivia, noting the girl's terrified eyes as the vines held her suspended over the ground. Her anger was feeding the vines, keeping them strong and steady against Olivia's fire.

"I'm tired of you bullying my friends, and March, and Sheila, and everyone else, for that matter," Sophie hissed. "I'm not afraid of you anymore. I'm not going to let you disrespect me anymore. I suggest you learn that now."

Olivia's eyes began to glow. She glanced around at the gathered students, who were staring at Sophie in awe. Some were tittering at Olivia.

The glow in her eyes faded, and she glared at Sophie dejectedly.

Sophie's anger ebbed.

"Put me down. Please," Olivia requested low so only Sophie could hear. "I can't feel my hands."

Sophie released her, backing away as Olivia massaged her purple fingers. She wanted to apologize as she watched Olivia bend to wake her toes up.

As she opened her mouth to do it, Olivia snapped back up and shot a fireball at Sophie's chest.

Sophie dodged it, but not quickly enough. It caught the sleeve of her shirt on fire and blistered her skin.

"Enough!" Professor Markel stepped between the girls just as Sophie gathered herself to retaliate. She hesitated, torn between obeying him and wiping the smug grin off Olivia's face.

Professor Markel smiled at her, then at Olivia, and took both their hands, raising them in the air.

Sophie gaped at him in confusion.

"These are your two main competitors in this year's elemental skills contest. Take note, people." He looked at the gathered students. "You want to be remembered on the plaque in Thicket Hall? You watch these two girls. See if they have any fault lines." He glanced at the girls, grinning like a madman. "I doubt you'll find them."

CHAPTER TWENTY

Sophie and her roommates headed back down the stone walkway after changing at the dorms.

"Dang, Soph," Bri kept saying. "Dang!"

Sophie rolled her eyes. "Would you let it go already? I'm not about to do some kind of death match with Olivia. I don't care what Markel says."

"But you so could!" Leslie pressed. "I mean, your power's grown overnight, and it wasn't weak to begin with, girl."

"Yeah," Janet agreed. "It would take all three of us to face off against Olivia, but you took her by yourself."

Sophie scoffed. "Come on, guys. You're not giving yourselves enough credit. I mean, Janet, you came to my defense that night in the bathroom."

The girls chuckled, reliving their first night in the dorms.

"Yeah, that was really something," Bri said wistfully. "The three of us making a shield around Sophie. That waternado, which has come in handy many times since then."

Leslie nodded in agreement. "Sure has."

Sophie just shook her head, smiling. "See? Y'all are amazing. And we won't even mention the you-know-whats last week."

The girls nodded soberly. They were approaching the river of students heading to Thicket Hall for supper. They couldn't afford to talk about that here.

They made their way to their table, where the guys had gathered around a meal of chicken pot pie and green beans with ham. Sophie chuckled as she watched Peter shoveling in heaping spoonfuls of the pot pie.

"Still haven't got your energy back?" she asked, pulling out the chair next to him.

Peter shook his head, then swallowed. "Nope," he answered. "I'm starving, like, all the time."

"Hmm." Sophie frowned. "Hope you didn't deplete yourself too much that night."

Peter shrugged. "Nothing for it now. Just gotta keep eating, I guess."

He turned back to his meal, and Sophie headed toward the drinks table.

She collided with a tall figure, and a rough buzz erupted in her mind as they made contact. It was as if the ever-present hum from Thicket Hall had tripled in volume.

"Hey! Watch it!"

Sophie glanced up at the person she'd run into.

Marcus glared at her from under his hood. His sleeves were rolled up, and his hands were tucked into his jacket's pockets. "Ugh. It's you." He gestured dismissively. "Get out of my way, princess."

"Watch it, buddy," Peter growled from his seat. Marcus rolled his eyes.

"What?" She shook her head, her mind rushing through questions faster than she could process them. Why did Marcus sound like the tree? Had he been the source of the buzzing all along?

Ignoring her reason, which was screaming at her to stop, she reached out as Marcus moved to leave and grabbed his bare arm.

Marcus gasped, and Sophie did too since the buzzing intensified, deafening in her mind. She gritted her teeth against it, fighting to understand.

"Sophie?" Leslie, who was seated closest to them, looked at her with concern. "What's going on?"

Sophie ignored her and stared into Marcus' black eyes.

"What do you have to do with Thicket Hall?" she demanded.

Marcus' jaw dropped open, his eyes pools of pure fear. He jerked his arm away.

"What are you talking about?" he hissed. Sophie looked at his arm. A small strip of green moss had formed where her hand had been. As he backed away from her, the moss turned brown, then fell off like a scab.

"I said, what do you have to do with Thicket Hall?" Sophie angrily took a step closer to him, her brows furrowed.

"Leave me alone!" Marcus sneered, then yanked his sleeves down and stormed over to his table.

Sophie watched him go in confusion.

"Dude, what's going on?" Bri asked. "You think he did something to the tree?"

Sophie wandered back to her seat.

"I don't know. He sounded like…like that humming sound I've been telling you guys about, but only when I touched him. I can hear Thicket Hall all the time." Sophie propped her face in her hands, blowing a stray strand of hair out of her face. "I think he has something to do with it. I don't know how much."

"I wouldn't put it past that egomaniac to try to kill the tree or something enormously stupid like that," Janet said.

"Seems like a real piece of work," Peter grumbled. He'd stopped eating and was glaring at Marcus across the hall. "Didn't even apologize for running into you. And why does he call you princess?"

Sophie snorted. "I don't know, to be honest with you. He seems to think I'm a sensitive, delicate little fairy and that it's much better to be an insensitive jerk. Don't get all jealous, okay?" She patted Peter's hand. "It's *not* a term of endearment."

"Yeah, he called her that when we played dodgeball," Leslie said. "Jerkiest person alive, that one."

"You're forgetting Olivia," Simon pointed out, and they all laughed.

Sophie ate her meal quietly, still pondering Marcus' connection with the tree. From the corner of her eye, she noticed a large figure at the food table.

"Roscoe?" she whispered. The caretaker had a large stack of peanut butter and banana sandwiches in his arms. He busily stuffed potato chips between the slices of bread, then took huge bites of the sandwich on the top of the stack.

"Be right back," she said, then leapt up from the table and ran to Roscoe.

Roscoe saw her coming and tried to smile, but his mouth was too full.

"How's the tree?" she asked quietly.

Roscoe held up a finger as he chewed, then swallowed with a loud gulp and gasped for air.

"No change," he said, then shoved more sandwich into his mouth.

Sophie frowned.

"Stop by tonight," Roscoe said. "Before curfew. Not after."

Sophie looked up at him hopefully, but he shooed her away.

"Go eat. You'll draw attention."

Sophie nodded and obeyed. She couldn't stop smiling. She was finally going to help the tree.

Marcus ate quickly and silently. The rest of his table talked softly around him, but he could feel their stares, their judgment. His arm still itched from the moss Sophie had grown after she'd grabbed him.

Most troubling, her big, brown eyes had seemed to pierce his soul and find him out. How could she know he'd had anything to do with Thicket Hall? Why did her question seem to confuse her or even anger her, as if it was a revelation she'd just received? Was she a psychic freak?

Why had she dared to touch him?

Marcus gulped. Why hadn't he stopped her when he'd knocked out other kids who had tried to get close to him?

She'd startled him, for one thing. For another, he'd felt a strange sensation like a surge of energy or a sugar rush when she'd touched him. It wasn't because Sophie was reasonably pretty, or that—he scowled at the thought—he tended to be girl-crazy.

It had been a physical sensation, and it had been accompanied by that weird moss. It was like nothing he'd ever felt before.

So, he'd just stood there and stared at her like an idiot while she had acted like a mind reader.

He picked at his food, anger growing within him. Why did she constantly have to embarrass him? Why was it always her, the doe-eyed little life princess, rubbing his nose in his failures and weaknesses?

He had to stay away from her. Not like he ever sought her out, but he had to be careful not to bump into her, not to speak to her. She knew too much, somehow. Marcus grimaced. She might be one of those psionics Professor Rogers had talked about. Or she just didn't like him and wanted someone to blame for the tree's sickness.

That would explain it all. Marcus felt a tightness in his stomach relax. Chance and her own bias had led her to the culprit, nothing more. Anyone with death magic could have made that spike, not just him... Though he thrilled in the knowledge that he was the only one powerful enough to make one by himself.

The thrill faded. The past few weeks had been chaotic because of him. The tree's sickness was causing weird things to happen. He didn't know why, but it was. And he'd never intended for any of that to happen. He'd thought Thicket Hall was just a giant tree—an important landmark, for sure, but just a tree all the same.

It had become clear he'd damaged more than he'd bargained for without causing the damage he'd hoped for.

He'd stay away from Sophie. Avoid her at all costs. Hopefully, the tree would heal on its own without any need for Headmistress Case or anyone else to hunt him down.

CHAPTER TWENTY-ONE

Sophie went to Roscoe's workshop that evening. She'd almost forgotten the caretaker's instructions to come that night. That interaction with Marcus and her roommates' heckling about the elemental skills contest had all but taken over her thoughts as the night wore on.

Mincemeat started meowing when she was several yards away, as usual, and Roscoe peered out his window, then unlocked the door and let her into the workshop.

The cat rubbed against her legs, purring like a motorcycle. Sophie grimaced. He was very pleased with himself for having left Roscoe a gift of two dead mice on his pillow. The gruesome images flashed in Sophie's mind, and she pushed them away in disgust, though not without scratching Mincemeat's ears. He was just being a good kitty.

"Glad you could make it, Sophie." Roscoe checked his watch. "We don't have much time before curfew."

"Sorry," Sophie said breathlessly. "It's been a crazy day."

"Look." Roscoe showed her a burlap bag that held

various objects—a tuning fork, a jar of a light-green viscous liquid, and a handful of transparent crystals. "We're gonna try several things tonight. One of them is bound to help the tree."

"What's the tuning fork for?" Sophie asked, eyebrows raised. "We're gonna tune the tree?"

Roscoe scowled. "No. Well, not exactly." He gestured impatiently for her to follow and hurried to the door. "I'll explain when we get there."

The two moved quickly down the path, trying to avoid looking out of place among the scattered packs of students wandering back to their dorms. Once they reached the back of Thicket Hall, Roscoe pulled the tuning fork out of the bag.

"Okay. First, we're gonna try this one." He handed Sophie the fork and placed her free hand against the tree. "Now, uh, *talk* to it." He moved his hands in a confused gesture. "I guess."

Sophie raised an eyebrow but did as she was told, reaching out with her mind to the tree's humming vibration and letting it wash over her.

Sapling. Return, you did.

The tuning fork began to vibrate in her hand, chafing her skin. She looked sidelong at Roscoe, who stared at the fork, a puzzled but intrigued look in his eyes.

"What am I supposed to do now?" Sophie asked. The vibration had become violent, and her palm began to burn. "This thing is hurting me."

Roscoe frowned and took the tuning fork out of her hand. "Darn. Okay." He handed her one of the transparent crystals. "See if you can funnel out the death energy, and..."

He moved his hands from one side to the other. "Transfer it, I guess, into the crystal."

"Roscoe," Sophie said with a frown. "I have the life gift, not death. I can't move death other than to push it out of the way."

"Well," Roscoe insisted, "Maybe you can push it, then. Push it into the crystals."

"It can't go through me," Sophie explained, her irritation rising. "It would take my life energy. You'd have to put the crystal—"

Roscoe yanked the crystal out of her hand and dropped it into the hole where the spike had been.

"Can you push it into the crystal if it's right by the source of the wound?" Roscoe asked, shaking his head in exasperation.

Sophie chuckled, letting her irritation fade. "I can try." She knew Roscoe was self-conscious about his lack of elemental knowledge. She closed her eyes, entered the hum with her mind, and began seeking the root of the death energy that pulsed, aching, through the tree's hum.

She found it in the same place as before. She realized, heart sinking, that it had spread and grown. More of the root had fallen to the disease, and it had gotten past the root and into the main trunk of the tree. There was so much of it. She looked hopelessly at the tiny crystal in the hole. It would take hundreds, maybe a thousand crystals like that to contain the sickness.

"Um, Roscoe? Do you have any bigger crystals like that?"

Roscoe shook his head.

"These are raw diamonds. These few cost the school thousands."

Sophie chewed her lip. "Well, it's not enough. Not nearly enough. The death sickness is in the trunk now."

Roscoe stared at her, his hazel eyes glistening.

"Tell me that ain't true."

Sophie just gazed at him sadly.

Roscoe paced, shaking his head.

"Surely it's not that bad. Those diamonds have helped heal horses and goats and all kinds of other animals. Even people." He put his head in his hands. "It's in the trunk. My heavens. Who would do something like this? How did it get that far?"

"Roscoe." Sophie stepped away from the tree and put her hands on his shoulders to stop his pacing. "I know you care about Thicket Hall more than anything, but you also couldn't feel the energy from that death spike."

She shivered. "It was horrible. It made me feel like every bone in my body was aching. And I've felt death magic before. I've never felt anything that strong. Whoever did this knew that it would take a lot to kill this tree. They haven't killed it, but they have caused a *lot* of damage."

Roscoe studied her, listening intently.

She took a deep breath.

"We have to keep trying, okay? It might take a lot of different things over time, but we can't pretend it's not as bad as it is." She gestured at Thicket Hall. "It told me this has happened before, and people died on this campus."

Roscoe nodded, blinking back the moisture in his eyes. He marched over to the burlap bag and pulled out the jar of green liquid.

"You're right," he said, opening the jar. "We can't give up."

Sophie channeled Roscoe's homemade healing compound into the damaged root of the tree for what seemed like hours. Every once in a while, Roscoe walked over and scooped another handful onto the bark. Sophie then placed her hand over it and channeled it into the most damaged parts of the tree.

Is good, sapling, but not going. Sickness stop it.

Sophie heaved an angry sigh. Bracing herself, she pushed her energy down through the damaged root, seeking the telltale oily presence of death. Her energy raced through it like a wildfire, consuming the traces of sickness that were encroaching upward.

When her energy met the oily resistance, it slowed, then stopped.

She gritted her teeth and pushed with all her strength. To her alarm, her energy was absorbed by the oily mass. She retreated, gasping for breath as she came back to herself.

"What's wrong?" Roscoe knelt at her side, mopping her sweaty forehead with the burlap bag.

"I tried to push past it," Sophie choked. "The tree said your compound was good, but it couldn't get through the worst parts of the death sickness. So, I tried to just…" She pushed her palm outward to illustrate what she couldn't say. She had to focus on breathing as the starry sky spun above her.

"Didn't work." Roscoe shook his head. "You have to be careful, Sophie. Remember what I told you about the ESCB."

"What is that, anyway?" Sophie asked.

Roscoe sniffed, looking away from her. "It's a regulatory board. If they suspect something is going wrong, or kids get hurt here--I mean, more than scrapes and burns here and there..." He rubbed the back of his neck. "They'll shut the school down."

Sophie gaped at him. "How?"

Roscoe made a noise like a growl. "It doesn't matter how. The fact is, they can, and they will. They've tried in the past. There's some not-so-nice folks among their ranks; I can tell you that." He looked at Sophie, his eyes narrowed. "Matter of fact, I probably shouldn't be telling you any of this. So don't you go and spew it around, got it?"

Sophie nodded but stopped quickly. Her vision still seemed to tilt.

"Do you have any food with you?" she asked.

Roscoe snorted. "No. Fine time to be hungry."

"I used up a lot of energy just now," she explained. "I'm still dizzy."

His look softened. "Oh. Right." He got to his feet, pulling her up and steadying her with an arm around her shoulders. "Here. We'll head back to the workshop, and I'll get you a bite to eat." He glanced back at the tree, slinging the burlap bag around his free shoulder. "We're done for tonight anyhow."

Sophie let Roscoe lead her to the workshop, her heart filled with worry, her head still reeling. She hadn't been able to push through that death magic to help the tree. Nothing they'd tried had worked. And Roscoe was the expert on Thicket Hall.

What were they going to do if they failed?

A week later, Sophie, her roommates, Charlotte, Peter, and the boys found themselves on the edge of the forest, looking out at Bardstown.

Bri shoved a snack cake into her mouth, looking nervous for once.

"You sure we should be out here?" she asked. "I'm all for playing hooky, but this seems a bit…much."

They'd hiked the winding road that led to the school into town, following the route their busses took them when they worked on their gardens.

"You sound like me," Janet said. She'd pulled her hood up and was biting her cuticles. "But I agree."

"It'll be fine," Vince said, as carefree as ever. He slung his arm around Leslie's shoulders. "We're allowed to do whatever we want with our lunch break. There's no requirement that we be present in Thicket Hall." He grinned at Leslie, who grinned back, a blush on her cheeks.

"Bri brought enough food for all of us," Luke said, reaching toward the girl's backpack. He withdrew his hand when she shot him a glare, then she rolled her eyes and relented.

Sophie took in a deep lungful of air. It had been her idea to come out here. She'd needed to get off campus, away from the constant buzz of the tree and the worrisome thoughts that pestered her like flies from dawn to dusk.

"Where to first, Soph?" Charlotte asked, hands on her hips.

Sophie squinted. The building across the street from

their gardens had drawn her attention several times over the last couple of trips to work on their project. She didn't know what it was about it, but maybe the building had some history that she could sense. Maybe there were parts of her psionic ability she hadn't experienced yet.

At least, that was her best guess.

"How about that?" She pointed at a yellow stone building.

"If you say so," Peter said, gesturing for her to take the lead.

The nine of them headed toward the building. A wooden sign announced its purpose as they got closer. *Jailer's Inn Bed and Breakfast.*

"That's an odd thing to do to an old jail," Simon commented.

As Sophie ascended the concrete steps, the buzzing grew. It was below her, or beneath the ground.

"Sophie?" Charlotte followed her as she jogged back down the steps and bent to touch the ground. The buzzing intensified. It wasn't quite like the tree or March or Peter, or anything else she'd been able to read.

"I think we need to go around the back," she said.

Peter shrugged. "Okay. If you think so."

She led them around the limestone building. The yellow stone looked older and more worn as they walked around. At the back was a side entrance to a basement.

A brown and gold plaque announced the entrance was the Old Nelson County Jail. Another sign beneath it said Closed to Visitors. As Sophie touched the door, the buzzing got louder, as if it were present in her mind.

"Creepy," Janet said, rubbing her arms. "These old rocks

are giving off weird vibes."

Sophie glanced at her. Maybe Janet could feel the buzz, too.

"It says on this plaque that this place is supposed to be haunted," Bri said, crunching through a bag of cheese puffs.

"Well, that explains it." Janet groaned. "Soph, if you wanted to come to a haunted house, why'd you have to drag me into it?"

Sophie frowned at the door. Was her psionic ability picking up on the presence of something more paranormal here?

"Well," she said with a sigh. "Let's check it out, I guess. We've come all the way over here." She tugged at the door, but it was locked. "Oh. Of course."

"I got this," Simon said. He pushed his way forward, then pressed his finger to the keyhole. Water began to trickle from the opening. He concentrated for a moment, then gave a couple of pushes with the tip of his finger.

The lock clicked open. He yanked the old door open, and it creaked eerily against its hinges.

"That was cool," Sophie said.

"I learned how to pick locks quite early in life," Simon said matter-of-factly. "My younger brothers locked themselves in cars and rooms too many times to count."

They all filtered inside, the pleasant air outside giving way to a damp and musty smell. The buzzing in Sophie's mind hadn't intensified, but it seemed more real now that they were inside the jail.

"Look how thick the walls are," Luke said, holding his hands on either side of the door jamb. There was easily enough space between his hands to fit two people.

"Well, you know," said Vince. "Can't let the prisoners pick through the walls to escape."

They walked further in. Old cells with bent metal bars lined either side of a short, dimly-lit hallway. Old-fashioned metal-grilled lanterns dotted the walls between each cell and gave off a yellow glow.

"Sure are wasting electricity keeping these on if no one's supposed to come in here," remarked Peter.

Something shifted in the light up ahead. Sophie felt Janet press close to her back.

"What was that?" Janet whispered.

Sophie put a finger over her mouth, then slowly crept forward, keeping her footsteps as quiet as possible.

A sudden breeze gusted down the hall. Sophie felt the buzzing sensation intensify, then taper back down as the wind died away.

"I'm outta here!" Janet squealed, heading for the door.

"Right behind you," Bri said past a mouthful of the snack cake.

"Hang on, guys," Sophie said. She continued to inch forward, using the light from the open doorway to guide her.

"You think it's still a good idea to keep going?" Vince asked. "I mean, whatever it is clearly doesn't want us here."

"It's not a ghost," Sophie scoffed, feeling out the buzzing sensation, noting where its volume seemed to increase—toward the left. "I don't know what it is, but it's not a ghost."

"How do you know?"

Sophie stepped across the hall to the last cell on the left, then pulled her phone out of her pocket and turned the flashlight on. She shined it into the cell, her heart pounding as a person raised their hand to block out the light.

"Whoa!" Vince and Peter jumped back. Sophie took a step back, too.

"Get out of here!" A raggedly dressed man, lying on the floor with bandages covering one leg, shooed them away angrily. "And get that light out of my face!"

Sophie lowered her flashlight, focusing it instead on his injured leg.

"Are you hurt?"

"What's it to you?" The man's eyes, a steely blue color, narrowed suspiciously at her. "Where did you come from?"

Sophie glanced behind her at the guys.

"Let's just go, Sophie!" Janet called from the doorway.

Sophie turned back to the injured vagrant.

"We'll go. I just want to help him first." She dropped to her knees near his leg and reached out.

"Don't touch me!"

She shrank back at the man's sharp rebuke.

"It's okay. I have the life gift. I just wanted to heal your leg."

The man made a low noise deep in his throat but didn't say anything else as Sophie touched the bandages on his leg.

The buzzing intensified, and Sophie recognized that it was pain she was hearing and feeling. She felt farther with her mind, judging the extent of the injury. He'd lacerated his leg at the shin and behind his calf, badly enough to render him unable to walk for very long.

Sophie grimaced. She didn't know if she'd have enough

strength to heal him completely, but she could speed things along.

"Okay. I'm just going to heal a bit." She closed her eyes, dripping her energy into the man's leg, one tiny piece at a time, targeting the areas most in pain and most vital to his ability to walk. She remained there for several minutes, hardly moving until Peter stepped forward and put his hand on her shoulder, strengthening her. Vince did the same, and with their combined energy, she pushed the healing faster until all that she could feel was a vague soreness in the man's muscles.

Releasing her energy, she took a deep breath. She wasn't swaying or dizzy as she'd expected, but her stomach growled.

"Geez, I'm hungry now," Vince said. "Bri, you got any more of them snack cakes?"

As the guys headed toward the doorway, Sophie smiled at the vagrant.

"I hope that helps—"

"Aargh!" The man leapt at her. A jet of water slammed into Sophie's chest, knocking her onto her back.

"Ow! What was that for?" Sophie sputtered.

"For not minding your own business," snarled the man, towering over her with a flame in his hand.

Sophie looked from the flame to the man in confusion. Hadn't he just—

"Yah!" Peter slammed into the man, his rocky body armor crushing the man against the wall. The next second, Peter fell to the floor, crying out in pain. A patch of black spread over his torso, and Sophie could feel the jagged, buzzing pain coming off him in waves.

She pulled Peter aside, focusing on healing his death wound, while Bri, Luke, Simon, and Leslie charged in with a massive waternado. Vince was hot on their heels with glowing eyes and two handfuls of flame.

"Get out of here!" the vagrant yelled. "Don't know how to keep your nose out of things, do ya? Useless kids, up to no good. I'll teach you. Right now. Unless you leave." He formed his fists into stone hammers, crossing them in front of him as the water vortex slowed.

Sophie glanced at them, her eyes wide. The man was a multi-elemental. He'd used water, fire, death, *and* earth against them. She'd never met anyone with more than one gift and putting her friends in any more danger from this strange man didn't sit well with her.

"Come on, guys. Let's go," she said, pulling Peter to his feet.

"Smart girl." The vagrant waved his stone hands in dismissal, watching them as they hurried to the door.

Have to get to the source of the power before the others. Can't stay here any longer.

Sophie paused in the doorway, glancing back at the squatter. Had she just heard...his thoughts? Like she had with March?

He narrowed his eyes, then shoved his open palms toward her. A huge gust knocked her through the doorway and slammed the door closed behind her.

She pressed her hands against the door, hoping to catch more of the man's thoughts. However, the buzzing had faded. She'd healed the man, after all. She couldn't hope to hear his thoughts through the three-foot thick walls.

What power had he been talking about? Who were the

others he was trying to beat? And why had he been staying here, to begin with?

It was clear he wasn't just some homeless man protecting a temporary shelter. He was the most dangerous person Sophie had ever met, having displayed nearly every elemental gift. Professor Rogers had never mentioned anyone like that.

Was it possible he'd been affected by the tree's sickness?

Sophie gasped, remembering a conversation she'd had with Nurse Bonnie about thugs and thieves looking for power. The power she now knew was leaking from beneath the sickening tree.

Maybe he was one of them.

"Sophie?" Peter put a hand on her back. "You okay?"

"Yeah." She pulled away from the door. "I've never met anyone with all those gifts."

"That *was* freaky," Peter said, letting his hand slip to catch hers. He squeezed her fingers tight. "That was too close."

Sophie nodded, giving Peter a grateful smile.

"Yeah, I vote no more random trips off campus," Bri said.

"Hear, hear," Janet added.

Sophie chewed her lip as they walked back to campus, all thoroughly shaken and noticeably quiet. She knew they were all thinking the same things she was—that bigger things were happening than they could have guessed, bigger than finals and exams and elemental skills contests.

They'd stumbled into the lair of a dangerous, power-hungry thug.

They'd been lucky to get out in one piece.

CHAPTER TWENTY-TWO

Marcus Jenkins wasn't going to lose himself now.

He took deep breaths to still the shaking in his hands.

It had taken him weeks to work up the resolve to do what he was about to do, not to mention several embarrassing encounters with Sophie and a rapidly deteriorating relationship with Olivia.

She'd berated him when he'd stupidly confided to her what he'd done—and his nebulous regrets.

"Only an idiot would back out now," she'd told him. "Plus, you know if you turn yourself in, they'll kick you out. Then what will you do?"

Marcus took another shaky breath. He could be sent home. He might not be accepted into any other elemental schools, either. He'd have to figure out another way to keep learning and growing his power.

But he had to do it. Things were getting *way* out of hand, and his worry increased as he saw the consequences of the tree's injury growing—kids' powers going haywire, rumors of weird creatures on campus, and gossip around

Bardstown, talking about thugs looking to take advantage of any weakness the school had.

He sighed and ran his hands back through his hair. He'd never meant for this to happen. He'd had no idea what his egomaniacal move would cost. He'd only allowed himself to think about winning the respect of everyone who'd put him down.

Including his father.

He scowled as he grabbed fistfuls of his hair. The last thing he wanted, now that he allowed himself to admit it, was to go back home to the scolding and ridicule of his dad. He'd ask why Marcus was such a failure. Why he'd been kicked out after losing what should have been an easy battle in the elemental skill trials. Why he'd been cursed with a lousy loser of a son.

But if he didn't reverse the damage he'd caused, he'd be just as big of a loser in his own mind.

He glared at the wall, regaining control of his emotions.

He wasn't going to let his father's opinion, or anyone else's, define him.

From now on, the only thing that mattered was how Marcus felt about himself.

Right now, he needed to make things right. If he didn't, he'd have to live with the knowledge that *he* had caused all this chaos in the name of winning.

Heaving up off his bed, he shrugged on his hoodie and headed out of the dorm.

As he jogged toward Thicket Hall, he noticed another figure near the tree. Heart racing, he slowed his pace, trying to appear casual as he approached. He studied the figure, noting its dusty green blazer and dark, curly hair.

It was Professor Lester Welby, an earth elemental teacher. He'd heard him speaking in the arena when he went to his death classes.

He watched Professor Welby walk around the damaged root, taking notes and nodding to himself. The professor then bent, curled his hand into a cup shape, and lifted.

The earth began to pile out on the sides of the hole the spike had been in. Marcus noted its oily blackness with dread. That was his death magic.

He glanced at what looked like a shadowed hill and nearly choked.

There were large mounds of diseased soil piled up around the base of the tree. Marcus stared at the piles in shock. He'd meant for the spike to kill the tree, but seeing it working left a bitter taste in his mouth and a chill running down his spine.

"Enjoying the view?" Professor Welby had stopped and was gazing at him pointedly.

Marcus fumbled his words. "Um, no, sir. Not really." He pointed with an open hand at the piles of dirt. "Is that…is that all from that hole?"

"Indeed." Professor Welby studied him with interest. "Don't you have somewhere to be?"

"No, sir. I'm on a lunch break."

"Hmm." Professor Welby tapped his pencil against his chin. "Maybe you could help me with something."

Marcus nodded vigorously. "Yes, sir." He stepped onto the grass and followed Professor Welby back to the tree.

"The dirt you see is not normal," the professor began. "It's diseased by powerful death magic. I need to know if there is any way someone with a death gift can reverse the process and return the soil to the ground clean."

Marcus frowned. "I'm not sure, but I can try."

"Good. I know you're among the most talented at this school," Professor Welby said. "It might be good luck that you crossed my path today."

Marcus nodded, his throat tight. He approached one of the massive piles of black dirt and touched it.

His death energy pulsed beneath his palm in response. It had grown, its raw power overwhelming him. He had to draw back.

He glanced at Professor Welby. "It's really strong." His voice shook.

"It certainly is," said the professor. "Do you know of any way to draw the death magic out of the soil?"

Marcus shook his head. "I can try, like I said before, but this is really strong stuff." He turned back to the soil, focusing on the small handful he had scooped into his hand. The power was much more manageable that way. He closed his eyes, but instead of letting his sooty energy infiltrate the soil, he focused on the magic that was present. Knitting his brow, he pulled on it, showing it his energy and tempting it to come back to him.

It took the bait, latching onto his palm and spreading across his fingers.

He sucked a sharp breath through his teeth, and it stung. He absorbed the death energy back into his body little by little until the pale skin of his hand re-emerged from beneath the ink-like black stain.

Inspecting the handful of soil, however, his heart sank.

He'd barely made a dent in the darkness seeping through it.

Professor Welby rubbed his chin.

"It was a good try, Marcus." He shook his head. "I don't think it will work."

"Me, either," Marcus said, dropping the dirt back onto the pile and massaging his hand. "You'd need a lot of life to get all this death out."

"That's not including the death magic still within the root. This is just the surrounding soil."

Marcus stared hopelessly at the tree, regret churning his stomach into knots. What had he done?

"Well, thank you for your effort, Marcus." Professor Welby turned back to his notes, scratching something off the list. "Hopefully, the next theory will work better."

Marcus reached out. "Wait."

The professor turned back to him, one eyebrow raised.

Marcus clenched his fists and took a deep breath. He had to say it, and it had to be now.

"I'm the one who did it."

The professor just watched him. Marcus continued. "I wanted my talent to be noticed. I wanted to do something so big that nobody could ignore me. I wanted to prove my dad wrong about me, but I took it way too far. I didn't mean for any of this to happen."

He gestured helplessly at the mounds of sooty dirt. "I didn't even know I was capable of doing something like that. The magic is beyond me now. I can't control it, and I can't stop it."

"How?" The professor took a step closer, peering at him as if he didn't believe him.

"What do you mean?" Marcus asked.

"How did you do it?"

"I...I made a spike out of death energy."

Marcus watched a sad light dawn in the professor's eyes.

"I see. It *was* you." Professor Welby closed his notebook and peered sternly at Marcus. "You know this will have consequences."

Marcus stared sadly at the ground. "Yes, sir."

Professor Welby put a gentle hand on Marcus' shoulder. "It took a lot of courage for you to tell me this. I know you want nothing more than to fix it, but you set something in motion that is beyond even the professors' ability to repair. As much as I respect your courage, I cannot protect you from the consequences of your actions. Do you understand?"

"Yes, sir." Marcus fought back tears.

Professor Welby let out a heavy sigh. "Let's go to Headmistress. She has to know, first and foremost."

Marcus' heart beat faster with fear, but he looked the professor in the eyes and nodded stoically.

"Yes, sir."

An hour later, Marcus sat in his room, his half-packed suitcase beside him. The meeting with Headmistress had gone about as well as he'd imagined. She'd told him there might not be a place for him at the school. That remark, even after she'd praised his courage and thanked him for the information he'd given her, had cut him deep.

He'd realized what he'd wanted when he'd come here—to be accepted and seen for who he was, not kicked to the side for not being talented enough like his father did.

He'd tried to prove his point and earn their acceptance by showing off.

Sophie had been right that day after the dodgeball game. He'd known it then.

There were *much* more important things in life than winning.

His phone rang, and he nearly dropped it in his rush to pick it up.

"Hello?"

"Marcus. This is Headmistress Case."

Marcus gaped. He'd expected a call from her secretary, not from the headmistress.

"Um, yes, ma'am?"

"I've taken everything into consideration about our conversation today," she said. "I've also spoken to your father."

Marcus gulped.

"I believe it's in the best interests of the school to suspend you for the rest of the semester."

Marcus choked out a relieved laugh. "Just the rest of the semester? You mean I can come back?"

"You'll be expected to keep up with coursework during your absence," Headmistress Case went on. "If you don't want to repeat your second year, that is."

"Yes, ma'am." Marcus could have jumped for joy. He was going to come back. He'd have to endure his father's jeering through the holidays, but he'd be *back*.

"It's a merciful punishment, Marcus. Keep in mind that I could expel you. If you ever do anything like this in the future, I'll have no choice but to do so."

"Thank you, Headmistress." Marcus could hardly speak

past the lump in his throat. "You don't know what this means to me."

"Unfortunately, I do," she said, her voice sad. "Please have your things ready to go. Your father will be here to pick you up this evening."

Marcus nodded soberly. "Yes, ma'am."

He dropped the phone after she'd hung up and fell back on his bed.

He was coming back.

This time, he'd do it right.

Norma hung up, a deep heaviness in her chest. She hated to send Marcus home. She knew who his father was. She knew the pressure the boy had likely faced growing up and how close he'd come to repeating the worst event in the school's history for the same terrible reasons.

But Marcus had to understand the consequences of his actions. Professor Welby had told her all about the boy's confession and his eagerness to help repair the damage he'd caused. She had no doubt his will was good. She just wanted to be sure that the lesson stuck.

While Marcus' information explained what had initially happened to Thicket Hall, it didn't explain who—or what—was still trying to siphon the power under the tree. That was the piece of the puzzle that most troubled Norma. There was also the ever-present problem of the tree's dampening effect lessening and unleashing chaotic elementals or causing the students' untrained abilities to go haywire.

Norma sighed, resting her face in the palm of her hand. She had to get to the bottom of that mystery.

The school—and the city of Bardstown—were counting on her.

Sophie muddled through her classes and evening routine that night. The man with multiple elemental gifts wouldn't leave her mind. Neither would the thought of what might have happened to them if things had gone any differently.

As she brushed her teeth, Olivia slid into the bathroom, phone pressed to her ear.

"I know. It's stupid," she was saying. She didn't notice Sophie standing at the sink. "He totally blew it. Told Headmistress Case and everything. I told him not to. I told him they would send him home, but did he ever listen to me?" Olivia stepped into one of the stalls and closed the door behind her.

Sophie stopped brushing her teeth and listened intently. She had a suspicion that Olivia was talking about Marcus.

There was a brief pause as the person on the other line spoke.

"No, he and I are over," Olivia spat. "He told me as much right before he left."

Sophie's eyes widened. She *was* talking about Marcus. What had he turned himself in for?

Was it something to do with the tree?

"Well, they sent him home for the rest of the semester. I'm shocked they didn't expel him. Good riddance, as far as

I'm concerned. He's turned into a baby all of a sudden. Said something about Miss Miracle Grow somehow figuring it out. As if."

Sophie's heart leapt. He'd told Olivia about that day in the dining hall when she'd grabbed his arm.

"I told you before, Adrienne," Olivia hissed. "He stuck a death spike into the root or something."

Sophie nearly gasped but remembered Olivia didn't know she was there.

It had been Marcus. He'd poisoned the tree. He'd caused the chaos they'd been dealing with.

Anger churned within her. Of course, he had. It made perfect sense. He was trying to prove he had the world's greatest death gift, so he could boost his ego and make up for losing the trials.

"No, he tried to help Welby fix it. I mean, he was in tears when he told me. He was so thrilled that he'd be coming back. Said his dad hates him, and he'd be mad that Marcus *didn't* kill the tree." Olivia's laugh rang out. "I mean, not what my parents would congratulate me for, but whatevs."

Sophie's anger softened. Maybe Marcus' stunt had more to do with a lack of self-esteem than with too much of it. Maybe he'd done it to gain his dad's approval. Not that that changed how much trouble he'd caused.

"No, I'm not giving that crybaby another chance," Olivia growled. "He's been talking so much about *Sophie* and how *kind* and *good* she is that he'll probably want to date her next. Even though it was her tree-hugging that made him 'fess up to Case and got him booted out for the rest of the semester. I *refuse* to compete with that twerpy little life fairy, especially not for a loser like Marcus."

She laughed humorlessly. "I mean, Sophie's dating that earth boy, so I don't see that happening in a million years anyway. I mean, can you imagine that tall emo dude dating little Princess Life?"

Olivia's laughter filled the bathroom again.

Sophie's face warmed, and she backed toward the exit. Her eyes welled with tears as she flopped onto her bed, though she wasn't sure why.

She couldn't believe she had made such an impression on Marcus, so much so that he'd risked expulsion to come clean about the tree. He'd been sent home to his judgmental father until after Christmas.

She squeezed her eyes closed, tears streaming down either side of her face. She'd misjudged him. She'd treated him like he was a bully, not realizing there was much more going on beneath the surface. She'd called him names and laughed at her friends' jokes about him.

What if she had tried to be a friend to him from the beginning? Would he have felt the need to hurt Thicket Hall as he had?

She wiped away her tears as her roommates' chatter filled the hall outside.

What was done was done. She couldn't change it, and she couldn't talk to Marcus until after his suspension.

She smiled sadly, imagining Marcus bravely confessing what he'd done and trying to heal the tree.

With that much courage and power on the right side, the dread she'd been carrying lifted.

If Marcus was now their ally, anything was possible.

CHAPTER TWENTY-THREE

The next morning, Sophie shook strange nightmares about the vagrant from her sleep-fogged brain. He hadn't left her thoughts the previous evening, and from the odd, ongoing silence from her friends, she guessed they had the same issue. She went through her morning routine, then headed to her multi-elementals class with Leslie and Bri. Janet had had a doctor's appointment.

As the girls passed Thicket Hall on their way, Sophie felt a prickling presence in her mind. It wasn't the hum from the tree, but something sinister.

Just get inside the tree, she heard.

She slowed down, turning her head in every direction. Why did the presence seem so familiar?

Sophie stifled a gasp as the buzzing materialized in her memory. It was the vagrant.

She stopped, and Leslie bumped into her.

"Soph, what's—"

"Shh." Sophie peered toward Thicket Hall. The tree

increased its humming to a frenetic pace as if it were shot through with fear.

Students passed them on the walkway. She noticed Headmistress Case leading a nicely-dressed gentleman into Thicket Hall—a parent, she thought. Hopefully not someone from the ECSB. That *would* explain the tree's fear and the strange thought she'd just heard.

She turned in a circle, scanning the campus, but nothing seemed out of place or unusual. The tree's hum was beginning to calm, ebbing away from her mind.

Sophie sighed. "I thought I felt that man from yesterday."

"Felt?" Leslie looked at her, puzzled. "What do you mean?"

"You know, like, how I can hear the tree or that humming noise it makes. I can do that with certain people, too. Like March and Peter."

Leslie shook her head, taking Sophie's arm. "Girl, I think you're just freaked out about yesterday."

Sophie chewed her lip. She wanted to agree with Leslie. It made sense.

Glancing at the tree, she wasn't sure.

CHAPTER TWENTY-FOUR

Homecoming weekend was upon Sophie before she felt she could blink. That Saturday dawned clear and bright, with a hint of autumn chill in the morning air. Her phone chirped early, letting her know her family was on their way, so she got up and hurriedly got ready to greet them.

"Sissy!" Amelia bounced into her dorm room forty-five minutes later, her beaming smile lighting up the whole room. "I've missed you *so* much! You just don't even know how much!"

Sophie laughed and gathered her little sister into a hug. She'd forgotten how much energy Millie had.

"Hey, Soph." Walter pulled Sophie into a hug, followed by Joyce. "Gosh, have we missed you!"

Her mother whispered in her ear, "We brought you something."

Sophie stepped back as her mother laid a garment bag across her bed.

"Go on," Joyce said, grinning broadly. "Unzip it."

"Yeah. You're gonna love it." Millie said, standing beside Sophie as she gripped the zipper and pulled it down.

Sophie pulled apart the seams of the bag, her mouth hanging open in admiration. The deep plum-toned taffeta and sparkling tulle overlay of the dress looked fit for a queen, and the sequins and crystals on the short-sleeved sweetheart bodice gave it a royal charm.

"Sophie, you're gonna look like a princess!" Millie breathed.

"Where did you find something so beautiful?" Sophie asked, running her hands gingerly down the fabric.

"As luck would have it, it was your Cousin Beatrice's first homecoming dress from this very school." Joyce smiled, tucking one of Sophie's long, dark waves behind her ear. "You wear her size, and she gave it to us."

"That's not all," Millie said. "Mom, show her the rest."

Joyce unloaded one of the large bags from Walter's shoulders. "Hon, you can probably put those down. You don't mind, do you, Sophie?"

"Of course not."

Walter nodded vigorously, seeming to snap back to attention. "Right. Of course." He deposited the bags at the end of Sophie's bed.

"You okay, Dad?" Sophie studied her father. His impatient posture and furtive eyes told Sophie he was nervous about something.

"Yeah, I'm okay." He rubbed his eyes. "Just...pollen or something, I guess."

Joyce smiled knowingly at him.

"Your father's indisposed at seeing his first baby girl going to her first dance."

Sophie laughed gently and touched Walter's arm.

"Dad. It's okay. There'll be chaperones, and everything is supervised."

"I know that." Walter patted her shoulder. "You're just... growing up, is all. Becoming a lady and all that." He gestured at the box in Joyce's arms while he took his glasses off to rub them clean on his shirt. "Go ahead. Look at what else your mother brought you."

Sophie smiled at him, then took the lid off the box. A dozen sparkling crystals caught her eye.

"It's a tiara," Millie said. "Remember when I said you'd look like a princess?"

Sophie laughed, holding the sparkling tiara up to the light. "It's gorgeous." She put it gently aside and took out the rest of the items in the box—a pair of taffeta gloves to match the gown, a deep purple silk-rose corsage, and a pair of kitten-heeled plum pumps.

"I know how you are with your flats," Joyce said, rolling her eyes. "I wanted to get you that pair of high heels that was *screaming* my name."

Sophie hugged her mom, unable to stop smiling.

"It's all beautiful and perfect. Thank you."

"So," Walter said, clearing his throat, "Who's this young man I hear about who's the cause of all this fuss?"

It was Sophie's turn to roll her eyes as Joyce and Millie laughed.

Sophie took her parents on a tour around the school, showing them the greenhouse, which was full of flowers for the homecoming dance the next evening, along with her other classrooms. Millie was awestruck by everything, and Walter made the occasional nostalgic comment or told them all about the professors he'd had who were featured on the plaques in the different buildings.

After that, it was game time. The school was competing in lacrosse against their nearest rival, Stonebridge School for Gifted Students. Walter perked up noticeably at the mention of lacrosse.

"Just so you know, Peter's playing," Sophie said, shooting her dad a sidelong glance.

"Well. That does change things," Walter said. "I see he's a respectable young man already."

Sophie laughed, and they made their way to the open arena, where dozens of bleachers had been set up around the field. Walter pointed out a spot closer to the edge of the field, and they all settled in as the players warmed up.

"This is all just so exciting," Joyce said, hugging Walter's arm and rubbing Sophie's back. "Takes me back to my high school days."

"That must have been when the dinosaurs still existed," quipped Millie.

Sophie snorted as Joyce rolled her eyes. "Very funny."

"So, which one's Peter?" Joyce asked, peering down at the players. "He must be pretty cute because you keep going on about him on the phone."

Sophie's cheeks burned. "Mom, stop."

"I want to know, too," Walter said. "That way, I know who to come after if you call home crying."

Sophie covered her face with her hands, but her mother giggled.

"Hey, Soph. I'm hungry. Will you show me where the hot dog stand is?" Millie tugged on her arm.

Sophie peeked through her fingers. Millie shifted her

eyes toward the concessions, then looked at Sophie pointedly.

Sophie smiled. "Sure, sis."

After they escaped the bleachers, Sophie pulled her sister into a hug.

"Gosh, I've missed you," she said. "My partner in crime."

Millie giggled. "I may have gotten you away from Mom and Dad, but I still need the deets." She pulled Sophie to an empty spot near the fence. "Show me which one is Peter."

Sophie grinned. "All right. I owe you that much." She leaned against the fence, peering at the players in hunter-green jerseys until she noticed Peter's sandy blond hair toward the sideline. He'd taken his helmet off and was guzzling water. When he noticed he was being watched, he flashed Sophie a grin and waved at Millie.

Millie smiled and waved back.

"His hair is so cute," she said, then twirled, the sweater tied around her waist floating around her like a skirt. "I wish I was going to a dance."

Sophie ruffled Millie's hair. "You will. Soon enough."

They returned to the stands as the lacrosse game started. Sophie watched and cheered alongside her parents as the school beat out Stonebridge by the slimmest of margins. Still, it was a great victory and created an atmosphere of school spirit as they had dinner that evening, crammed into Thicket Hall with the rest of the parents who'd come to visit their kids.

"So, I hear Thicket Hall has taken a beating this year," Walter said.

Sophie nearly spat out her tea. "Wha...what do you mean?"

He leaned forward. "I heard from one of the alumni—one of my old classmates—that someone tried to hurt Thicket Hall, and now things are going haywire."

Sophie just stared at her dad. How had her dad's classmate found out? Headmistress Case had said not to tell anyone what was going on, but at this point, it seemed everyone knew.

"Um, yeah," Sophie said, trying not to look so shocked. "It's under control, though. They found out who did it and took care of it." She grimaced, thinking of Marcus sitting at home.

"I just can't believe anyone would try and hurt this big old tree," Joyce said, gazing around in awe at the multitude of rings along the walls. "What a treasure this place is."

Sophie nodded her head in agreement.

"Well, it made me wonder if some of the old stories are true," Walter said. "There's a blip in the history of this school, you know. A time when magic got really wild, and people even died."

Sophie's memory flashed back to what the tree had told her, the images it had shown her of lifeless bodies on the lawn. She forced herself to swallow her food and look incredulous.

"Wow. That sounds…crazy."

"What's even crazier," Walter said, leaning toward Sophie, "is that the rumors say it had a lot to do with Thicket Hall. Can you believe that? Hurting a tree caused all that magic to go haywire?" He shook his head. "I don't see how, but the rumors and connections certainly abound."

Sophie nodded, swirling her tea in her glass. "Interesting."

Walter finally leaned back, crossing his arms. "It really is."

Part of the way through their meal of chicken tenders and mashed potatoes, Headmistress Case stepped onto a hastily rigged platform and tapped a microphone.

"Attention, honored guests, parents, and students. We have prepared a presentation to honor exceptional students, as well as a mosaic performance by our seniors." Several more professors filtered onto the platform and smiled at the crowd as Headmistress Case began reading the students' names and accomplishments.

It wasn't long before Sophie heard her name. Her parents and sister beamed at her, clapping and, in Millie's case, whistling.

"For outstanding talent and improvement in life elemental skills." Headmistress Case lowered a medal around Sophie's neck and smiled warmly at her. Leaning close to Sophie's ear, she whispered, "Keep up the good work."

Sophie grinned at Headmistress Case and shook hands with the professors who'd lined up to greet the awardees. Professor Rogers handed her a decorative certificate and nodded.

"Well-deserved, Miss Briggs."

Sophie retreated to her table, passing the medal and certificate for her family to see.

"Always knew you'd do well, Soph," Walter said, patting her back.

Sophie couldn't help but beam with pride.

A little while later, Thicket Hall's humming increased in frequency. Sophie looked away from the senior's mosaic recital and gazed out the window. Maybe she could slip out to check on the tree.

"I'm going to go grab something from the dorm," Sophie told her parents.

"You want me to go with you?" Millie asked eagerly.

"I'm fine. I don't want to be too long," Sophie said, smiling as she ruffled her sister's hair, then slipped outside and rounded the tree.

"Hey, Sophie!" Sophie glanced over toward the path. Kelly, her mentor, was headed toward the greenhouse. "What's up? You enjoying homecoming?"

"Yeah." Sophie sighed. "Can I tell you something?"

"Sure." Kelly hurried over. "What's going on?"

"Well…" Sophie glanced at Thicket Hall. "I really need some help. Thicket Hall is…you know. Not 100% right now. And it's actually…told me what's wrong."

Kelly stared at her, surprised. "You mean…it spoke to you?"

"In a way, yes." Sophie twisted her hair as she continued. "It's been asking me to get help. I'm trying to, but there's a huge blockade of death magic deep in the root. Roscoe and I have been working on it, and the tree has told me if I could just get past that blockade, maybe Roscoe and Headmistress would be able to help it heal."

"Hmm." Kelly adjusted her round glasses. "Sounds like a big task. Probably too big for one person."

"Maybe if I had help…" Sophie looked at her.

Kelly frowned. "I don't know, Sophie. It sounds dangerous." She gazed at Thicket Hall, though, and her brown eyes hardened. "But I want to help, so we can try." She put down her books and stood in front of Sophie. "What do you propose?"

Sophie thought for a moment. "Roscoe had me channeling life energy to the tree. If I had more energy, or the two of us tried together, we might break past that death barricade."

Kelly pursed her lips. "Sounds plausible." She stood shoulder to shoulder with Sophie, putting one hand on Thicket Hall and the other on Sophie's arm.

Sophie nodded at Kelly. "Ready?"

"Ready."

Both girls closed their eyes. Sophie leaned into the tree's hum and let it form words in her mind.

You here, sapling. Bring someone else?

She just nodded so as not to break Kelly's concentration and felt deep into the tree's damaged root. The blockade was still there and had grown since she'd last dealt with it, but she felt Kelly's energy flowing through her, strong and practiced.

Taking a deep breath, she let their combined energy surge through the roots until the golden magic appeared like a fireball in Sophie's mind. It had to be big and powerful, and it had to hit with enough force to obliterate the blockade without the death magic pulling their energy away.

Kelly's hand trembled on her arm. "You sure about this?"

"Trust me," Sophie replied. She pushed the energy faster and farther until it abruptly impacted the blockade, slowing but not stopping this time.

Hope surged through Sophie. She fed it more energy and felt it tearing through the oily blackness.

Suddenly, the death blockade was gone, and their energy ricocheted back up through the roots.

Sophie felt it channel through her like an electric shock.

Kelly screeched and fell on her bottom.

"You okay?" Sophie knelt beside Kelly. She was rubbing her eyes, and a dribble of blood leaked onto her lip from one nostril. Sophie put her hand on Kelly's forehead, seeking the injury, but the woman pushed her hand away.

"It's all right," she said, pulling a handkerchief from her pocket. "It was life energy that hit me, so it's just got to dissipate. You add more, and it might do more harm than good."

Sophie lowered her hand. "Sorry about that." Her heart swelled, and she reached toward the tree, feeling for the death blockade.

She smiled, then laughed. It was gone without a trace.

"Did it help?" Kelly asked, getting up.

"Definitely," Sophie said. She jumped up and down, then spun Kelly in a circle. "We did it. I can't believe it! Wait until I tell Roscoe!"

Kelly laughed despite the tissue stuffed in her nostril.

"That's awesome! I'm so glad it worked!"

"This was just the first step," Sophie said. "It'll need time to heal, but it doesn't have that massive block anymore."

"I better go take care of my nose, then," Kelly said, laughing nervously as she gestured at the dorms.

"For sure!" Sophie said. She pulled Kelly into a hug. "Thank you."

Kelly stiffened, then patted Sophie's back. "Of course."

Sophie went back to dinner with her parents, enjoying the rest of the presentation with hope reigning in her heart. They'd removed a huge obstacle to the tree's healing.

If they could just help it heal, everything would be perfect.

CHAPTER TWENTY-FIVE

The next evening, Sophie stared at herself in the bathroom mirror, turning from side to side and watching the sequins on her dress shimmer. The purple fabric brought out the warmth in her brown eyes and dark hair. She adjusted her tiara on top of her crisp waves and touched up her makeup.

"Wow," Janet said as she entered the bathroom. "That purple is a great color on you."

Sophie smiled, taking in Janet's beautiful midnight blue gown and carefully curled hair, strewn with blue crystal pins.

"You look amazing, too," she said, straightening Janet's diamond pendant.

"We *all* look like rock stars," Bri said, walking past in a shiny little black dress. She tossed her blonde waves behind her shoulders, then bent toward the mirror and smoothed on red lipstick.

"Going for the classic look, I see," Leslie said, curling the last section of her short black hair. Her mermaid-silhouette teal gown accentuated her height and gave her a Twenties-era vibe.

"Of course," Bri said. "I don't have time to come up with fashion ideas. Therefore, I steal from the best."

They giggled as she clicked away in her high heels.

The girls waited in the lobby of their dorm building for their dates to pick them up, as was the custom at the school. Sophie glanced at the other girls, noting Olivia in a white, glittering sheath gown that slit at her mid-thigh.

"Bold choice," Bri said with an admiring nod.

Sophie rolled her eyes. "I'll say." She looked for March, smiling as she saw her in a princess ball gown, in a beautiful light blue that matched her eyes. March met her gaze and smiled, giving a little wave as Vincent turned up, handsome in his pinstripe suit with matching blue tie, and tugged on her arm.

"Oh, here he is," Bri said, smiling as Luke approached, all black and white to match Bri. He offered her a small bouquet of white roses and gave her a gentlemanly bow.

"Cool," Bri said. As she sniffed the flowers, her eyes lit up, and she pulled a white chocolate candy bar from the arrangement. "Oh, you know me so well."

Sophie giggled and waved as they left. One by one, her friends dispersed, Leslie with Vince, who offered her a teal daisy corsage, and Janet with Simon, who'd slicked his hair back and approached Janet like a mouse would approach a cat, his bouquet trembling in his hands.

"Oh, stop it," Janet had said. "Of all the people to be nervous around, I'm like, the last person."

Simon had smiled in relief and offered her his arm.

Sophie kept an eye out for Peter. She couldn't help but

feel impatient, especially when she watched Charlotte take Reggie's arm, looking glorious in an asymmetrical gold dress.

A tap on her shoulder made her turn around.

Peter, his sandy waves neatly combed, gazed at her in awe, the purple rose bouquet in his hands forgotten.

"Wow," he murmured.

Sophie blushed fiercely, smiling like an idiot.

"You look great yourself," she said, noting his tie matched her dress perfectly.

Peter gathered himself, clearing his throat. He handed her the roses, then bowed and offered his arm.

"Sorry. I just...you look amazing. I mean, you always look amazing, but tonight, you look...extra amazing." Peter slapped his forehead.

Sophie took his arm and giggled.

"Thank you." She looked purposefully into his eyes, and he smiled back, relaxing his shoulders.

"I'm glad you always understand what I'm trying to say," Peter said, leading her toward the door.

They walked in an amiable silence up the stone walkway, which had been decorated to the nines with the flowers they'd been growing all semester, wrapped around each lamppost and potted at regular intervals along the way.

"You'd think they'd have a carriage service. You know, since all you ladies are in these impractical gowns with high heels," Peter remarked.

Sophie stuck her foot out, showing off her kitten heels. "Reason Number One I refuse to wear high heels."

Peter laughed.

As they entered the open-air arena, they gazed around, their mouths hanging open. Sophie hadn't remembered there being that many flowers in the greenhouse, but here they were, growing up trellises, hanging from gold string lights crisscrossed above the dance floor, and decorating the edges of the floor.

"You really grew a lot of stuff," Peter remarked.

"I guess so!" Sophie laughed.

Charlotte waved them over to where she and Sophie's roommates were dancing together as a group to a boppy, fun electronica mix.

"You ready?" Sophie asked Peter.

He smiled and patted her arm. "You bet."

They joined the group and let loose, Sophie dancing with her roommates from time to time as the songs changed, their high-energy vibe remaining the same for several songs in a row. Reggie showed off his breakdancing skills, much to everyone's delight, especially Charlotte's.

A song with a Latin beat came on, and Vince glanced at Leslie.

"Let's make some steam," he said, and everyone erupted into laughter as Leslie took his hand, their touch literally creating steam. They performed a salsa dance they'd learned, drawing applause from the small crowd that had formed around them.

Sophie laughed and glanced around, content to people-watch as Leslie and Vince had their moment in the spotlight. Olivia had snagged a cute third-year instead of Marcus, and her face was lit up with genuine laughter. Sophie smiled despite herself. Happiness looked good even on Olivia.

In a corner, a girl hopped into the air with a shriek. Another girl, not in formal garb, laughed and ran away, her fingers smoking. Sophie watched as one of the professors apprehended her and sent her away.

She rolled her eyes, though she couldn't help but chuckle.

The Latin dance song ended, and Leslie and Vince took a bow. The lights dimmed, and a slow, romantic song came on.

Sophie watched as her friends paired off, awkward at first, but soon the girls were laying their heads on their dates' shoulders, and the guys were giving each other a subtle thumbs-ups behind their dates' backs.

Peter took Sophie's hand. "May I have this dance?"

Sophie laughed. "Of course, good sir."

She put her hands on his shoulders, and he shyly put his hands on her waist. They turned with the music, avoiding each other's eyes. Sophie was amazed she hadn't stepped on his feet yet.

"So. You ever dance like this before?"

Sophie looked at Peter, shaking her head. "Nope."

Peter chuckled. "Me, either. I have no idea what I'm doing."

Sophie shrugged. "I don't think that's the point." A gust of wind hit her back, blew her hair around her face, and nearly knocked her tiara off, pushing her into Peter's arms. He stumbled back a few steps but managed to catch her.

Sophie sputtered, trying to get the hair out of her mouth. "What the—"

"Prankster," Peter said. He held her up with one arm, parting her hair with his free hand so she could see. His face was inches from hers, she realized. Her cheeks warmed.

Peter smiled tenderly at her as he straightened her tiara. "You okay?"

"Yeah." She got her balance and attempted to fix her wind-blown hair.

Peter took her hands, still smiling. "Don't worry about it. You look great."

Sophie smiled as he pulled her back into the dance, and this time, he didn't stop gazing at her with his deep emerald eyes.

Sophie stared back, unable to quit smiling, her heart racing despite the slow tempo of the song. Her head spun and she stopped turning, though she didn't let go of Peter's shoulders.

"What's wrong?" Peter asked.

"Just dizzy, that's all." The ground beneath her feet seemed to vibrate, though she wasn't sure if that was due to her dizziness or because Peter hadn't stopped staring at her. He hadn't let her go, and he was moving closer.

"Me, too," he said, his voice low and his eyes on her lips.

Sophie's heart kicked into overdrive, and she closed her eyes in anticipation.

The ground was *definitely* vibrating, and both of them opened their eyes, their faces so close their noses almost touched.

"What's going on?" Sophie whispered.

Peter looked down at the ground, his brow furrowed. "I don't know, but I don't like it."

The tree's low hum suddenly increased in volume,

practically shrieking in her mind, and Sophie instinctively put her hands over her ears.

"You okay?" Peter took her arms. "Sophie?"

"It's the tree," she growled past gritted teeth. "Something's wrong."

Peter glanced at their group. The slow dance had ended, and another upbeat song had taken its place. Sophie slowly uncovered her ears, realizing it wouldn't do any good, and jerked her head at Leslie, who'd paused to give them a concerned glance. She took Vince's hand and hurried over to Sophie.

"What's up?" she asked.

"Sophie thinks something's wrong with the tree. And we felt the ground vibrating," Peter explained.

"Hmm. Yeah, I felt that, too, but I was sure it was just everyone stomping around," Vince said with a lighthearted chuckle.

"The tree's in trouble," Sophie said. The hum hadn't lessened in volume, but she was adjusting to it. "We need to go check it out."

Leslie shrugged. "All right. We can all go." She glanced around at the chaperones. "But we'll need to be sneaky."

"There's a table down near Thicket Hall for an after-party," Vince said. "If we just tell them we're going down there to help..."

"Perfect," Sophie said. "Let's grab everybody. We need to hurry."

One by one, they pulled their gang from the dance floor and headed down toward Thicket Hall. Sophie and Leslie went first, a girl with a girl to avoid any teacher's suspicions, and the rest of the group likewise paired off, citing the excuse of either a bathroom break or seeing about helping at the Hall.

Sophie noted that as she and Leslie hurried down the stone pathway, the vibrations increased in strength, and the tree's distress call amplified in volume.

"I'm coming, I'm coming," Sophie hissed into the hum, trying to project her presence toward the tree to calm it.

It seemed to have some effect, and as she came closer, the humming began to take on the stilted words she was used to hearing from Thicket Hall.

Sapling. Need you. Person here, below me. Leave, they will not. Hurt me.

Sophie shook her head, bewildered. What did it mean, below? As far as she was aware, the Hall where they ate their meals was on the lowest floor.

"We'll need to go inside the hall, I guess," Sophie said, pulling Leslie toward the entrance.

"Man, these vibrations are strong!" Leslie said, clicking after Sophie. "Makes me wish I hadn't worn these heels."

No one was guarding the entrance as Sophie and Leslie entered the hall. Tables decorated with balloons in hunter-green, black and white were scattered around. Sophie took in the silence of the hall. It seemed so much bigger now that she was seeing it empty of people.

As she pressed forward, the vibrations died. Puzzled, Sophie backtracked. The vibrations increased again, but this time, there was a buzzing in her mind, seeming to flow toward the right side of the hall.

"I think we need to go this way," Sophie said. Footsteps echoed behind them and Sophie whirled, but it was Peter, Charlotte, and the rest of her friends catching up.

"Any luck?" Bri asked, panting for breath. She'd taken off her heels and thrown her blonde hair into a messy bun.

"We're onto something here," Leslie said, following Sophie as she gingerly picked out the path of the vibrations.

Sophie followed the flow around the side of the room and into a stairwell she'd never gone in. The vibrations were almost audible now, and Janet shrunk away, clinging to Simon's arm.

"I don't like this," she said, glancing around. The rest of the gang looked similarly uneasy.

Sophie continued to follow the flow, going around the bottom of the staircase to the other side, closest to the tree wall. The space between the wall and the staircase amplified the vibrations until Sophie thought her whole body was quaking.

But out of the corner of her eye, metal flashed in the light. She turned toward it, noticing a doorway beneath the staircase.

"I found a door," Sophie called. She moved forward, placing one hand on the doorknob and another on the door.

The vibrations coursed through her now, and a deep, buzzing energy filled her mind, crowding out even the tree's frantic hum. She tried turning the doorknob but to no avail.

Peter rounded the staircase first, grimacing against the eerie vibrations. He sheathed his arm in stone.

"Might want to stand back," he warned Sophie. He then raised his stone arm and struck the door, sending splintered wood and the metal doorknob flying. Sophie covered her head but smiled as the door swung open.

"Thanks," she said. Peering into the open space, she could see another set of stairs leading down into a dark, open space.

The others came around the staircase.

"Do we really want to go down there?" Luke asked, eyeing the doorway warily. "I mean, remember what happened last time we barged into someplace we shouldn't have been."

"Yeah." Janet shuddered. "No fun."

Sophie steeled her will. "I have to try and help the tree. If you guys want to help, that's great, but none of you has to come with me."

"Like heck, we're gonna let you go down there by yourself!" Charlotte retorted.

Sophie glanced back at her friends. They exchanged worried glances, but their eyes were determined.

"Char's right," Bri said. "We've got your back, Sophie."

Sophie smiled, hauling up her skirts. "All right. Let's go."

They traipsed down the stairs, lighting the way with their cell phone flashlights. The vibrations grew steadily worse as they descended, and by the time Sophie reached the floor, it was rattling her teeth.

She swept her phone light over the wall, searching for a light switch. Instead, she saw a string dangling from the ceiling and pulled it.

The single yellow lightbulb gave off a sulfurous light, illuminating a large, mostly unfinished room with a cracked concrete floor.

"Look," Simon said, pointing toward the far wall, which looked chipped and deteriorated. Sophie noticed a pick and hammer lying near the broken spot.

"Someone's been chipping away at this wall," she said, edging closer. She stooped to pick up the hammer but instantly jerked her hand away. Energy pulsed through the tool in waves, an enormous amount of energy. She reached out to put her hand against the wall, steadying herself, but the wall, too, sent waves of ferocious energy pulsing through her, and she stumbled back, trying to catch her breath.

"Are you okay?" Peter hurried to her side, supporting her arms.

"Yeah." She struggled to slow her breathing. "Just…don't touch that stuff."

"Who in the world is down here trying to tear down a wall?" Leslie asked.

"Seems kinda pointless to me," Charlotte added.

Sophie shook her head. "It's not pointless." She gulped down a few more breaths before she spoke again. "Someone's trying to get down under the tree. There are these channels of energy, like, elemental energy. And the tree protects all of that. Now that it's sick…"

"It's vulnerable," Reggie said, his eyes alight with understanding. "So, someone is trying to steal the leaking energy."

"Exactly."

"Do you think they're still down here?" Janet asked, her voice trembling. "I don't want to be caught down here with a magical burglar."

"Wait. How do you know all this?" Luke asked Sophie.

"Well," Sophie said, "I ran into the wild elementals that appeared right after Marcus hurt the tree. Headmistress Case told me not to tell anyone."

"Wait. Marcus did this?" Janet's voice went up an octave.

Sophie covered her mouth. She hadn't meant to let that slip.

"Of course he did it!" Charlotte fumed, pacing. "Only a massive, selfish jerk like him would even think to hurt Thicket Hall."

"Figures," Peter grumbled.

"Guys, Marcus didn't do this." She gestured at the chipped wall. "He's not even at the school anymore. At least, not right now."

"Once again," Luke asked, giving Sophie an incredulous look, "how do you know?"

Sophie sighed. "I overheard Olivia talking about it in the bathroom. She said he's been sent home for the semester. She also said he's changed a lot." She stared thoughtfully at the wall. "He turned himself in, apparently."

"Whoa." Vince shook his head. "If that's true, that would have taken a huge change of heart."

"Unlikely." Bri huffed. "That dude's heart is frozen in some death-y, gross coffin in his chest."

"Anyway," Sophie said firmly, "we're getting off subject." She glanced at the wall. "Someone's been down here, trying to get to the energy channels. They could be trying to steal it, or they might just be trying to cause more chaos."

"Or both," Peter put in.

"Or both," Sophie agreed. "But I don't think they're still here, and I don't think we can get much farther than this. I can't touch that wall without feeling like I'm gonna explode."

Janet nodded. "So, we're heading back?"

Sophie sighed. The tree's hum was calmer, and there were no other signs of the person who'd been here.

"Yep. Let's go back."

CHAPTER TWENTY-SIX

"Today," Professor Nelson declared, "we'll be creating robots." She clicked her remote, and an image of a robot appeared on the screen.

Sophie stared bleakly at the projected image, her eyes sleepy. She and her friends had stayed up too late last night, talking about the homecoming dance. Why on earth was Professor Nelson expecting them to do actual work the day after the whole school had stayed up all night?

"You'll be provided with spare parts to get things up and running, but the fewer parts you use in your creation, the more points you'll get."

Sophie heard the excited murmurs of her classmates, but all she could muster the energy to do was turn to Janet with an incredulous glance. Maybe they'd all had steaming mugs of coffee—an unusual offering for the students—from the dining hall this morning.

Sophie had never liked coffee, so she'd opted for tea instead. The two glasses of sweet tea she'd downed to wake up had done little for her stamina.

Janet, similarly exhausted, shrugged and slid her glasses up the bridge of her nose. "We'll be lucky if our robot even looks like a robot."

Sophie snorted.

Professor Nelson sorted them into their usual groups. Sophie's always included Janet, Sheila, Vincent, Luke, and a fire elemental girl named Rosie. Sophie had been relieved to find that Rosie was a lot more like Vince than Olivia, with her casual t-shirt and jeans and Southern drawl.

"All right, y'all, what kinda robot do you wanna make today?" Rosie asked as they shuffled over to a workstation.

"Preferably something easy," Sophie mumbled, propping her head on her hands as she sat at the lab table.

"Well, what could our robot do that's unique? Could it hula hoop? Can it water your garden?" Luke asked.

"Could it kill bugs in your garden? Like, a pesticide robot scarecrow." Vincent put in.

"Ooh!" Sheila squealed. "What about a water fountain? Decorative and quirky."

"Interesting idea. I was thinking more along the lines of a flame-throwing robot." Rosie chuckled. "Maybe that's too selfish, though."

Sophie managed a laugh.

"Guys, I found these gears. We won't have to use them in our robot, though, if I use them as a template and make one out of stone or crystal," Janet said, bringing a box of parts to their table.

"Great idea," Luke said, high-fiving Janet.

"Hey, Sophie, you okay?" Rosie peered at Sophie, whose eyelids had begun to close against her will.

"You know they put something special in that coffee this morning. That should have perked you right up."

Sophie looked at Rosie, bewildered. "What do you mean?"

"My mom said it's an annual tradition," Luke said. "The Morning-After-Homecoming coffee. It tasted like hot cocoa, but I wasn't tired after I drank it."

"Ugh. Of course. I chose not to drink it because I don't *like* coffee," Janet said, slapping her forehead.

"Me, too," Sophie said.

"Wait." Rosie lowered her voice and dug in her backpack, pulling out a small red thermos.

"It was really good, so I got some for later. Y'all can have some if you want."

Sophie gratefully took the lid of the thermos filled with still-warm coffee Rosie poured her. After taking a tentative sip, sweet chocolate flavors exploded on her tongue. She downed the cup with a few gulps, licking her lips.

"That *was* good." She gave the cup back to Rosie, who refilled it for Janet.

"You said it," Janet added, wiping her mouth on her sleeve.

The coffee worked its magic. Sophie felt life returning to her, much like energy moved through her when her friends put their hands on her shoulder. She was able to rejoin her group, making vines with hollow insides to substitute for the pipes Janet had brought over.

Vincent shyly offered to kill the shoots of the vines they didn't need, stopping the growth at the edge of the vine so it could be more easily handled as they assembled their robot.

Janet and Sheila worked together to make a strong, muddy glue for attaching parts to the inside wall of the robot, and Luke blasted the glue with air to speed dry it onto a test piece of Sophie's vine pipes.

"Looks great," he said, trying—and failing—to tug apart the two vines he'd joined.

Rosie worked with a pair of sunglasses and one ignited finger, welding together the metallic pieces of the robot's frame. Luke worked beside her, channeling air into a tiny stream to fuel Rosie's makeshift welding gun.

Sophie and Janet paired off, Sophie making belts from woven grass to power the gears Janet had made. The end result worked like a bicycle chain mechanism and would guide the water up Sophie's vine pipes and through the robot's open mouth.

Rosie and Janet joined Janet's handmade copper wires to the circuit board and battery. Janet jumped back several times as the wires shocked her.

"So that's why they put that plastic over them," she said, grumbling as she rummaged through the box for electrical tape.

Sophie heard a screech from the other side of the classroom and glanced over. Olivia's hair was standing on end, and smoke rose in tendrils from her fingers and hair. The girl holding their circuit board began to back away from Olivia, and Sophie chuckled.

As they worked, the robot slowly came together, and Sophie realized their group was having a lot of fun. There'd been much laughter and joy during the construction. Even Vincent was open and amiable despite his shy, introverted nature.

As a finishing touch, Vincent put his hand on every spot they'd used their mud glue, making sure there were no living seeds that could sprout and destroy their infrastructure.

Professor Nelson examined their robot, making notes on her clipboard and nodding in approval.

"Very well done. Now, let's see it in action."

Sheila filled the robot's reservoir with water, and Janet flipped the crystal switch she'd created. The robot sputtered to life. They could hear the gears turning and whirring.

Luke plopped a bucket in front of the robot as water trickled, then spouted from its mouth, alternating between the two functions.

"Hmm. I'd thought it would have a steadier flow," Rosie said, scratching her head.

"Well, it's good for watering gardens," Vincent said with a dry chuckle.

"Let me see if there's something caught in the pipes." He opened the back panel and reached inside, squinting as he felt the vines Sophie had made.

"Ah!" His eyes lit up, and he held still for a moment.

The water flow increased. Water spouted from the pipe at the same pressure, creating a fountain as they'd intended.

"Random sprout inside the pipe," he told Sophie.

She smiled at him. "Thanks for that."

Professor Nelson scored them and moved on to the next group's robot. Sophie stood back and marveled at their creation. It was homemade, and that showed in every inch.

As everyone patted each other's shoulders and beamed with pride, she realized they'd done it together. Not one element had been a solo endeavor.

She grinned, warmth welling in her heart. She wished things could always be this way.

CHAPTER TWENTY-SEVEN

Sophie discovered that things didn't stay rosy for long. She was in Professor Ann Shuyer's elemental art class a few days later, in a temporary setup in Professor Roger's classroom. It was the first time they'd had art class since Vince's accident a few weeks before. The professor still seemed distraught over the destruction of her studio. She paced pensively in front of the projector screen, cringing when Vince made his appearance. He smiled nervously at her and gave a small wave.

Sophie and Janet took seats closer to the back of the classroom.

"No way am I getting my backpack roasted again," Janet said, hugging her book bag protectively.

Sophie rolled her eyes.

"Today, we'll be working on mosaics, as in our last class," Professor Shuyer said, her voice tight. "However, we have some additional precautions in place, which I hope we won't have to use."

She gestured to several rows of fire extinguishers, and a

dozen senior students and faculty filtered through the left-hand door. "They have varying gifts, though most of them have water."

Sophie stifled a snort.

She dismissed the students and faculty and picked up a remote. "Anyhow, before we begin, I'd like to show you some of the most intriguing and beautiful pieces of elemental art in existence."

She clicked her remote, and a glittering mosaic appeared on the screen. The tiles and vines formed an intricate portrait of a woman in a silk dress, cooling herself with a detailed, delicate fan.

"This piece is known as *La Vie un Belle* or *Life of a Beauty*. It represents a French debutante in the late 1800s."

Sophie studied the portrait, noting the use of dead leaves and scorched edges to give the colors a feathery, faded effect. She smiled. It made her heart feel complete to see each gift contributing, especially historically, since she knew death had long been stigmatized.

"Here's another piece that took the artists several years to complete." When Professor Shuyer clicked the remote, Sophie gave a soft gasp. At first, she could barely make out that it was a mosaic and not a painting. Tiny gems sparkled, blending into one another so carefully and thoughtfully that their individuality faded into the overall image.

"The use of fire to darken the gems and hone the metal frame is noteworthy, as well as a special adhesive made by firing clay and sap from the gum tree."

Murmurs of wonder bubbled up from the class, and Professor Shuyer grinned.

"If you like these, just wait until I take you to the Elemental Art Museum right next door in Louisville." She clapped her hands, looking gleeful for the first time that day. "I'm sure you'll all *love* it."

Sophie exchanged excited smiles with Janet. It would be awesome to leave campus for a while and go enjoy themselves.

When the hum from the tree intensified in Sophie's mind, her smile faded. There was still so much they didn't know about Thicket Hall, like whether it would survive after Sophie's and Kelly's destruction of the blockade and how long it would take to heal if it did.

The elemental skills trials were coming up fast, too. Yet another thing Sophie had to worry about, in addition to the tree they were trying to grow for their group project.

Sophie's joy all but vanished. She was *very* stressed. She had done nothing but study, practice, fight with Olivia about growing their tree, and carry the ever-present weight of uncertainty about Thicket Hall's fate for weeks now.

Well, there had been a few bright spots, homecoming being one of them. She smiled, remembering Amelia twirling at the lacrosse field and her dance with Peter that still made butterflies flitter in her stomach a week later.

They still didn't know who had been trying to get to the tree on homecoming night or if they'd been successful in reaching their goal. The tree's hum had been steady since then, but Sophie hadn't had a spare minute to go visit.

As they paired off to start on their mosaics, Sophie made a mental note to visit the tree soon. Tonight, if possible.

Norma buttoned her hunter-green blazer. She sighed, then took deep breaths.

Everything would be fine, she thought, repeating it like a mantra. It worked, at least for the few moments of peace she got before a sharp rap on her door made her pulse spike.

She heaved another sigh, then rounded her desk and answered the impatient knock.

She plastered on a smile and greeted the familiar beady-eyed woman and her two male companions. The willowy blonde woman clutched a black portfolio to her chest. Norma noted the official ESCB badge on her tartan blazer with distaste.

"Darla. So nice to see you again."

"Likewise." The woman sniffed as she strolled through into the office without being asked and plopped down on the loveseat. The two men behind her followed her in, though they remained standing, flanking Darla like bodyguards.

Norma gritted her teeth but said nothing. She closed the door, then locked it. One of the men took the liberty of creating a soundproof seal. It was thicker and darker than Byrne's, and his narrowed eyes never left Norma as he finished his work.

Norma sat behind her desk and folded her hands to keep from fidgeting.

"May I ask what brings you here today?" Norma began. Darla glanced up sharply from her tablet.

"Don't play the fool with me, Norma. We know something is going on here at the school. Word has gotten back to us about injured students, accidents involving out-of-control powers, and dare I say it..." she shuddered in a gross exaggeration of concern, "I hear Thicket Hall is weakening."

"I assure you that it's all under control," Norma replied. "A one-time incident, if you will, which I reported promptly to your department if you'll recall."

"Yes." Darla's voice was emotionless as she flicked through documents on her tablet. "I do recall, but what I don't recall coming across in my records is a report about students encountering free elementals."

Norma raised an eyebrow. "I thought I was quite clear in my report that there was a student involved."

"Not that one," Darla snapped. She tapped the tablet, then handed it across Norma's desk. "This one."

Norma scanned the page, noting that the reporter had opted to remain anonymous. Sophie and her friends had run into more elementals early in October and hadn't bothered to report it to Norma. She noted that the incident had occurred after curfew, which would explain their reticence.

One of them had leaked word to someone who wanted to get the school in trouble. Someone who didn't have enough guts to put their name on their tattling. Someone who was probably a former student. One of the parents, perhaps.

Norma fumed silently. Typical alumni cowards. She'd been dealing with them for years, but this year, of all years, was *not* a good time to get on her bad side. She'd track down the tattletale and give them a tongue-thrashing they'd never forget.

"I see," she said, using all her restraint not to throw the tablet at Darla as she passed it back.

"News to you, huh?" Darla asked, a smug grin on her dainty pink lips. "Interesting. I thought you had everything under control." She sighed, her eyes large and worried. "Well. It looks like you might need more help. Maybe a few officers on campus could help solve this problem you seem to have with supervising your students—"

"I do not now, nor will I *ever,* require your officers on my campus," Norma hissed. Wind swirled through the room despite her best efforts to contain her temper. Darla's eyes widened with real fear, and the two men with her straightened, watching Norma carefully.

Norma took a deep breath. "I will handle this in-house, as I always have. I would hate to *inconvenience* your officers, whom I'm sure are needed for much more important matters." As she spoke, noting Darla's fear with some pleasure, the winds dissipated.

Darla shook herself, then tapped in something on her tablet.

"Well." She sniffed. "Handling it in-house is an option, though we will need extensive documentation of your procedures." She paused, giving Norma a steely glare. "And we will need to hear about any further incidents from *you* first, with written documentation and all the proper forms turned in."

Norma stifled the urge to roll her eyes.

Darla stood, approaching Norma's desk, and leaned over it on her hands.

"Mark me, Norma. I will be back at the first *inkling* of unusual activity. And next time, I *will* bring my officers to make sure nothing...*tragic*...happens to your school. Or to you, its *revered* leader. Do I make myself clear?" Her beady eyes flashed onyx, and Norma saw the succulent on her desk wilt.

She glared at Darla defiantly. The woman smirked, and Norma felt a stinging sensation in her hands.

Darla wasn't strong enough to hurt her, but the woman had the entirety of the ESCB to back her commands, and they both knew it. Norma had no choice.

She forced herself to nod politely. "Understood," she said tersely.

"Wonderful." Darla turned abruptly and snapped her fingers. The soundproof barrier disappeared and the newcomers filed out, Darla's stilettos clicking on the floor.

One of the men leaned back into Norma's office and gave her a polite nod.

"You have a nice day, ma'am."

Norma didn't bother to reply. Though she'd fended them off, for now, there was only one misstep, one tattletale, between her and losing the school to the ESCB for good.

Though Darla's death threat had been more antagonistic bluff than reality, Norma didn't doubt that the board could—and might—find a convenient reason to send her to the afterlife sooner than she bargained for. They'd done it with others less powerful than her, and she was approaching eighty. It wouldn't be hard to find a believable excuse. The only reason they'd held off for so long was that Norma had always run her school like clockwork, as well as because of the persistent memory of Norma's immense power.

She couldn't afford any more missteps. She couldn't afford to be weak or to let her age show. Her power was as great as it always had been, and if there was ever a time it was needed, it was now.

She had to keep going.

Sophie made good on her intention to visit the tree. She cut out of dinner early and rounded Thicket Hall, noting the piles of diseased soil lying around the roots with a frown. She'd have to ask Roscoe if they'd found any way to purify it and put it back. It wasn't doing the tree any good to have a gaping hole near its root system.

She stepped up to the massive trunk and spread her arms, leaning into the hum with her mind until the tree's familiar speech materialized.

Hello, sapling. Better, I feel. Still, not good.

Sophie's heart rose and sank in rapid succession.

"What's going on?"

Sickness still spreading. Not as much as before. Other trees help me. Bring nutrients. Bring life. Take away sickness in little parts. Not fast enough. Get sicker, I do not. But heal, I do not.

Sophie nodded grimly. The network of trees had been able to assist more easily since the blockade had been taken down. Although Thicket Hall was not getting worse, it couldn't fully recover, either.

"We're trying to figure out a solution," Sophie said. "But I've been kept so busy with classwork…"

Know, I do. Do all you can, you are. The tree's amiable warmth washed over her, then changed to a prickling sensation. *Scared, Norma is. Bad, selfish people come. They ask her about me. I hear it.*

Sophie's eyes widened. "That organization Roscoe was talking about." She huffed angrily. "Just waiting for something to go wrong."

Yes, sapling. Bad people want what I protect. Why person try to break my walls?

"That's right," Sophie said, recalling the hidden basement. "Who were they? Are they part of that organization?"

Know, I do not. Left before you came. Strong, they were. Strong as you, more even.

"I know." Sophie shuddered, remembering the intense energy pulsing off the walls and tools. If she'd had to guess, the stranger in the basement was many times stronger than she was, based on the power they'd left behind.

Need to try everything, sapling. Roscoe and Norma have ideas. Tell them to try. Help, it will. Cannot do this, just trees. They help, repay me for many suns and moons. But not enough.

Sophie nodded. "Okay. I'll tell them."

She reluctantly pulled away from the trunk. Everyone was finishing dinner, and she had to get back to her dorm soon.

"I'll tell them. Just hang on. We'll find a solution."

Glancing up the hill, she saw Roscoe's workshop silhouetted against the sunset. Her eyes narrowed.

She'd go back, but not before at least Roscoe heard what the tree had to say.

"I'm coming! Give me a second."

Sophie heard Roscoe's irritated grumble from behind the workshop's door, as well as Mincemeat's excited meowing. Roscoe looked unsurprised to see Sophie.

"Yeah, I figured it was you. Cat wouldn't shut up."

Sophie giggled and stepped inside.

"What do you want, besides bothering me at supper time?" Roscoe pointed at a seat at the wooden table. Sophie was glad to see the death spike was gone.

"I just talked to Thicket Hall," she said, sliding into the chair.

Roscoe sat down and picked up his spoon, then set it down again and frowned at Sophie.

"You know, I'll never get used to that as a conversation starter." He batted his eyelashes, mimicking Sophie with a high-pitched voice. "I just talked to a tree. You want to hear all the *oakiest* gossip?"

Sophie snorted. "Yeah, gossiping is the last thing Thicket Hall wants to do. Though it did tell me some interesting things about Headmistress."

Roscoe raised an eyebrow. "Like what?"

"Well, it implied that she has been really nervous, and people came to ask her about the tree."

"Yeah." Roscoe stuffed a spoonful of ravioli in his mouth. "ESCB's been breathing down her neck lately."

"The tree says they're bad, selfish people," Sophie said. "They want what it protects."

Roscoe nodded soberly. "That they are, and that they do. At least that's what Norma—I mean, Headmistress—

always says. The tree might just be parroting her thoughts or emotions."

Sophie remembered the prickling sensation and rubbed her arms. "No, it seemed pretty worked up about that. It also got really angry when it talked about the thing that happened in the past."

Roscoe studied her while chewing another bite. "You mean to tell me this tree has full-fledged, human-like emotions?"

Sophie nodded. "Yeah. Doesn't seem much different, does it?"

"But how do you know or understand how a tree *feels*?" Roscoe waved his spoon as he talked, dripping tomato sauce on the table. "I mean, does it use words like, 'I'm angry,' or whatever?"

Sophie drew to mind her first conversation with the tree. Its warmth, which felt like affection, could transform into heated, fiery anger very quickly during a conversation. She also felt less concrete concepts like power, wisdom, and majesty that she didn't know how to explain.

"Well…it's hard to talk about. I just get a…" She moved her hands, trying to find the word she wanted. "A feeling, or a sensation. Like, love is warm, but anger is hot. Fear is this prickly feeling."

"Interesting," Roscoe said past a mouthful of food.

"More importantly, it wanted me to tell you something. It was saying that there's a really big network of trees all around from Bernheim, and since Kelly and I unblocked the death clot—"

"Wait. What?" Roscoe dropped his spoon.

Sophie grinned, proud of herself. "Yeah. You remember

when we were trying to get your healing stuff down into the tree, and I tried to push past that blockade of death energy, but I couldn't? Yeah. My mentor and I busted through it. The tree says it's been doing better, but it can't fully heal because the sickness is still spreading."

"Hold on a sec." Roscoe patted his mouth clean with a napkin. "You didn't tell me?"

Sophie's heart sank. "I know. I'm sorry. I've been so dang busy—"

"That is great news." Roscoe got up and started pacing. "With that thing gone, we could try the compound again. If we got the trees to keep doing what they're doing, and we try some things again, it might help."

"Exactly," Sophie said. "The tree said to try everything we thought of and that everything helps."

Roscoe clapped his hands, then went to his bookshelf and pulled out a well-worn spiral-bound book.

"This is great. This is..." He went to the stove and started putting bottles on the counter, almost knocking several over in his excitement. "Sophie, I'm glad you came. Now, why didn't you tell me this *sooner*?" He shot her a playful glare but quickly went back to his recipe book.

Sophie chuckled, scratching Mincemeat behind the ears. He had come up and started rubbing against her legs. An image of his canned food repeatedly appeared in Sophie's mind like a blinking alarm. Sophie sighed.

"Roscoe, did you forget to feed your cat again?"

Roscoe grumbled under his breath, then reached into the cabinet for Mincemeat's food.

"Dang it. Not again."

Sophie relished the hope rising in her chest and got up to open the can Roscoe had abandoned on the counter.

It was possible now. They could heal Thicket Hall and reverse Marcus's damage. They could stop the crazy accidents.

And most of all, they could protect the energy channels from whatever—and whoever—was trying to steal them.

CHAPTER TWENTY-EIGHT

The elemental skills trials finally arrived on a Saturday in mid-November, much to Sophie's chagrin. Ever since her little battle with Olivia during practices, she'd had to endure Professor Markel's constant thumbs-up in the dining hall or stupid jokes during combat class.

"Can't wait to see how far you go at the trials," Professor Markel had said one day at lunch, elbowing her and nearly knocking the tea out of her hands.

"Listen. Is there a way to opt out of this?" Sophie had asked, more out of frustration than a real desire not to compete.

"Nope." Markel's jubilant smile never budged. "Name's already on the roster. You're representing your element, you know. Gotta go make 'em proud."

Sophie had rolled her eyes and returned, disgruntled, to her table.

Today, though, she had to put on her game face. She brushed her teeth and dressed early that morning, then headed down to Thicket Hall for a generous breakfast and some civilized conversation with her friends.

To her chagrin, though, nearly everyone at her table was wearing Team Sophie t-shirts. The bright green letters were emblazoned on goldenrod fabric. They cheered as she approached with her plate. Simon gave a couple of good-natured "Boos," and Sophie rolled her eyes. Simon was competing too, though she noticed no one was wearing a Team Simon shirt except Janet.

"Sorry, Soph," Janet said with a shrug. "Gotta support my guy, but I hope you two tie."

"I tried to tell her, Sophie. Sisters before misters. She wouldn't listen." Bri said past a mouthful of blueberry muffin.

"Guys." Sophie couldn't help but smile. "How did you do all this?"

"My mom has a cutting machine," Leslie said. "I just put in a request for the shirts, and she mailed them to me, like, a couple weeks ago."

"And you didn't tell me?" Sophie sat down and took a deep gulp of her Earl Grey tea.

"Well, I made one for you, too. Don't be jealous." Leslie pulled a shirt out of her messenger bag and plopped it on the table in front of Sophie. "Plus, you would have freaked if you knew beforehand."

Sophie just shook her head.

After breakfast, they headed to the outdoor arena. The weather had blessedly decided to trend warm, though she noted a breeze that might make her task harder was blowing. She waved goodbye to her friends—Peter stopped to give her a good-luck kiss on the cheek—and headed toward Professor Garver at the life station.

"It'll be different today, Sophie," Garver said, throwing her arm around her shoulder. "Each student competes with the full attention of the panel of judges. So, it'll be more like your exam and less like the practices we held a while back, as far as that goes."

Sophie gulped. This would be a solo performance.

"The first years are competing separately from the rest of the school, which is open to second through fourth years. It'll be you against each first-year student who placed first in their elemental trials practice round."

Sophie nodded, her hands suddenly cold. She knew it was nerves and rubbed them together, hoping the friction would keep her fingers loose.

"First years will go first, of course, followed by the general trials with the rest of the school. Life and death go last, so you'll get a chance to see your competitor's work before you perform. That can be a blessing or a curse, depending on how you look at it."

Sophie groaned. "I think it's a curse for me." That was the last thing she needed—have Olivia's high score in her mind while she was trying to focus on not spilling her bowl of water.

Garver laughed and shook Sophie's shoulders. "I'm not worried. I know you. You'll do just fine." She smiled earnestly at Sophie, then hurried off to meet with the life competitors from the other grades.

Sophie sat on a bench near life's competition station and hugged herself. Although she'd been telling herself for weeks not to take it seriously, she couldn't help it. She wanted to beat Olivia badly enough that her stomach tightened thinking about it.

But thinking about Marcus, sitting at home and listening to his father berate him, lessened some of the tension in Sophie's abdomen. She didn't want to end up making a stupid mistake like that. She didn't want to let winning and competing become more important than just doing her best.

She took a few deep breaths, slowly through her nose and out of her mouth, and the tension eased more. She'd do her best. She'd ignore the scoreboard as much as possible. She'd root for Simon and focus on the task in front of her.

That was the plan, anyway.

An hour later, Sophie found herself wadding up her sleeves as she watched a first-year girl named Galeria spin her pinwheels in a perfect pattern, putting on quite the show. Her score came back nearly perfect—a 9.6—and her friends applauded raucously from the sidelines.

Next came Trevor, an earth elemental. He closed his eyes and moved his fingers in an intricate pattern, making his rocks balance without a single wiggle. A ring of displaced dirt slowly began to form around his tower of rocks. There was one movement—a single, tiny jiggle in one of the base rocks—and the stones tumbled down. Sophie frowned, watching him leave the station with disappointment painted on every feature. While her heart ached for his misfortune, she secretly thrilled, knowing there was one less competitor to worry about.

Next came Simon, and Sophie was able to relax for a

moment. He flashed her a grin, then set to work lapping waves together around a pile of sand. She watched as it slowly formed an intricate structure, complete with turrets, a drawbridge, and a working moat.

"It's a scale model of Bodiam Castle in England," Simon said as Janet whistled, and polite applause rained down from the spectators. Sophie noted his score—a 9.75 out of 10—and smiled despite herself.

"You did good," she said.

"I know. Beat that, Sophie." Simon said, grinning like a madman.

Sophie grinned back and rolled her eyes.

Next came Olivia with her paper maze. She only glanced at Sophie once before starting, but Sophie could tell by her body language that she was tense and trying hard *not* to focus on her.

Sophie pried her sleeve loose from her hands as she watched Olivia's tiny flame trail make its way through the maze. It made it almost to the end when a stray spark flew, aided by a sudden gusty breeze. Olivia froze and Sophie did too, but the spark disappeared without scorching the paper. The flame continued, and Olivia let it go out as soon as she reached the finish line, releasing a shaky breath.

Applause erupted from the sidelines, and Olivia's score flashed on the judge's panel—another 9.75.

Olivia crossed her arms and huffed. "Ugh. A tie."

Sophie saw Professor Garver waving at her from the life station and realized it was her turn. She headed over, taking deep, steadying breaths as she walked. She had to beat two nearly perfect scores to take the trophy.

"You got this, Sophie," Garver said as she approached,

positioning Sophie at the starting line. Sophie watched Garver pouring water into the bowl around a flickering candle, then closed her eyes, drowning out the sounds from the crowd, even her friends chanting her name. She tried to find a place within herself that just wanted to succeed in her task with no other pressure.

When she felt grounded, she opened her eyes and placed her hands palm-down above the dirt, letting her power trickle in to form strong, steady roots beneath the soil. Then she turned her hands over and lifted them, and thick, hearty vines snaked their way out of the ground. She wove a basket around the glass bowl as she had before, then slowly and carefully began to grow her vines to lift it. The bowl rose into the air without any rolling or movement, and Sophie released a breath. That was the hardest part.

Next, she focused on keeping the growth of her vines even and strong, weaving latticework supports under the two main vines that held the bowl steady. As it grew taller, she thickened the vines from the bottom up, drawing on all the nutrients and water in the soil that she could find nearby.

Finally, the bowl climbed up to the thirty-foot mark, and another sudden gust blew past, making the flame inside the bowl flicker. Sophie held her breath, but the flame burned strong.

"Complete!" Team Sophie roared from the sidelines. Sophie let go of her power, stumbled, and sat down on the bench, waiting anxiously to see her score from the judges. After a moment of scribbling, they raised their whiteboard: 9.75.

"Unbelievable! There is a three-way tie between life, fire, and water!" called an announcer. "This is exciting stuff, folks."

Sophie frowned, recognizing Markel's chipper voice. Her heart thrilled. Her performance had been on par with Simon's incredible castle and Olivia's precise fire maze. If the death elemental student did as well, would there be a rematch?

The last competitor stepped up, a stocky, copper-skinned young man named Diego. He rubbed his hands together, his brows furrowed in focus. He studied Sophie's vine tower, his eyes traveling down the lattice she'd created. He then bent to the ground, starting at the root. Sophie watched as the tower shrank and withered little by little, bringing the bowl down steadily. Halfway down, Sophie saw that one of the support vines looked very brittle. As she reminded herself that she couldn't say anything out loud, the tower collapsed, sending the bowl and candle to their demise on the packed dirt.

Diego kicked at the vines and broken glass and stomped off. Garver beckoned Sophie closer to the winner's stage and left her next to Simon, who looked ecstatic, the fuming Olivia, and the shy, smiling Galeria.

"Well, there you have it, folks. A worthy effort by Diego and Trevor, but unfortunately, their tasks were not complete. They have been disqualified from the trials." Markel seemed at home with the microphone, his booming voice echoing across the arena. "We have, in second place, Galeria Noble for air—"

He was cut off by thunderous applause from the sidelines. Galeria stepped up to the second-place platform, and a silver medal was placed around her neck.

"And, in a first for the school in over a decade, a three-way tie between Simon Green for water, Olivia Wright for fire, and Sophia Briggs for life."

The crowd went bonkers, and Sophie smiled as she saw Janet giving her two thumbs-up. They all stepped up onto the first-place platform, having barely enough room to stand without touching each other.

"Get me out of here," Olivia hissed close to Sophie's ear as Markel put their gold medals around their necks.

"Congrats, guys!" Simon said, turning to give Sophie and Olivia a high five. Sophie gladly accepted, but Simon's smile withered under Olivia's glare. He quickly withdrew his hand and turned away, focusing on the person with a camera taking their photo.

"Sourpuss," Simon coughed toward Sophie, and she chuckled.

"What are you laughing at, Miss Miracle Grow?" Olivia snapped.

Sophie shrugged. "Just happy we all won."

"Sheesh. Can you be any purer? It's annoying." Olivia stormed away as soon as the photographers were done. Simon and Sophie met their friends on the sidelines. Janet gave Simon and Sophie huge hugs.

"I wanted you to tie, and you did! Now I don't have to pick."

Simon and Sophie laughed, and Sophie realized, as she watched her friends cheering and laughing, that it didn't matter that none of them had won. They'd done well, and it was the best outcome she could have hoped for. She and Olivia had nothing to tease each other about, and her friends didn't have to feel divided between supporting her or Simon.

She smiled. It was the best of both worlds.

CHAPTER TWENTY-NINE

Sophie reluctantly woke late the next morning to a high-pitched humming in her head. She groaned, massaging her sore muscles. The trials had taken it out of her.

She rolled over and grabbed her phone from the charger. The clock read 8:45. Several missed messages showed up, from Peter, Janet, and Leslie. The common thread of the messages made her heart pound, and she paid closer attention to the humming that had woken her.

Peter's message read, **Are you up yet? Where are you? They have that coffee again at breakfast.**

The next one was from Janet. **Roscoe keeps poking his head in the Hall. I think he's looking for you.**

Then Leslie's. **Girl. You better get down here before the coffee's gone. I'll save you some. BTW, Roscoe looks really worried. He's been in to get banana bread like five times now. Might wanna see what's up.**

Sophie shook herself awake and leapt out of bed, hurrying through her morning routine. She tucked her phone into her jacket pocket, then wrapped a scarf around her neck, took off down the stairs, and burst onto the path toward Thicket Hall.

The tree's high-pitched humming was laced with prickling fear, and Sophie pushed herself faster. She sprinted past Olivia and Sheila, who were trudging up the path, looking tired.

"Where's the fire?" Olivia shouted after her. "Sheesh."

"It's the tree," Sophie called back, unwilling to stop and explain.

"What tree? Our class tree?" Olivia broke into a run after Sophie. "It had better not be dead or something."

"No, Thicket Hall!"

Olivia slowed to a stop.

"Ugh. Miss Tree Hugger's at it again. Freaked me out for nothing."

Sophie rolled her eyes but kept running. As she approached the entrance, she saw Roscoe's hulking figure near the double doors. He saw her coming, and his eyes lit up.

"Sophie! Thank goodness."

Sophie paused at the doors, panting for breath.

"What's going on?" she asked once she could breathe. "I can hear the tree. It seems scared."

"It's getting worse," Roscoe said, eyeing the tree with concern. "Even with the bulk of the sickness gone, it's just not getting rid of the infection quick enough. It's kind of like when a person goes into sepsis." Roscoe shuddered. "But I think I know what's missing." He looked at Sophie, a rare twinkling hope in his eyes. "We've been going about it all wrong. We've been doing stuff little by little as individuals or using people we think are the strongest. And it's helped, but not enough. Listen, the trees have it right."

Sophie raised an eyebrow. "What do you mean?"

Roscoe gestured in frustration. "Don't you get it? The tree has a network, a really big network of other trees, but Thicket Hall is also a really big tree. It's the bulwark of the whole forest, and it takes more to maintain this lovable monster than all the trees combined."

He slapped the tree's bark lovingly. "That's why even though the whole network is working to help, it's not enough. If *we* create a community or network, just like the trees, you could be the conduit, with your…" Roscoe searched for the word, "unique abilities!"

Sophie's heart rose. "Then we can save Thicket Hall."

Olivia and Sheila reached the doors, and Olivia crossed her arms.

"What's all this 'save Thicket Hall' business?"

Sophie, her heart still buoyed with Roscoe's discovery, turned to Olivia.

"Listen. We can save Thicket Hall if me and you, and everybody else we can find… If we all work together, just like we do with our class tree, we can reverse the death magic."

Olivia stared at her dubiously.

"Why do I care?" She gestured at the double doors Roscoe and Sophie were blocking. "I just want breakfast."

Sophie heaved a frustrated sigh. "If we don't help Thicket Hall, there won't *be* a school for much longer."

Olivia's brow furrowed, and Sheila gasped. Olivia looked at Roscoe and Sophie.

"You mean Marcus's stupid spike worked? Like, it's killing the tree?"

"Yes," Roscoe answered, his features serious. "And without Thicket Hall, there is no School of Roots and Vines."

Olivia still looked incredulous. "No way that crybaby pulled it off."

"Look," Sophie said. "Let's go eat breakfast. Just think about it, okay?"

Olivia frowned, brows furrowed as she thought.

"All right. Whatever." She and Sheila disappeared inside the hall.

"Sophie, we need to help the tree," Roscoe urged, fidgeting nervously. "Like, *now*."

Sophie bit her lip. "Well, you know the old saying. Something about putting on your own life jacket first." Her stomach grumbled. "If we don't eat, we'll be pretty useless."

Roscoe sighed. "Fine. Just make it quick, and recruit as many as you can." He held the door open for Sophie and followed her inside. "As for me, I'll be gathering up the professors."

Sophie smiled as Roscoe headed for the stairs. "Good luck!"

"You, too." He saluted, then ascended the stairs and went out of sight.

Sophie reached her table, and her friends greeted her warmly.

"There's Sleeping Beauty!" Bri said. She poured Sophie a steaming mug of coffee from a stainless-steel decanter. "Good thing I was here. These hooligans might have drunk the whole pot."

"Um, actually, pretty sure that was you," Janet said, rolling her eyes.

"Guys, listen." Sophie took several gulps of her coffee, then continued. "We need to help Thicket Hall. It's getting worse, but Roscoe thinks if we all work together and grab as many extra people as we can to help, we can draw out the sickness."

"I thought you and Kelly blasted it," Leslie said. "What's going on?"

"Roscoe explained it was like an infection," Sophie replied. "The thing that caused it is gone, but it spread into a lot of the tree's systems and whatnot."

"That's not good," Peter said softly.

"What do you need, Soph?" Bri asked, standing.

Sophie smiled. "We just need a network."

After Sophie had eaten, her roommates hurried around the hall, recruiting people to their cause. The guys followed Sophie toward the door, and Sophie saw Roscoe heading down the stairs, several professors following him.

"The cavalry is coming!" Roscoe said, giving Sophie a thumbs-up. She grinned and returned it, and they all headed outside and around the back to the tree. Sophie noted with dismay that the tree had dropped several soot-colored leaves. Its hum deepened as she approached, and she leaned into the trunk to listen.

Others you brought, sapling. They help?

"Yes," she said aloud. The professors looked at her, puzzled, but she ignored their questioning stares. It was the first time she'd used her psionic ability in front of anyone besides Roscoe.

"You'll get used to it," Roscoe told them with a snort.

Sophie spread her arms around the wide trunk.

Worse, the sickness is. I fear... The hum shifted, and a surge of shrill, prickling pain washed over Sophie.

Tears rose in her eyes. "You have to hold on," she told the tree. Her friends had joined her, along with half the cafeteria. Even Olivia was there, arms crossed and looking irritated. Still, Sophie smiled at her. She'd come after all.

"Let's hurry this along," Olivia said when she saw Sophie smiling. "I have a nail appointment later."

A figure appeared around the curve of the trunk—Headmistress Case, her wrinkled face looking more weathered than usual.

"What's going on?" she asked, taking in Sophie, Roscoe, and the professors and students gathered nearby.

"We're going to save the tree," Sophie said triumphantly.

Headmistress raised one eyebrow. "How?"

"Community, Headmistress," Roscoe said, stepping forward. "That's what the tree's been lacking. It needs more than just one person's efforts at a time. It needs us all together. And Sophie here...well, she can be the conduit. She's been able to...communicate with the tree."

Olivia snorted. "You mean she not only hugs trees but talks to them, too?"

Roscoe silenced her with a stern glare.

Headmistress Case looked at Sophie dubiously, but she came closer and gently touched the tree, her eyes wet.

"I suppose anything is worth a try at this point." She nodded at Sophie. "I know how strong you are, and Thicket Hall favored you for a reason. Perhaps this was the reason—so you could save its life."

Sophie smiled, proud but also embarrassed by the wondering glances her classmates were giving her. Even Olivia was staring at her open-mouthed, though Sophie figured she was just angry that Sophie was in the spotlight and not her.

Headmistress Case nodded at her colleagues, who linked hands.

"Join hands, everyone." Roscoe walked among the students, making sure they were following directions. "The tree needs *all* our power."

The students did as they were told, and soon there was a large circle looping back around to Sophie.

Peter smiled. He was at one end of the circle. He put one hand on Sophie's shoulder and connected the circle on his end.

Sophie smiled back and placed her hands against the tree. A hand grasped her other shoulder, and her eyes widened in surprise when she noted the perfectly manicured nails resting on her shoulder.

Olivia avoided eye contact, but there was a small smile as she rolled her eyes.

"All right, Miss Miracle Grow," she muttered under her breath. "Let's save the tree."

Sophie couldn't contain her grin, and her heart surged. She closed her eyes and began channeling energy into the tree drop by drop like Kelly had taught her, seeking the death magic poisoning Thicket Hall. She found it quickly; deep in the root, where she'd removed the blockade, tendrils of putrefaction greeted her probing mind. She grimaced.

"Olivia. I need you and any other fire elementals. We have to purify the diseased root."

"Got it."

Sophie felt an unfamiliar energy flow through her, bold and bright like lava. She aimed it at the rotting root, letting it flow in carefully. She didn't want to accidentally destroy anything healthy.

The fire did its job. Soon, there was nothing left of the rot. Only the healthy parts remained.

"Great," Sophie said breathlessly. "We did it. Now I need life and earth."

Peter squeezed her shoulder. "On it."

Energy like crystal and sunlight mingled in her body. She worked it into the root, slowly rebuilding what the fire and disease had taken. After a few moments, she pulled back, marveling at what her mind saw—a brand new, healthy piece of root, almost like a tree prosthetic, deep within the ground.

Water, sapling. It will not survive without water.

"We need water now," Sophie said, and a cool, rushing sensation filled her. She let it flow down through the tiny capillaries and smaller roots of the tree until it reached the new piece they'd just made. It worked almost too well—the still-growing root sprouted too many channels, choking off the main one.

"Death," Sophie said, her voice frantic.

"You sure?" called a timid voice Sophie recognized as Vincent's.

"Positive!" she replied, and an oily, uncomfortable surge of energy filled her. She gritted her teeth, struggling not to push it away. It was moving slower, like a viscous syrup, making it easier for Sophie to target just the roots she needed to pare back. She let them decay into their minerals and nutrients to feed the new growth.

"Okay, enough of that," she said when the job was finished. She shuddered as the eerie death magic left her.

"Not pleasant, huh?" Olivia asked, smirking.

"Nope," Sophie replied. She took a deep breath, then plunged back into the tree's hum, following the trail of infected parts. These weren't as bad as the main root but would need a good bit of life, like she and Kelly had used, to reach up to the diseased lower branches and leaves.

"All right. Need life again."

Familiar golden energy filled her, making her breathless, but she pushed it into the tree, targeting the diseased capillaries, branches, and leaves with furious comets of life energy. She pushed the magic up, watching in awe as it devoured the lingering traces of sickness.

The magic suddenly stopped, only partially entering the veins before rebounding back with enough force to knock everyone onto their behinds, breaking the circle.

"Ow!" Sophie reached up to massage her pounding head, noting that her chin was wet. She touched her chin, then drew her hand back to look at it. Her fingers were red with blood.

"Sophie!" Peter scrambled over to her. "Are you okay?"

Sophie's head swam. She never had tolerated the sight of her own blood very well. She mopped her nose with her scarf, trying not to look at the large crimson stains on the light blue fabric.

"I'm...fine." She fell onto Peter, closing her eyes against nausea rising in her throat.

"Oh, my gosh. Headmistress! Roscoe!" Olivia's shrill cry rang out. "Sophie's hurt! She's bleeding!"

Sophie couldn't fully appreciate Olivia's gesture of friendship while she was trying not to vomit on Peter. She heard hurried footsteps come through the grass, then a cool, wet hand on her forehead.

"Soph. You all right?"

Sophie smiled at Leslie's voice, then burped, covering her mouth. "Could be better."

A snort sounded nearby, and Sophie felt a gentle breeze flow across her face.

"You're telling me," Bri snarked. "It's gonna take a lot of bleach to get that out."

"Miss Briggs," said a sharp voice, and Sophie opened her eyes. Headmistress Case stood over her. The woman's gray eyes were turbulent. "What happened?"

Sophie blinked to stop her vision from blurring. Headmistress Case bent and felt her wrist.

"Nurse Bonnie," she called, her voice shaking.

"I'm here," Nurse Bonnie said. "Roscoe said I might be needed." She hurried over and knelt beside Sophie, clicking her tongue nervously as she checked the girl's vital signs. "Magic snapped back like a rubber band, and since Sophie was on the front lines, as it were..."

"She got blasted by everyone's energy," Headmistress Case finished. "But why did it stop? Why did it bounce back, I mean?"

"It stopped at the leaves," Sophie whispered hoarsely, pointing up. Everyone followed her pointed finger, taking in the still-blackened leaves on the lower branches. "I don't know why."

"Shush," Nurse Bonnie said, putting a hand on her forehead. Sophie felt a bright flow of energy in her nose and head and the pain eased, along with the dizziness.

Headmistress Case paced.

"What do we do now?" Olivia asked. "I mean, did it work? Did we save the tree?"

"If we let any part of that death magic stay, it'll reinfect the tree," Roscoe said.

Sophie noticed the tree's humming was buzzing urgently in her mind. She opened up to it, letting the tree's words in.

Would destroy leaves. Too much power. Something gentle, like wind.

Sophie nodded. "That's it. We have to use air." She recalled the butterfly she'd healed with her breath and why that had felt like such a natural choice. It was because her power would have been too much for the butterfly. It would have exploded it like the caterpillars she and Charlotte had learned about in class, and some instinct inside her had known that without being able to put words to it. "We have to use life and air together. That's how we'll heal the leaves."

Headmistress Case's eyes lit up. "Brilliant. That's a smashing idea."

Sophie smiled. "Well, it was the tree's idea."

Headmistress Case glanced at the tree. "I suppose it does know best." She then looked at Sophie. "Are you well enough?"

Sophie shook her head. "My job is done. I don't want to push myself anymore."

Headmistress nodded. "That might be for the best."

"I know someone who could help you." Sophie looked around, spotting Charlotte and Sheila chatting worriedly back toward the path. "Charlotte!"

Charlotte looked over, saw it was Sophie calling her, and dashed to her side.

"You okay, Soph?"

"I'll be all right, but I need you to help the tree."

"Yeah, of course." Charlotte's brown eyes were wide and earnest as she nodded. "What do you need?"

Sophie smiled at Headmistress Case. Charlotte looked at her, too, fiddling with her braids nervously. "Headmistress will show you."

A few moments later, the circle formed again, except for Sophie, who curled up in a root near the base of the tree and watched. Headmistress Case and Charlotte were in the center this time.

"Life and air," Headmistress said, and Sophie watched in awe as the lower branches began to move in a gentle wind. As the air rushed through leaves with a soft rustling, amplified by the sheer size of the tree and the number of branches, the leaves turned from spotted brown and black to a deep, healthy green. It took several moments for all the leaves to return to health, and as they neared completion, Sophie gently leaned into the tree's hum, now musical and deep and lively in her mind.

"How are you?" she asked Thicket Hall.

In response, a friendly warmth spread through her.

You did it, sapling. Knew you could, I did. No sickness left. All deep breaths, all sunlight.

When the wind died, people clapped and cheered and patted each other on the back. Roscoe wiped a tear from his cheek, and Headmistress pulled him into a hug in a rare display of affection that made his eyes go wide. Even Olivia seemed happy as she bragged to Sheila about her role.

"No," Sophie said, smiling broadly. "*We* did it. All of us."

The tree's hum dipped to a deep rumble, almost like laughter.

Right, you are sapling.

CHAPTER THIRTY

"Well." Peter stood in front of Sophie, hands in his jacket's pockets, as he stood beside his older brother's car. "I guess this is bye for now."

"Yeah." Sophie chuckled at Peter's nervousness. He probably didn't want to do anything his brother might embarrass him for. Still, she couldn't let him leave for winter break without a hug. "Come here." She grabbed his hands and wrapped her arms around him, and he gingerly returned the embrace, smiling despite his red cheeks.

"Ooh, Pete's got a girlfriend!" Sophie heard from the car. Peter sighed and rolled his eyes.

"Shut up, Max!" He shook his head but smiled at Sophie. "Sorry about him. He's a jerk."

"Siblings are like that sometimes." Leaning forward, she gave him a quick peck on the cheek. "I'll call over break. Promise."

Peter, grinning from ear to ear, nodded as he headed toward the car, nearly falling off the sidewalk as he maintained eye contact with Sophie. "Yeah. Ditto."

Sophie giggled and waved as they pulled away, noting a familiar vehicle approaching. She could see Millie waving through the van window from a football field away.

"Hey, Soph!" Bri, Leslie, and Janet were hurrying toward her. "We got something for you, but don't open it until Christmas."

Janet and Leslie held up a hastily wrapped package, their eyes twinkling.

Sophie put her hands to her chest. "Guys. You seriously didn't have to."

"It's Christmas," Leslie said matter-of-factly, pushing the package into Sophie's arms. "It'd be against my Southern raisin' to send you home without somethin'."

"Yeah," Bri said. "Besides, if it weren't for you, we wouldn't be coming back to the school next semester."

Sophie shook her head. "You know as well as I do that we *all* helped."

"But without your…weird hearing the tree hum thing," Bri said, struggling to find the words, "we wouldn't have been able to help."

"You mean her psionic ability?" Janet asked.

Sophie started. She'd been using the word to describe her second sight, but she hadn't said it out loud to anyone. She certainly hadn't heard anyone else describe it using that word.

"Yeah." Bri looked as surprised as Sophie felt. "I guess that makes sense, huh?"

"I'd wondered, but you know, Professor Rogers said it's really rare, and it's hard to test," Leslie said.

"How much more of a test did we need? She healed the tree using *everybody's* gift, not just her own. She could hear the tree telling her what to do to help it. I mean, it's obvious to me." Janet said as she pushed her glasses up the bridge of her nose.

"Says the girl who kept telling Sophie she needed to get her ears checked," Bri snarked.

Janet glowered at Bri.

Millie burst out of the minivan and tackled Sophie with a bear hug. "Sissy!"

Sophie laughed, nearly dropping her gift.

"She's so cute! I wish I had a sister." Bri said.

Millie smiled bashfully at Bri. "I can be your honorary little sister."

The girls laughed. "This is Millie," Sophie said. "And Millie, this is Bri, Leslie, and Janet. They're my roommates."

"I remember. They were all there when we came the first day," Millie said.

Joyce and Walter joined Sophie and Millie on the sidewalk, and Sophie repeated her introductions, smiling as her family and friends chatted happily.

She looked toward Thicket Hall, taking a mental picture of the campus. A gentle breeze moved toward her, and a single, dark green leaf landed in her hair. She retrieved it and slipped it into her pocket, letting her mind greet the happy buzz coming toward her from the tree.

Stay safe, sapling. Come back soon.

She nodded with a smile.

After a prolonged session of goodbyes, she climbed into the minivan and settled next to Millie. She tucked her friends' gift under her seat.

"Buckle up, girls," Walter said. "We'll be celebrating the occasion with lunch at Tiny's Chicken."

"Yes!" Millie pumped her fist.

Sophie peeked at the tag on the gift, noting that all three of her roommates had signed it—Janet in her neat cursive, Bri in her all-caps lettering, and Leslie in her practical yet feminine script. She'd have to text them pictures of her opening the gift on Christmas morning.

As she sat up, something cold and heavy settled in her chest. A familiar yet subdued sensation of buzzing encroached on the edges of her consciousness.

Glancing around warily, she pressed her face against the window as they rounded the circular drive. Nothing seemed amiss near the tree, just people milling around, kids greeting parents, and Headmistress Case sweeping the top of the steps, just like on the first day.

She took deep breaths and tried to calm her nerves. Maybe she was so used to looking out for Thicket Hall that she was getting worried about leaving. Not that Headmistress and Roscoe couldn't take good care of it. They'd been here since before she had been born.

She peered out the rear window. Thicket Hall looked healthy. Feeling for the tree's hum, she could just barely hear it as they pulled away. It was the same happy hum she'd heard since they healed it a couple of weeks ago.

Still, the odd sense of dread wouldn't leave her. She itched to warn Headmistress or Roscoe, but what would she tell them? That she had a vague sense of fear? That they should be on guard against...what?

Sophie sighed.

"You okay, sissy?" Millie was staring at her, concerned.

"Yeah. I'll just miss this place," she said, looking at Thicket Hall in the rearview mirror as they exited through the iron gate.

"I know the feeling," Walter said with a nostalgic sigh. "But you'll be back before you know it. In the meantime, we're gonna enjoy our break."

"Yeah." Sophie pushed the dread away and took another deep breath. She smiled at Millie, who grinned back.

"Yeah, we are."

Get sneak peeks, exclusive giveaways, behind the scenes content, and more. PLUS you'll be notified of special **one day only fan pricing** on new releases.

Sign up today to get free stories.

Visit: https://marthacarr.com/read-free-stories/

AUTHOR NOTES - MARTHA CARR

AUGUST 17, 2022

I've started a project answering questions for my son about my life. I realized after last year's fifth round of cancer, and then chemo this time that he was expecting me to die sooner rather than later. It's been a lot for him to deal with and there isn't much I can do to make it better, except tell him stories that I can leave behind – eventually. Hopefully, a long time from now. I'm going to let you guys listen in as well.

So, my author notes for this year are going to be answers to questions and all of you can get to know me better, too. Maybe inspire, maybe give you a laugh along the way.

Today's question is: Have you ever pulled off any great pranks?

I don't know that anything I've done rises to the level of 'great pranks' but I've pulled a few fast ones in my day, mostly in college. At Virginia Commonwealth University I worked in what was then the new library. It was so new that a lot of the stacks were still empty and when visiting prospective professors would visit, they'd steer them around the library, hoping the teachers wouldn't look inside.

I hear the school is tearing it down to build a new one. That's when you know you're old. You've outlived concrete and steel.

I worked in a department where all we did was check to see if we had books that were listed as necessary for a university level library. If we didn't have them, we ordered them. This was 1980 and well before internet and computers and everything was done by hand staring at small type of titles with long names. April 1st was rolling around that first year and to liven things up, I posted signs around the campus that there were free drinks and put our room number in the library as the destination. Students showed up all day long as my boss pointed to the water fountain.

Another prank was the time I put those silver strips the insert in the spines of books in her coat pockets. The strips make the alarm go off if you try to leave with a book without checking it out. I watched from a little ways back as she kept setting off the alarm and the guards kept looking at her, searching her bags. It only took a minute before they let her go.

Since I was the only student in their midst, I was always the prime suspect for these pranks - go figure. And my boss good naturedly tried to get me back by sending me memos about the library with alarming news like payroll would be delayed or the building was closed for construction. But I was on to her and none of them ever worked.

Knowing me, there were probably other jokes I pulled off, but they're lost to the past.

Two I'd still like to do (and are borrowed from someone else) and just might are:

1. Put in a medicine cabinet in the guest bathroom. Behind it glue a lot of marbles in various stacks. Attach a small sound box so that when it's opened by a nosy guest, the loud sound of falling marbles erupts. Everyone in the house will know the cabinet was opened. You have to hope the guest peed before they looked inside.

2. Place a dressed up mannequin in the back of a closet so it looks like someone is hiding in the back of the closet. Again, you want everyone who visits to have a solid, hard-working heart. It's probably why I haven't done those yet but I still might...

You know how you like to say the entire house will be your office when I'm gone. Imagine a fun house for an office! (Also, I'd like to add that I hope you're very old and retired when you get the house.) Think about it..

I haven't had a lot of time or energy lately to come up with any elaborate schemes, but quarantine is over, chemo is done and books are selling well. Maybe I can go big with something. You never know. Stay on your toes, Louie. This has got me thinking. Love, Mom. More adventures to follow.

AUTHOR NOTES - MICHAEL ANDERLE

AUGUST 22, 2022

Thank you for not only reading this book but these author notes as well!

Have you ever pulled off any great pranks?

Dammit, this isn't a great question for me. I am not fond of making others feel bad (which is what a prank is all about), and I have a horrible poker face.

(*Editor's Note: I'm right there with you, big guy. May I also say I hate surprise parties! They fall into the same category for me. Well, I hate surprises in general, so...*)

In short, I suck at pranks and rarely, if ever, was a part of one. Since my father STILL is into pranks in his…70s? 80s? (b. 1941), I'm sure I was a bit of a disappointment.

Darryl, my older brother, would occasionally pull a prank, but my younger brother Paul was absolutely born from my father's loins. Paul is nine (9) years younger than me. I was out of the house before he really got into playing pranks.

Thank God.

As his closest older brother, I'm thankful my younger

sister Nicole took the lion's share of his creative hackery. From what I've learned, she gave as good as she got.

The worst I did in my youth was walk around our senior high school (Jersey Village HS in uhhh…Jersey Village, TX) using two paperclips to pop electrical light sockets. Sure, I might have fried myself (it was stupid, but isn't that what teenage boys are?), but it wasn't a prank against others.

The last question I had to answer had to do with vegetables. This question was pranks. I swear Martha's book of life better have something better soon, or I'm going to start making shit up.

Then I'll be cool. My life will be a lie in the far future, but I won't be around to know the results. Wouldn't that be the ultimate prank?

I look forward to chatting with you in the next book!

Ad Aeternitatem,

Michael Anderle

MORE STORIES with Michael newsletter HERE:
https://michael.beehiiv.com/

GET SMOKED OR GO HOME

They say she's not good enough for the family business. Maybe it's because she was meant for something better.

Sometimes what looks like the worst day ever, is the beginning of our best adventure.

Idina takes that first step into a new life and gets the hell away from them to forge her own future.

But her calling is the one thing they are the most against. She joins the military just like Uncle Rick. The other family outcast.

A new Warrior is about to find out the true roots of the Moorfield name. Nothing will ever be the same.

AVAILABLE ON AMAZON AND KINDLE UNLIMITED!

BOOKS BY MARTHA CARR

THE LEIRA CHRONICLES

CASE FILES OF AN URBAN WITCH

DIARY OF A DARK MONSTER

THE EVERMORES CHRONICLES

SOUL STONE MAGE

THE KACY CHRONICLES

MIDWEST MAGIC CHRONICLES

THE FAIRHAVEN CHRONICLES

I FEAR NO EVIL

THE DANIEL CODEX SERIES

SCHOOL OF NECESSARY MAGIC

SCHOOL OF NECESSARY MAGIC: RAINE CAMPBELL

ALISON BROWNSTONE

FEDERAL AGENTS OF MAGIC

SCIONS OF MAGIC

THE UNBELIEVABLE MR. BROWNSTONE

DWARF BOUNTY HUNTER

ACADEMY OF NECESSARY MAGIC

MAGIC CITY CHRONICLES

ROGUE AGENTS OF MAGIC

CHRONICLES OF WINLAND UNDERWOOD

WITCH WARRIOR

OTHER BOOKS BY JUDITH BERENS

OTHER BOOKS BY MARTHA CARR

JOIN THE ORICERAN UNIVERSE FAN GROUP ON FACEBOOK!

BOOKS BY MICHAEL ANDERLE

Sign up for the LMBPN email list to be notified of new releases and special deals!

http://lmbpn.com/email/

For a complete list of books by Michael Anderle, please visit:

www.lmbpn.com/ma-books/

CONNECT WITH THE AUTHORS

Martha Carr Social
Website:
http://www.marthacarr.com
Facebook:
https://www.facebook.com/groups/MarthaCarrFans/

Michael Anderle

Website: http://lmbpn.com

Email List: http://lmbpn.com/email/

https://www.facebook.com/LMBPNPublishing

https://twitter.com/MichaelAnderle

https://www.instagram.com/lmbpn_publishing/

https://www.bookbub.com/authors/michael-anderle

www.ingramcontent.com/pod-product-compliance
Lightning Source LLC
LaVergne TN
LVHW091708070526
838199LV00050B/2309
9798885418478